Jenn LeBlanc

The Spare and the Heir

BOOK FIVE IN THE LORDS OF TIME SERIES

Dedication

PURPLE

RHONDA STAPLETON :
EDITING

PRODUCTION :

KATI RODRIGUEZ :
ASSISTANT OF ALL THE THINGS
POKÉ WRANGLER

SHELLY DAS :
ASSISTANT ARTISTIC DIRECTOR
SWAG COACH

KIMBERLY DISTEL :
MAKE UP / HAIR
H20 WRANGLER

PRODUCTION INSPIRATION :
BRITNEY

a note about the illustrations:

*These illustrations are meant to be
a work unto themselves.*

They aren't meant to depict the scenes with perfect accuracy in setting, costuming or design. They're meant to accompany the text and evoke the emotions of the scenes in the same way the words do.

More of a companion than a direct visual translation.

Certainly you will notice discrepancies between the scene and details in the images, but that's the nature of creation, some things don't work visually when they do work with words.

Thank you for understanding and I hope you enjoy this illustrated version of Calder.

Hugs n' smooches,

Jenn

Epigraph:

SELFISHNESS IS NOT LIVING
AS ONE WISHES TO LIVE,
IT IS ASKING OTHERS TO LIVE
AS ONE WISHES TO LIVE.

~Oscar Wilde

PROLOGUE

London, 1876

Quinn

Quinn suppressed a groan as he followed Calder from the Serpentine, deeper into the trees that hid the rest of London from the park. The sloughing of bark and loss of leaves made for a nerve-rackingly loud carpet for them to stumble over, but it was a sound Quinn would now associate with this moment forever. He knew he would. Because the farther they got from the public, the closer they could be to each other.

Calder had to mind his footing because the underbrush was thick with the detritus of fall—but Quinn's attention was on Calder. He breathed deeply to cast every bit of this moment to memory, knowing there was something special about it. He didn't know what it was, but there was something… the air around them buzzed as though a thousand invisible bees wished he were a flower.

"Slow down," he said in a low voice, and Calder stopped and turned to him with a crooked grin. Quinn walked right to him, running his nose up the edge of his jaw and just breathing him in as he wrapped a hand around the edge of his coat and held him still. Calder smelled delicious—gabardine and boy, soap and sweat—and Quinn wanted to taste him.

"Not here," Calder groaned, and his voice trembled softly as it blew across Quinn's ear. Calder turned and marched much more determinedly; his muscles shifted under his pretty new bespoke coat, his arms stressing the breadth of the fabric as he reached out to steady himself on various trees. A gentleman would never have need to spread his arms so far, and so gentlemen's coats were not made for such activities.

Calder would soon be a true gentleman with a gentleman's responsibilities and thus needed a new wardrobe to suit. In a few years he'd walk in much more exclusive circles than Quinn ever had. They still had some time to themselves before Calder was expected to truly take up the rein of his current title, and it would be years beyond that before he was to take up his father's title of Duke, God willing. For now, he was simply Marquess of Canford, but to Quinn he was Devil.

Quinn had never felt less than Calder until recently. Until this particular trip to London, really. Calder's family was beginning to expect so much more of him, and Quinn's family…well, they had Wilder, who'd take the rein of his father's Marquessate, and so Quinn was left to himself while his brother and older cousins were trained up. Quinn would be free to do whatever he pleased—within reason.

All Quinn cared for was today—the future could go hang for all its importance to him. All he wanted to do was follow Calder as he did now. Wherever he went. Do whatever he wanted. Simply bask in the glory of this bit of wonder they'd found. Particularly after the past week together.

They'd always been close—closer than the rest of the cousins. So close they trusted each other with their very bodies. Done certain things beside each other, with each other, to each other. Nothing that would be perceived as beyond a boy's natural curiosity, not truly. But this week something had changed, something else happened, Quinn had become much more brave and Calder had allowed for it.

Quinn was still afraid to consider it overmuch, still concerned that this—whatever this was—was coming to an end. He didn't want it to; he wouldn't let it. He couldn't because Calder—Devil—was everything to him now.

Calder

The light shifted from dappled sun to shade and from there only deepened in the dense copse. Once the sound of London was muffled by the thickness of the leaves, Calder stopped again—and once again Quinn didn't. Quinn pushed into his back, forcing his feet forward as they stumbled together until his body met a large old tree that leaned to one side, the trunk of it bigger than the both of them in circumference.

Calder allowed it. Truth be told, Calder loved it. He loved this new power Quinn had found, this boldness he hid from the rest of the world. This bravery that brought them both to this new place they found themselves.

Calder leaned into the tree, the bark biting his palms and cheek. He closed his eyes as the heat of Quinn's hands sank slowly through his coat. He was still so tentative against his back, through all the layers of fabric. As if, after all these years, he wasn't certain. How could he not be, at this point, after everything? Then again, that was part of what he loved about Quinn— though he'd never tell him—this beautiful shyness that was so prevalent, even with him.

Calder loved this part—Quinn's lingering reticence. The part where Quinn would explore and only grow more and more bold, and Calder would wait patiently until it happened. Until there was no turning back and Quinn had to do something about what he felt. Until they had to finish what they'd started. Just as they'd finally done only a few days before. It felt as though they'd drawn out this tease for years. And certainly Calder had. He'd waited patiently for Quinn to come to him, to match his level of passion and want—he'd refused to push him. To discover what Calder already knew to the depths of his soul, that Quinn had been made for him.

Prior to this trip to London, they'd done naught but a lot of mutual tugging and touching of each other, but they'd never…not until that night. And that night was seared into his memory as clearly as his own name. The heat and pressure once he'd managed to get inside Quinn's body, the newness of it, the discovery of something he hadn't known would be so very much. Just lying there against his back, attempting to savor every moment, trying not to move—as his body was demanding he do.

Calder would never forget those moments, what had led to them. What happened then, and what happened after. Quinn was his, he forever would be.

The nervousness Calder felt now at being discovered here in London only heightened his senses. It was easier for them to sneak around in the country; nobody ever looked for them until they missed supper. But here in London it seemed they were constantly being scrutinized for where they'd gone off to and what they were doing.

It was primarily his own family, because he had things to do, things to learn. Things that made him want to be the spare and not the heir. It was a mere stroke of luck, a matter of a mere few minutes, that had made him the first and his brother the second, but there was no changing that fact now. Calder was jealous of Quinn in that respect—as the spare in his own family, Quinn would never have to deal with so much scrutiny.

Lately, though, Quinn's mother seemed to look at him askance a bit more than she had in the past, but what could she know? She couldn't possibly know that he'd ruined her second son in his childhood bed just days before. She couldn't possibly know that Quinn had ruined him right back. How could she? She was busy doting on the heir. Quinn was naught but the second son—he was needed only if something happened to his brother, Wilder.

Quinn's hand slid inside the back of Calder's trousers, his fingers playing with the valley of his arse and—just like so—all of Calder's maundering ceased, the words becoming pinpricks of light too bright to look at directly and capture. "Oh God, Quinn. Quinn," he mumbled, his hot breath deflected back at him off the bark of the tree.

They stayed like that for a while. Quinn teasing and Calder doing nothing but heating the bark of the tree with his breath. Calder anticipated the pleasure they could bring each other and shifted against the tree as his cock rose between his legs. He tilted his hips in invitation, and Quinn slid his hand, searching, as his breath warmed the back of Calder's neck. As if a flashpoint, goose bumps ran his flesh, out across his shoulders, and down his arms even though they were bound by the sudden stifling heat of this coat.

They needed to stop before they got too far, because they couldn't do this—not here. Here was too dangerous. Here they could too easily be caught. But Calder wanted him here. He wanted the temptation, wanted to feel that edge of the knife.

"We shouldn't," Quinn said against his neck, sending new chills through his system. Something in him had shifted, and Calder had yet to figure out what it was. Calder heard a distant child shriek in joy, and he pushed away from the tree, breaking Quinn's hold and moving sideways so his hand slid from his trousers with a stiff complaint from Quinn.

"You only just said—"

"I know what I said," Quinn replied, taking up the space against the tree Calder had abandoned.

Calder leaned into him. "We have to stop. We're too close to the rest of London," he whispered, but he did it against Quinn's ear and watched as the words shuddered through his body.

"Nobody comes back here," Quinn argued, and Calder knew he needed to quit teasing him, because he was torn enough as it was.

He leaned his shoulders back against the tree and crossed his arms over his chest. "Men looking for other men doing what we're doing come back here, Quinn. We can't be found."

"Fine. Later, then. Come to my house tonight." He turned to catch his gaze and almost acceded from the look in his eyes alone.

"No," Calder said, "your mother makes me nervous. Come to my house. You can climb to the balcony—I'll let you in."

"You'll have me scaling walls to see you?"

"Is that a problem?" Calder asked as he wrapped one arm around Quinn's waist, pulling him closer, his hand holding tight to the round of his arse as though he owned it. And he did. Just as Quinn owned him. He pulled him in until he breathed nothing but Quinn, and he watched Quinn's reticent gaze, his own body hesitant regardless of how much he wanted this.

Calder swayed toward him, brushing his lips against Quinn's. It was something they hadn't yet done in all they'd done, and Calder had only just realized it. He held his breath as Quinn's stilled. Is this intimacy too much for him? This meant something entirely different, somehow. This wasn't just two boys exploring—this was so much more, and he was suddenly, entirely, too nervous. His raw ends were exposed.

He let his gaze travel Quinn's face, the strong jaw and mostly straight nose. The heavily lashed eyes that were trying to figure out what he was doing just now. Calder's stomach trembled, tying his nerves into loose knots. He wasn't sure why this was what made him nervous. He kept his eyes open, his gaze on Quinn's as he reached out and teased Quinn's lips with his tongue. Calder saw the moment Quinn gave in to this strange intimacy, when he allowed his eyes to drift shut and he dropped his mouth open, the tip of his nose nudging his, and Calder was lost.

He closed the space between them again, brushing gently, simply sharing their breath to and fro as Calder attempted to steady his heart. It raced between his lungs, and he couldn't seem to settle it enough to be slow. To savor the moment as he wished to.

Quinn's hand came up between them and fisted the edge of his waistcoat, pulling him closer and sealing their mouths together in the warmest of bliss, and Calder lost all train of thought. There was nothing but the smell of the freshly torn bark against Quinn, the linen smudged with dirt, the heat of the sun on the trees above, and the cool of the ground beneath their feet. They were caught in their own small world between hot and cold, light and dark, happiness and pain.

The sweat of his skin slid down the center of his back, and he heard a whimper and thought it might have been him. He pressed Quinn back against the tree and explored his mouth with everything he had, learning the texture, the taste. It wasn't as if he hadn't his own tongue in his own mouth to explore, but he hadn't ever realized how soft the underside of a tongue was, how rough the surface, how slick their teeth as they bumped awkwardly together.

Calder reached up and held Quinn's head steady so he could delve deeper, explore more, but Quinn pulled back. "Devil, stop. We'll be found. We aren't so far..." he said.

"Devil?"

"Yes?" Quinn questioned softly, and the crease between his brows made Calder's fingers itch to smooth it away. "You still like it?"

"I do, I think...I like it very much, in fact."

"Will you live up to it?"

"I hope to live up to every thought you have for me," Calder said as he leaned again toward Quinn's mouth, refusing to back away just yet. Refusing to let go just yet. Refusing to return to the rest of the world just yet.

"You already have," Quinn said.

Quinn

Calder leaned away from him, his bright eyes playfully excited in the single beam of sun that filtered through all the trees in the park. Quinn couldn't catch his breath; he seemed to be rather short of it and he knew if they continued down this path that he was likely to embarrass himself by having off in his trousers, right here in the park.

Because this was so very different. This wasn't just playing around, exploring bodies—fucking. This was something else, something more, and Quinn didn't know what, and he wasn't sure Calder felt it in the same way he did and that truly frightened him.

Quinn had been able to feel that kiss all the way through his veins, as if they'd filled with sunshine and brandy.

"Call me that again," Calder said.

"Devil," Quinn sighed.

"Again," he said, and his gaze dropped to Quinn's mouth.

Quinn's muscles vibrated with restraint. "Devil."

"Never stop," Calder begged.

"Devil."

Calder smiled his half-cocked wicked grin and pushed his body into him, shoving his hand against Quinn's hardness. He pressed against him through the rough fabric of his trousers, cupping his bollocks then sliding away. "Later," he said breathlessly, a promise to Quinn. "Later," he repeated as though he had to promise himself as well.

Quinn could do nothing but nod because of the euphoria that sank into him with that touch—as though he was now allowed to drink that sunshine and brandy. He let his head fall back against the tree and tried to catch his breath, tried to calm his blood, tried to soften his cockstand in his trousers. God, he really was the Devil—Calder. The nickname truly fit.

When Quinn looked back up to Calder, he nodded and smiled again, but his eyes were glassy and far away, and Quinn knew this had affected him as well. Calder grabbed him by the lapels and yanked him forward, kissing him one last time, and Quinn bit his lip—he wasn't sure why, wasn't sure what had come over him—and Calder pulled back as he watched him, one hand on his chest between them.

Quinn wanted to beg forgiveness, dropped his mouth open to do so, but Calder touched his mouth, and Quinn was mesmerized. Calder pulled his hand back and they could both see the small streak of blood. Quinn stilled as Calder's eyes went black, his fingertips on Quinn's chest holding him at a distance as Calder licked the rest of the blood away from his mouth. "Later," Calder said again and it sounded feral, powerful, like a promise Quinn definitely wanted him to keep.

When they turned from the thicker copse of trees, Quinn heard a distant noise and something in the pit of his belly dropped, like a lead weight dragging his stomach down. He reached out and grabbed Calder's elbow.

"What—" Calder said. He turned, but when he saw Quinn, he said, "Are you well? Quinn?"

His look of fierce concern overwhelmed Quinn, but the weight in his belly didn't lessen. "I have to…" Quinn shook his head. He felt as though he should be somewhere else, as though he were missing something terribly important, as though he'd forgotten the most crucial thing in his life.

But here he stood gazing at Calder, soaking in his troubled expression. There was nowhere else he'd rather be than with Calder, and even if he had forgotten something, it was menial in comparison to this boy. Quinn took a deep breath and tried to shake the feeling off then Calder took his hand, pulling him forward as they walked back toward the park proper.

When they emerged from the tree line, the noise Quinn had heard transformed into a terrible clatter—too many hooves scraping, wood splintering, the shriek of a horse and women screaming. Quinn jolted, his stomach twisted, and without a second thought, he ran toward it as Calder chased. They came up over the rise to find a man on the ground holding a girl while women huddled and pointed uselessly. Several footmen attempted to control a horse as it tripped and struggled against its tack, still bound to an overturned phaeton.

Quinn paused to assess then ran for the girl—he couldn't take his eyes from her. Something pulled at him, an unwound spring returning to its curl. Blood streaked her face and her white dress, matted her dark curls. Surely she'd been killed. His heart thumped against his chest. Quinn dropped to his knees at her side and took her hand, and whatever heaviness had been in his belly seemed to bloom like the headiest rose presenting itself for inspection as one finger curled against his palm.

She was warm, though her fingertips chilled while he held them, so he chafed them between his hands. "Has someone fetched a doctor?" he asked.

"Yes," the man said, his eyes on Quinn.

Quinn felt Calder's hand tense on his shoulder. He stared at her, sprawled in the man's lap. Calder pulled his coat off, and Quinn laid it over her small figure. She was still young, but one of the most beautiful people he'd ever seen. Her eyes fluttered open, and every single one of Quinn's muscles froze on his frame and his breath stilled as her gaze met with his.

Her eyes were shades of green rimmed with gold, like the sun through the trees they'd just left. Quinn couldn't breathe and he felt Calder's discontent without ever taking his gaze from her. His heart reached out and gathered hers to him, as though it needed shelter. He wanted to take her from this man, pull her to his chest, and protect her forever. But her eyes closed, and he managed to drag his gaze away.

He looked up to Calder, helpless in the face of something so wildly foreign to him, but Calder stood over them, confused. "Devil?" Quinn said as he turned back to the girl. *Why doesn't Calder feel it?* Her soft brown skin, her black hair tangled with blood and flowers, her long, perfect eyelashes surrounding those wide eyes. He shook his head.

Calder pushed his shoulder, and Quinn saw Calder point to the man.

"I'm sorry, sir, what?" Quinn asked, but the man didn't answer as his gaze narrowed on Quinn. "Should I alert anyone for you? Her mother?"

The man cut a glance to a woman who sat nearby on a bench, much calmer than the rest of the women and several of the men. He turned back to Quinn. "No, son, thank you."

"The physician is here. Let's go," Calder said, and Quinn turned to see the doctor jump down from a cart, followed by a couple of men with a stretcher. She seemed so small, it really wasn't necessary. He could pick her up and carry her to the cart himself. He almost reached to do so, but the man—her father?—tightened his grip and glared at Quinn as though he didn't belong there. Because he didn't, even though it felt as though he did, like a lost memory of her was wedged in his brain and wouldn't come loose.

"Just a moment, Devil," he said to Calder. His gaze floated back down to her again and he realized he'd been holding her hand the entire time, because she squeezed it and opened her eyes. She caught his gaze with the sharpness of a blade, stealing the air from his lungs.

"My head hurts," she said, her quiet, breathy voice the tiniest sound he'd ever heard.

"A physician is here. He will care for you," he replied and started to let go of her hand, but she tensed and he stayed. Tears formed in her eyes, her lip quivering as she looked around, clearly terrified. Quinn reached out and swept one tear from her cheek with his thumb before Calder took hold of his shoulder, breaking the small contact.

"I'm frightened," she said to him, but he was already being pulled away again by Calder.

"Wait," Quinn begged.

"Don't leave me," she murmured to Quinn as she looked up to the man who held her with a wild panic in her eyes.

"Quinn, we should go—they'll take care of her. Come on, give them room," Calder said.

He nodded, but everything in him rebelled. "I have to go," he said finally.

"She'll be fine," Calder said.

"You'll be fine," Quinn repeated to her blindly.

"Please," she begged, and he knelt as close as he dared, leaning toward her so he could hear her.

"What's your name?" he asked.

"Grace."

"My name is Quinn," he said as Calder grabbed his arm and dragged him away.

"What was all that?" Calder asked, bumping Quinn's arm to gain his attention again.

"I don't know," Quinn answered. "I just needed to help her. I had no choice. It felt as though I knew her…I—I don't know." Calder stopped, and Quinn turned to him. "Didn't you wish to help?"

"Of course, but there were others there—her father, the physician. What more could I do but—damn," he said, looking back to the melee. "That was my new coat."

"We can go—"

"No, I don't want to return," Calder snapped, then turned away.

"Why are you so upset?"

"I don't know. I don't like seeing you looking at someone else that way, Quinn. I find myself a bit jealous of a sudden and I don't particularly appreciate it. It's foreign to me. It isn't something I've ever considered. It's only ever been you and I."

"It's still just you and I, Calder. She was but a child," Quinn said, trying to calm him.

"Yes, and so are we, but in ten years we will be men and she—"

"She won't matter to me then. I won't even remember her then. I don't know why—" Quinn watched Calder, waited until he looked back up so he could see his face. He wanted to take him in his arms and comfort him, but out here in full view of London society, that wasn't going to happen. "I'm sorry," he said quietly. "I don't know what came over me. I've never—" he stopped; he didn't want to finish what he'd begun to say. He reached out and wrapped a hand around Calder's arms, squeezed them in a brotherly fashion, then dropped his hands. It was the most comfort he'd be allowed to give him. "Let's go back to the townhouse, yes?"

Calder agreed, but was still frustrated. As they walked away, Quinn couldn't help but sneak one last glance over his shoulder at the wreck. The girl was gone, the carriage back on its wheels, the horse unhitched. As if nothing had happened here. As though it were just another bright London afternoon in Hyde.

But something had happened here; something had changed. Quinn could feel it, he just had no idea what it was. Grace, he thought. Grace—a lovely name.

Grace

Time slowed as the two boys disappeared from view. She was losing something terribly important. Her physical pain was inconsequential to that loss. She was aware of the pain, in the way she'd always been aware of her cat circling her feet for dinner as she tried to answer the front door.

She looked up to the stranger who held her, the doctor who prodded her, the two men who waited to move her, the people who milled around her, and wondered if she was dreaming. They all looked so strange, their clothing like something from that old-time photography studio at Casa Bonita.

"Is the horse okay?" she asked.

"The horse..." The man looked past her, focusing his eyes on the distance. He frowned. "The horse will be fine," he said. He was lying.

She wanted to get up and chase the boys and realized when hands on her shoulders pushed her back down that she'd tried to do just that. She'd wanted to hold Quinn's hand and never let go. She wanted to touch Devil, to see if he were real, because he was just so very pretty with his bright yellow hair, his fancy clothing and his big eyes.

They lifted her to the stretcher, and a sharp pain lanced through her head and down her spine, her vision dimming at the edges.

Quinn and Devil. She conjured their faces in her mind and held on to the coat that smelled of them both even as they tried to take it from her.

"Where is my mother?" she asked.

"She's gone to the townhouse. I'll send word once we arrive at the hospital," the stranger said.

"Who are you?" she asked, and the man frowned, and the hurt in his eyes almost made her take it back, but she couldn't, and now she was even more frightened. Her voice trembled. "I want my mom."

"I'll send for her," the man said. "Until then, I'll be with you."

"But—I don't know you and I want my mom." She closed her eyes, and tingles chased up her shoulders and the sides of her neck. She swallowed against them then lifted one hand and pushed on the tip of her nose with one finger to stop the tears before they started.

They lifted her suddenly, and her stomach dropped to her spine, her hands flying out to the edges of the stretcher. Her eyes opened wide on the bright sky above her, and a butterfly flew past as though nothing were wrong.

She closed her eyes and clamped one hand on Devil's jacket. When she opened her eyes, the stranger was next to her again. His brows creased as he followed her up into the back of the wagon they put her on. "Why are there horses in the park?" she asked.

"There are always horses in the park."

"For the Stock Show—but it's spring. There shouldn't be horses in the park. They aren't police horses."

"Celeste, try to rest. We can talk more when you're feeling better."

"My name isn't Celeste." She almost gave him her real name, but you weren't supposed to give strangers your name—except that he was helping her. Was he a stranger if he was helping her? She needed her mom.

The doctor glanced from her to the stranger then back to her. He said something to the driver up ahead of them, and the cart jerked, then started, swaying through a turn.

"Celeste," the stranger said.

"I'm not Celeste," she said again, but her head hurt, and she didn't want to think about it anymore. She closed her eyes and pulled the coat up to cover her face, but the doctor stopped her, forced her hands back down to her chest. "My name is Grace," she said. "I want my mom. Please get my mom. Her name is…" She had to think. "Her name is Debbie."

"I will have her brought to the hospital," he said quietly.

The stranger was shaking his head.

"She lives in the duplex between Lafayette and Marion. Close to Cheeseman. Not the fancy one with the big pillars, the small one across the alley next to it."

She heard him reply but her head hurt too much. She closed her eyes as tears warmed her cheeks, and hoped her mother would find her soon.

Celeste leaned back against the wall by the window seat of her hotel room, her journal on her lap, her gaze out the window on the Place du Palais-Royal. She remembered the day she'd come here as though it were yesterday. She'd completely forgotten about it until recently.

Once she'd recovered from her physical injuries, they'd taken her to the Royal Earlswood Asylum, where they'd begun to teach her what her memories *should* be. Celeste had been taught to write down all the things *they* had told her were true. All the things they'd said were *real*. They'd forced her to learn a new past by rote memorization, sitting next to children who had trouble learning. Children they'd called idiots and imbeciles. Words she'd been taught were hateful and inappropriate were bandied about like simple descriptions. Categories. Names even.

Bring me that imbecile there…

Take that idiot back to her room…

She shuddered and closed her eyes. Her childhood became a fright of violent terms, and occasionally violent actions.

They tied her to tables and hooked her up to machines or took her blood, and they told her she'd remember or they'd have to do this again. She didn't want them to do this again. She set her mind to learning the past they gave her. She took notes whenever the man she called Father came to visit her.

She called him Father.

She passed their tests.

She still begged for her mother—the last thread of hope she had—but

her mother was gone, and the woman who took her place…she wouldn't see nor meet her until the day her new father took her home.

Once she was sent home, she started keeping a second journal. She left the one with their lies on her secretary, and the one with her truth she hid in the back of her wardrobe. At one point the journals were irrelevant and frustrating because she didn't believe any of it. She couldn't tell what was right and what was wrong anymore. It was all wrong, all of it. Nothing was right; it all felt impossible.

Eventually her mind shifted and what they told her was true made everything about her life easier—so she accepted it. She did as she was instructed and she worked hard to forget the rest. Her life was difficult enough without fighting for a world she couldn't reach out and touch.

But she never could quite forget.

Eventually she abandoned the journal in her wardrobe—the one with the past they said was wrong. She even forgot it was there, until one day, while digging out a shirtwaist that had fallen from a hook, she found it. But she left it. It had been spending time with Quinn that had sent her searching for the old journal again. She hadn't understood why she wanted to read it so desperately.

She stopped fighting her memories and began to believe in them, to trust them. The things she'd forced herself to forget but never quite had. The things all the physicians had said were lies. She read that journal, and every word of it clicked in her brain like separate tumblers in a massive lock. Every word rang true to her, every word felt like it belonged in her story. Reading those words loosed a splinter in her mind that had rested there since she'd been forced to remember memories she hadn't forgotten to begin with—because they'd never been hers.

A violet puddle of ink dribbled across the page. She hadn't even realized she'd been pressing the nib so hard into the paper. She set the pen aside and tilted the journal to separate the page. She meant to remove it, but when she lifted it, the ink ran in the opposite direction, a rill sliding down the crease. She pressed the journal closed to trap it before it dripped to her skirts, and when she opened it again, she found what looked like a moth with the body of a girl.

She picked up the pen and finished her moth, adding flowing hair and tiny toes at the bottom of her legs between the outstretched wings. Then she blew across the paper to help it set.

That day in the park, the one that was so vivid, the first memory she'd been told to erase—there had been butterflies that day, but she couldn't remember if they'd been here or there. They'd flitted around the flowers and grasses. Resting then flying off when she'd chased them.

Even with that quiet memory, she hadn't yet remembered the boy. She'd dreamed of those butterflies, had thought about them constantly whenever she'd seen him, and finally she'd given in and uncovered the deepest of the memories. The first of them. The most powerful of them. There in her very own handwriting. That had been when she'd remembered the boy, and his name—Quinn.

At first she'd thought it couldn't possibly have been him, but every time she'd closed her eyes, she'd known the truth of it. Her Quinn, now her husband, was the boy from the park, and his Calder…he was that beautiful Devil. He was still that beautiful Devil.

He and Quinn had been the first thing in this world she'd remembered. Not the man who'd held her, the one they called her father. Not the woman who claimed to be her mother.

Quinn and Devil. They'd been her first connection, ripped from her much too soon. Finding Quinn again had felt to her like coming home, and she hadn't understood why. It was an odd sort of feeling, as though a piece of her had gone missing and the first time their eyes had met again it had shifted back into place.

She set her new journal aside and inspected the pen; she'd need a new nib. She touched the prongs, leaving a streak of purple at the tip of her finger. She set the pen aside and leaned her forehead against the cool pane of the window. She missed him. She wanted him here. Not because she wanted for her husband, but because she wanted for her friend. She wanted for his companionship. She loved him, and she'd sent him away to follow his heart, because how could she not?

Quinn and Calder belonged together, and it was what she'd planned for all along—that Quinn should have a lover, that he should be happy with someone else, that she wouldn't have need to visit his bed. She hadn't planned to love him so very much.

But what he had with Calder—it was a magnificent thing to see. They were much more than mere lovers. Quinn wasn't himself without Calder in his life, and she couldn't live with herself if she came between them. So she'd wait for him to return and she'd take him and his love however Calder was willing to let her have it. She'd bend to Calder's wishes, for Quinn's sake.

She stood and went to the desk, placing her journal on it. They'd return to England as soon as her dresses and her portrait were finished. Days maybe, a week at most. It frightened her because she didn't know how she'd be received. Of course, she was to stay with Perry and Lilly at Westcreek, so really she wouldn't have to deal with any of society, and hopefully her family would stay away. Perry had made it quite clear her mother wasn't welcome in his home.

And yet…returning and not coming out into society in itself was a message, was it not? Turning away from society, from their judgment, refusing to be called out and to accept their ire. Simply bypassing the ton and pretending they didn't even exist? When they did eventually return to London, it'd be even more difficult, of that she was certain.

She went to the desk and pulled a sheaf of paper from the drawer. She wanted to send another telegram, but she needed to think it through because she wanted Quinn to know she loved him, wanted him to know he had her support, wanted him to know so many things. She wrote two pages of thoughts, the sorts of things she needed to tell him, things they needed to discuss. In the end, when she went down to the telegraph office, she left it quite simple. She told him all he could possibly need to know at the moment. She told him just enough.

Quinn

Quinn paced the forward deck as they approached Alexandria, unable to contain his excitement. Calder could be here. He could be here. He could be waiting for him at the dock. Quinn could be mere moments away from seeing Devil again. The man he loved, the man he wished to spend the balance of his days with. Somehow. He didn't yet know how they'd manage it, how he'd explain Celeste and their marriage, but he knew they'd find a way.

Or perhaps Calder wouldn't be here. Perhaps he hadn't been told soon enough, perhaps the telegrams missed his arrival…but he could be here. He could be. Quinn closed his eyes and tried to make it true with the only thing he had—his hope.

The ship swayed as they lay anchor, and the crew prepared the ferries for transport to the docks. Quinn was first aboard the ferry, settling close to the bow as the rest of the passengers funneled onto the deck.

What if he's not here? Quinn leaned against the rail and scrubbed his hands through his hair, trying to restrain this feeling, trying to keep himself from having—what had Lulu called it? A panic attack. He tried to keep himself from panicking, because there was no one here to help him.

It was one of the reasons he'd kept to his cabin for the first leg of the journey, though it wasn't the only reason. He didn't feel at all sociable. The ferry jerked as it pulled away from *The Lady Celeste,* and he lifted his head to watch their approach to the small wooden docks. He wasn't even sure where he was going, but if Calder had received the message he'd asked Warrick to send, then Calder would be here. Unless he didn't want to see him, but why wouldn't he? He'd come all this way; certainly that would say something about his dedication.

Quinn had no way of knowing where to look if Calder wasn't at the dock. Surely if he were in Alexandria, Calder would come find him. If Calder wasn't here… His hands shook, and he tightened a fist on the side rail and closed his eyes as he steadied his breathing. He should have sent someone else to retrieve his telegrams, but he wanted them quickly. He wanted them in his hands. And part of him believed Calder would be here waiting for him.

He scanned the docks, all those hopeful faces waiting for the ferry to approach. Looking for their friends, family, lovers who arrived. He didn't recognize any of them.

The telegraph office had to be close. He shouldn't have to go far to find it.

He walked the gangway to the dock and stumbled with the solid ground under his feet for the first time in weeks. He threw his hands out at his sides and stood straight, watching as other passengers walked a crooked line on the solid dock like a group of ants following a trail. He hadn't expected this.

He took a few slow steps until he had his footing, then he wove through the welcoming crowd as he looked for any sort of sign that would lead him to the telegraph office. He found it rather quickly, close to the main street that led from the docks into the city. He walked in and stood in the line— which was what he'd been trying to avoid by disembarking first.

He couldn't keep himself still, and other people in the office cast disapproving glances his way. He finally approached the window and gave his name.

"Three, sir," the man said in heavily accented English.

Quinn handed him several coins, not paying any mind to what he gave as he took the papers and walked out. He folded them before he could see anything that would be upsetting, then stood outside for a moment to catch his breath.

The hard-packed dirt of the streets led to the dirt-colored bricks of the buildings as though there was no break between what God made and what man did.

His hands started shaking and the paper crinkled, the sound loud to his ears. Calder could be coming later; it could be that he didn't know when to come to the dock—after all, travel times weren't specific. They'd actually managed to arrive on the day they were scheduled, but that was nearly unheard of, so perhaps Calder waited for word before coming down to the docks. In which case he'd be here soon. So Quinn should return to the ship.

Only, Quinn would have been here waiting on the dock for a boat to arrive. Like a lovesick dolt. Calder was much more reasonable.

Quinn turned back to the long wooden docks leading to *The Lady Celeste.* He should return to his cabin before reading anything—he needed to be safe. He should also be there should Calder arrive. What if he missed him somehow, and Calder was already aboard the ship? Quinn closed his eyes for a moment to still his nerves then he gazed up to the windows that lined his private suite, hoping to see a familiar form.

The glare of the sun off the water was so blinding his eyes watered, so he turned his gaze to the gangplank of the ferry as he walked. His vision narrowed, sweat beaded on his forehead, and his heart raced. He'd had two weeks of sitting and wondering and considering and waiting and now that he was here—all that time, all that patience, everything he'd repressed flooded his system. He hated this. He hated that he was so weak. He hated that he had no way to contact Calder. He hated that he had no idea where Calder was.

Quinn stood at the base of the gangway, another boatload of passengers making their way ashore from the ferry. Once the last of them stepped off, he put his hand on the rope that was meant to keep people from falling to the water and walked aboard. He jumped to the deck and went to the bow, keeping his sights on his ship.

He made it to his cabin, locked the door behind himself, and slid down the wall, letting the panic pass. Letting his nerves calm.

He looked down to his hands.

Three telegrams.

He straightened the folds then broke the tape on the first and unfolded it.

> *Return to Paris*
> *Warrick*

Quinn closed his eyes, then read the telegram from his cousin once again before he opened the second telegram.

Keep Going

I love you

Celeste

He let out a breath and smiled as he checked the date—she'd sent it yesterday, which meant she was fine. She was still in Paris, and he could reply to her—just as soon as his nerves settled. He held the final telegraph in his hands.

You are no longer welcome here

Brianna Cheshire

Brianna Cheshire. Not "Mother" or even "Adeleine," her preferred name. She'd used her formal name and title to sign this telegram. It wasn't the response he'd expected to the telegram he'd sent her before leaving Marseilles—the telegram in which he'd informed her he would no longer deny his love for Calder, for a man.

Quinn knew she wasn't amenable to him being in love with Calder, but he'd hoped she'd see his dedication. He'd hoped she'd support him, somehow. Particularly since she'd managed to force a marriage between him and Celeste, a marriage that could lend credence to his public life.

He'd been wrong to hope for so much.

Quinn's fingers tightened on the paper, tearing it at the edge before he loosened his grip and set them all aside. He looked down to the stack and slid the top one over. He picked up the telegram from Celeste and read it again. And again.

Quinn was suddenly exhausted, as was typical after an episode. He needed to reply to Warrick and Celeste, but all he wanted to do right now was sleep.

He had two more days in port to gather his thoughts. He stood and went to his bedroom and leaned the telegraph from his wife against the

lamp on the side table. He stripped bare and crawled beneath the sheets and let the exhaustion have him.

Q

"No peace for the wicked, Quinn."

The whisper sank past the sleep that trapped his brain in his unconscious mind, waking his thoughts. He opened his eyes in the dark, listening for more words as he stared out the windows at the moon and stars reflecting off the black water. He hoped it was more than a dream. He concentrated on the reflection of the stars, the way they and the moon danced upon the waves—coming and going in the dark.

It lulled him and his eyes started to drift closed again, but a form shifted in the glass, walking from the waves like an ancient sea creature—half man, half fish. Quinn's vision blurred behind the salt and he sat up in bed, letting the tears slide down his cheeks as the form solidified in front of him. He'd know that shape anywhere. *Anywhere.*

He went to Calder, his hands shredding his clothing as if it made no difference. He backed him up against the windows. As if it didn't matter. Because it didn't. Nothing that kept Calder from Quinn mattered anymore. *Nothing.* Quinn clenched the edge of his waistcoat and shirt and pulled hard, sending the buttons flying in all directions as Calder's laughter vibrated through his fingertips and skimmed the hair at his ear.

"Quinn," Calder said, and the words danced over the edge of his ear, breaking his movements and pausing his fervor. He tightened his fists in the fabric against his chest, refused to let go of him.

"Devil," Quinn said, and his voice broke on the word.

"Shhhh…it's all right."

"I'm sorry. I'm sorry. I've told them all. I've—"

Calder's hands came up to his wrists and held him tight. "Breathe, Quinn, breathe," he said, then cupped his cheek, and Quinn rested his face in Calder's hand, just soaking in his warmth. "You need to calm yourself."

Quinn paused, closed his eyes, and let go of the ruined clothes as he spread his fingers against the two great planes of Calder's chest, and the knuckles of Calder's hands pressed into his. Quinn's breath hitched, the whole of his body shaking. He caught his gaze, refused to let go. "Fuck calm, Devil, I want you in me. I need you—that will calm me. Only that."

Quinn shoved the fabric down Calder's arms and pulled at the trousers that hung on his waist. He wanted to be as close to him as he could. He wanted that stiff friction. Quinn shook so badly he needed something solid to hold him in place, so he pressed him against the window.

Calder's back bowed away from the glass. "Oh God, it's cold, the glass—" Calder said, the words stopping when he hissed a breath through his teeth at the shock of the cold against his back. He pushed into Quinn, bringing

their bodies together, and Quinn knew he smiled. The jerk of Calder's body didn't slow him down. Quinn concentrated on his skin against his hands, on the goose bumps rising across Calder's flesh from the chill.

He followed that flush of heat down his chest to the edge of his trousers as he toyed with one of his nipples with his teeth and tongue. Quinn had always loved how Calder's trousers slid a touch lower on one side because of the shape of Calder's round arse, the large divot of his abdomen to his hip, just the sharp shape of him. They could never get him fitted quite right. Every flex of muscle changed the shape of him.

Fitting him was chasing a rainbow, like fitting metal to a stone; it would never be perfect. They were familiar with softer people, his tailors. His bespoke suits never quite suited, were never bespoke enough. He would always be a bit unkempt, a touch wild beneath, somewhat unrestrained. No matter how much they attempted to make a gentleman of Calder, part of him would always remain unruly and a bit savage.

Quinn slid his thumbs along those heavy ridges of muscle as Calder groaned hot against his neck and moved, those thick ropes flexing into Quinn's fingers as Calder shifted, tried to get more. He pushed Quinn back with his chest and brought his hands between them.

"The cuffs, Quinn. Remove the studs. I want to touch you." Calder's voice shook—probably from the chill, possibly from the moment, hopefully from excitement—Quinn didn't know, didn't care, because he loved to hear this man unravel, and so Quinn would serve as valet.

He carefully removed the cufflinks then dropped them to the floor, then he took Calder's shoulders and turned his back to him. Quinn pulled the waistcoat and shirt from Calder's arms. He meant to put the clothes over a chair, but when that broad back and all of its rippling skin took over Quinn's field of view, conscious thought of clothing left, and all that remained were thoughts of heat, and friction, and slide. Grabbing and clawing. Pushing and tearing. Holding and keeping.

Quinn's gaze skated down Calder's back, and the cool of his shoulders where they'd touched the glass sank into the pads of Quinn's overheated fingers. He pushed Calder against the glass again, heard the "oof" as Calder's breath left his body from the force of it, felt the shudder of his skin at the tips of his fingers as Calder's chest met the cold window this time.

"Don't ever do that again. Don't ever leave me again, not like that. Do you understand?" Quinn said.

"There's my Quinn. Where have you been all this time?"

"What do you mean?"

"You Quinn, this Quinn, the one who tells me how it is. Bends me to his will. Informs me of how he's going to handle me with action and will. The Quinn who has no questions and happily gives answers by sheer force of movement. The Quinn who never questioned what he wanted and whether or not I wanted him. That Quinn, the Quinn I fell in love with those many years ago. Where've you been? I've been waiting for you, so very patiently."

"I've always been here," Quinn said as he tried to wrap his head around the words. Had he truly changed so much? His heart sank as he considered it. He had changed, it was true, and it hurt that Calder pointed it out, that he said he'd been waiting, left wanting. At what point had Quinn turned into this man who didn't know what to do? When did he become this person who was so lost and unsure of himself and where he stood with Calder? When was it that Quinn had become so much less than himself? He knew the answer to that question as he thought it, but that wasn't something he wanted to consider just now, so he forced the old memory aside.

Quinn pressed hard against Calder's back, his cock fitted into the crease of Calder's arse so perfectly, just as it always had done.

"Yes," Calder groaned, his breath so hot it marked the window in quick bursts of condensation. "Yes, Quinn, like this. However you wish, whatever you want."

"Promise me you won't leave me again, Devil. Say it aloud, so I know you understand."

"I understand, Quinn."

Quinn slid his hand into the too-long hair at Calder's nape and held him tight against the glass, listening to the creaks of the window from the pressure. "Tell me what it is you understand, Devil."

"I understand what you said."

Quinn watched the words form in Calder's throat, watched his throat slide as he swallowed against them. He pressed him harder, pinning him there, feeling his muscles shift and settle in the force of Quinn's movements, and Calder groaned, knowing he had to give more.

"I won't leave you like that," Calder said. "I'll never leave you like that again. I won't do it, Quinn. I won't," he said softly.

His hold on Calder's hair loosened but he didn't back away, fitting his hips to Calder's arse. There was something so decadent about the slide of naked flesh over fabric. He relished the rise in Calder's breath as he continued. The slight tremor in the muscles beneath his skin. The way his hands pushed against the glass, only to bring his body closer to Quinn, the cold glass chilling his hot skin creating a temporary outline in fog that streaked with every movement.

Quinn tucked his face into the crook of Calder's neck, his cheek resting on that hard ridge of muscle on his shoulder as it flexed, like a caress waking his nerves. He stayed there, relishing in the tremors that coursed Calder's spine, as if his body fought against the heat that poured from inside against the cold at his skin.

Quinn licked a streak up his neck to just behind his ear, then blew across it gently, and Calder's knees buckled, hitting the wall below the window before straightening again. Quinn nudged the back of his ear with the tip of his nose, and Calder shivered against him. "Touch yourself," Quinn said, and the sound that came from Calder's throat had no corresponding letters to define it. Deep, and raw, and real.

Quinn scraped the sharp of his teeth up and down the edge of Calder's ear, his tongue darting out between them occasionally. Calder pulled one hand from the window, the print left behind dissipating slowly. He slid that hand between himself and the wall below the windows, forcing his arse back into Quinn even more because Quinn didn't give him the room. He didn't move; he held himself still. He wanted Calder to work for it.

Calder moved against himself. The sound of his knuckles bumping against the wall and the scrape of fingernails on fabric filled the room above the heavy breathing that drifted like a fog to their feet.

Calder tried to shift one leg, needing better access to his bollocks, and Quinn kicked his feet wide, still keeping his torso tight against the glass, letting the slide against the glass burn his nipples as Calder grunted and tensed and Quinn bit the soft edge of his ear.

"Do you think someone on the docks is watching us?" he asked.

Calder drew a sudden breath, the quiet of which stunned Quinn and sent blood rushing to his already hard cock. Then Calder's body jerked once, twice, his hips pressing forward against his trapped hand.

"Oh God, Quinn, I—"

"Have you embarrassed yourself, Calder? That's all it took for you?" His hair tickled Quinn's cheek as Calder nodded.

"Well, then," Quinn said. "I suppose it's my turn." Quinn turned Calder without moving back, rolling him between himself and the glass until they were nose to nose against the bordering wall, leaving nothing but smudges and dissipating handprints on the window. He looked into Calder's eyes and tore the fall of his trousers away, the buttons popping as they fell to the floor to join those from his shirt and waistcoat.

Quinn pressed his bare skin against Calder's slippery belly, Quinn's cockstand against Calder's satiated penis. He felt it twitch, and Quinn grinned. "I would hope you aren't done quite yet. There's so much more for us tonight."

"Quinn," was all he allowed him to say before his mouth covered Calder's, silencing him. His tongue licked into him, his lips sucked between Calder's, their teeth clashing like a champagne toast to the future, and just like that, all the anger and hesitation and loss were gone between them.

Quinn slid his hands up Calder's arms and held his neck, cupped his face, relished every lick, every bite, relearning the feel of his man. Calder toed out of his shoes and bent as he pushed his trousers off, and when he straightened, Calder wrapped his hands around Quinn's back and his arse and lifted, and they moved toward the bed.

Quinn was carried along on the wave that was Calder, allowing him to concentrate all of his attention on him, his too-hard face, his too-strong neck, his too-bright eyes, his too-soft hair. All of his too-muchness struck Quinn in that moment like an explosion, and his heart skipped as he clawed at him. He needed more—more contact, more heat, more wet, more everything. He didn't want to ever let go again.

He wrapped his legs around Calder's waist, and they crashed to the bed, a tangle of bodies, as Calder crawled over him. The both of them pulled and pushed and shoved until they were all the way on the bed, supported and safe in this space Quinn had built for them.

Quinn brought one hand to their joined mouths and shoved a finger between them. Quinn wrapped it with his tongue, then Calder's, then his again as Calder rocked his hips against him. Quinn took his slick finger and wrapped one hand around Calder's hip, then slid his hand at the crease of his arse, found the sweet spot of Calder's entry, and pressed inside to a peace he hadn't experienced in weeks. Months. And he could finally take a full breath.

Calder was on top of him, in his arms, his tears streaking and dropping on his face now like rain—and Quinn wanted to let it rain, to let it bathe him, let it cleanse them both and let them start anew. It hurt, this cleansing. It pulled at his soul in tiny pricks that bled as he realized how much he'd hurt this man.

The room lightened, allowing Quinn to see the deep shadows of Calder's eyes, and Calder's cock pulsed against his. Quinn hadn't changed his mind; he knew what he wanted. He wanted him inside, where he belonged. Quinn had felt nothing but his own hand for weeks now. He wanted the heaviness of Calder, the thick press of his blunt cock at the gate. The burn of the first stroke that led to a fire he couldn't control for the want of it.

Quinn dragged his legs up, hooking them around Calder's waist and grabbing his arse to guide him.

"Quinn, it's a dream," Calder breathed. "Quinn."

Quinn shook his head in disbelief. "No, Devil, I want you. Please."

"Why did you come?" Quinn watched as Calder's eyebrows pinched together, and he wanted to smooth the wrinkle away with the rest of his confusion.

"I haven't yet—"

Calder shook his head slowly to and fro. "No, Quinn, why are you here?"

"Because I love you. I've always loved you." A streak of light burst over the water from the horizon, and Quinn realized the sun was coming before he wanted the night to end. He closed his eyes tight against the sunrise. "Please, Calder, I need you." He dug his hands into the soft round of his hips.

Calder nodded against his forehead. "But why, Quinn? You don't follow me. You wait for me. Why didn't you wait for me?" Calder was pulsing the soft tip of his cockstand against Quinn's arse, just tiny teases of promise.

"I couldn't, I couldn't wait any longer," he said, and as if his heart hadn't raced enough yet tonight, it picked up even more, threatening to spill. Did he want to hurt him? Couldn't they talk after? Why was he—

Calder pulled back, suddenly cold. "No, you didn't wait, did you?"

"No—I'm here, I didn't—"

"That's not what I mean, Quinn. I mean her."

"Her?" His heart dropped like a lead weight to his belly, and Quinn let his legs fall away, framing Calder's body. "Celeste?" No. No, no, no. He couldn't…how could he know? He hadn't even had a chance to explain. "Let me—"

"No. I don't need excuses from you. You promised me you'd always wait. You promised me this one thing, Quinn," Calder said, and Quinn watched him, knowing he wasn't finished speaking, knowing he couldn't stop the words. "You broke your promise," he whispered finally, and Quinn's heart jumped, squeezing his chest until he choked on a sob he couldn't restrain.

"Devil, you don't understand." Quinn forced the words out, but Calder pushed back, sitting on his knees between Quinn's widespread legs.

"I only need to understand one thing," Calder said, and his body started to fade. "Are you truly married?"

"Yes."

"You broke your promise, Quinn. You didn't wait. Why didn't you wait for me?"

"I couldn't," Quinn said and reached for him, but his hands met with empty space as the sun came fully over the horizon, flooding his room with light as he opened his eyes—and Calder was gone. "No."

Something inside him shifted, a knowledge that Calder wasn't here to meet him because someone had told Calder about his marriage to Celeste. Quinn knew with a suddenness that took his breath away that Calder wouldn't be in Alexandria waiting for him—because the man knew. That was why Warrick wanted him to return. Because Quinn had, in fact, broken his one promise to Calder. He hadn't waited.

He stood from the bed, his legs shaking as he made his way to the secretary in the main room. He pulled a sheaf of paper from the drawer and uncorked his ink, dipped his quill.

> *How could you think to interfere*
>
> *Why would you do this to us*

Quinn sealed the paper and wrote the directions for the telegrapher on the outside then rang for service and slid it beneath the door and into the hallway. He wanted it gone before he could change his mind.

Calder

The moment the horses trudged up the slope and entered Jodhpur, Calder could breathe again. The air in the city was sharp with the tang of spices, the powder floating on the breeze as if color were a tangible thing in the dusky air around him. They arrived at the haveli late, and Calder left his cases in the entry to the rooms that had always been his. He was filthy, but sleep was absolutely going to come first. He stripped most of his clothes on the way to his bed, leaving them strewn about the floor of the main room. After a week in France waiting for an acceptable berth, followed by a month on a ship and several days on trains and in saddles to get here, *that* was all he wanted. Sleep and a shower—which wasn't as likely as a bath—and some clean clothes.

He stopped at the door to his room. The air smelled of oranges and cardamom. It certainly wasn't unpleasant, but it also wasn't his. Someone had been here—his gaze swept the darkened room cautiously—correction, someone was here now. He cast his gaze to the corners as he kept an eye on the great lump on the bed. Finding unwanted people in his private spaces was getting to be tedious.

He took the corner of the bulky linens and pulled, slowly uncovering a tall, beautifully naked body.

"Calder?" the man said as he rolled toward him.

"And who are you?" Calder asked, his tone low and purposefully menacing.

"A wedding gift, my lord," the man replied, his voice now uncertain.

"A—excuse me?" Calder narrowed his gaze as his skin tightened.

"A wedding gift for you…my lord," he repeated.

Calder cast his eyes down the long, lithe figure, his brown skin absorbing all the light in the room. Nobody knew he was here, save Rakshan. As far as he was aware, nobody knew of his rooms in Jodhpur. He told anyone concerned, including Warrick, that he stayed in a well-known haveli across the city. One owned by a prominent British family.

His fingers twitched against his leg as he tightened his muscles, forcing his body to still.

He heard Rakshan moving toward him from the main room and shifted, allowing him access to his bedroom. Rakshan picked up what was ostensibly a robe or tunic from the floor and crooked a finger at the man, rousing him from the bed. "Do you wish to speak with him further?" he asked Calder, pausing for a moment so Calder could consider him.

He looked away. "No, I've no use. The message is understood."

Rakshan led the man to the door and asked if he'd been paid in advance. He said he had, but Calder heard Rakshan hand over several more coins before he bolted the door and returned.

Calder stared at the bed—part of him had hoped it was Quinn. His logical mind knew there was no possible way it could have been, and yet…

"Is anything else amiss?" Rakshan asked from behind him.

Calder shook his head as his gaze searched the room. Nothing had been touched. The man had walked in and crawled into his bed, and Calder knew it had been done recently, because they'd only just spoken with the owner of the haveli—his rooms had been prepared for him late this afternoon.

"What did he mean by it?" Rakshan asked.

"By what?"

"That he was a wedding gift."

"Warrick didn't tell you?" Calder asked.

"He tells me only what I must know, and even that is somewhat vague."

"Ah," Calder said as Rakshan continued to watch him. Calder looked away. The dent in the middle of his bed remained and would remain until the mattress was turned and fluffed. "Quinn is married," he said finally. Just saying it made his skin crawl as though it attempted to reject the notion bodily.

He turned and gave Rakshan the best fuck-it-all smile he could and closed the door between them. His hand wouldn't release the door handle, the tension of his muscles locking him in place. He let his head fall forward to the wood of the door, his other hand resting there for a moment as he concentrated, forced himself to calm. Thinking of Quinn married was a knife to the gut every single time, and the wound had yet to heal fully before he seemed to be reminded of it.

Rakshan cursed through the heavy wood. Thankfully he didn't knock or try to convince him of anything. It was something he appreciated about Rakshan; the man knew when to push and when to walk away. He was a brilliant strategist, one of the reasons Warrick was so fond of him.

Calder stilled, then took a deep breath and turned from the door. He wandered his room, checking the corners and wardrobe and drawers to be certain, but not a single thing was out of place. He knew Rakshan would be arranging for men to watch the haveli, and he also knew it didn't matter who it was who'd sent the man. There wasn't anywhere safer for him to go in Jodhpur. If Madoc had managed to discover these rooms, he'd find any others.

Wedding gift, my arse. That was a painful reminder and a bald threat. The entire incident was foul with the scent of Madoc. He'd always been one to push buttons in the most sadistic of ways. There really was only one possibility—that Madoc was truly alive. Warrick's older brother hadn't died tragically as they'd previously believed. It meant Madoc had sent that letter to Warrick, Madoc had baited Warrick to come to India…and Madoc now had the upper hand because he knew Calder was here in his stead. Calder only had to wait for him to show his face. Calder didn't like feeling as though he'd walked into a trap, but he'd known when he'd left London he was doing exactly that. Whether it had turned out to truly be Madoc or not. He had hoped, however, that he wouldn't be discovered this quickly.

Calder pulled the linens from the bed and tossed them off the balcony to the central courtyard. He did not sleep on used sheets. He flipped the mattress over and covered it with new linens from the wardrobe then crawled into bed.

Perhaps it was because he was back in India, and perhaps it was that *in that moment* he'd be happy to welcome death to ease the pain of losing Quinn, but Calder slept that night better than he had in a very long time.

Quinn

By the time they departed Alexandria, Quinn had a stack of telegraphs from Celeste. She told him the dresses were beautiful; she and Lilly had been to the opera every night they could manage, and Perry had slept beside them in the box. As hard as it was for Quinn to smile, that had made him laugh. Her first sitting with Sargent was wonderful, and she was to see him again in a couple of days. She sounded happy.

His beautiful wife was in Paris, and as much as he wanted to be there to watch her enjoy it, he wasn't. He was aboard a steamship traveling through the Suez Canal on the way to India to attempt to find the man he wanted to spend his life with. A man who knew he was now married and had cut off all communication. Warrick had admitted that he'd told Calder of the marriage. He also told Quinn he'd heard nothing from him since. Quinn saw no reason to reply to Warrick either, yet he'd received several more telegrams from him.

Warrick had finally accepted that Quinn had no intention of returning before finding Calder, even if the trip was dangerous. He wasn't going home without talking to Calder, trying to explain. He'd already cut ties with his immediate family, so he had nothing to return to anyway, and Warrick knew it. Everything that mattered was ahead of him in India, except Celeste. She was in Paris having the time of her life. On her own.

Where did he belong? With the wife who wouldn't touch him, or the man who now hated him?

When he arrived in Bombay, he'd find the guide Warrick had arranged.

Tarak would take him as far as Jodhpur in Rajpootana. From there he'd be on his own again, because nobody knew where Calder was, and Quinn refused to ask for further help from Warrick.

Quinn had had nothing but dreams of Calder since the first night in Alexandria. He sat in the chair and watched the water as it disappeared behind the ship and he prayed that if he found Calder, he would listen. Quinn didn't want to sleep because he knew the dreams would come, and while he loved feeling that Calder was close for those moments, the second he woke up was so painful it made him wary.

In theory it would be nice to sleep through the trip, but Calder...the dreams were akin to having his heart opened and warmed only to be once again cut from his chest. Nights had become the worst sort of torture for him. Of course he'd eventually sleep simply because there was no way to avoid it.

Quinn couldn't think beyond what he wanted or needed from Calder and with so much time and not much to do, it was all he did—think. Most of the time in circles.

It would be two mind-numbing weeks of waiting and watching the ocean fade behind the boat with Calder invading his waking thoughts as

well as his sleep. Quinn considered the relationship he and Calder faced. He thought about everything Calder had said their last night together. He considered the dreams even when they came, because somewhere in them Quinn knew he was attempting to tell himself things he refused to see when he was awake. Things that Calder had tried to say but Quinn hadn't heard. Why else would they be so painful? Quinn tried to listen now, endeavored to give all of his attention to figuring out what it was that had gone so terribly wrong.

When they'd been younger, bolder, Quinn had never had problems with these panic attacks that threatened. He hadn't really considered it before, where they'd originated, because it had become his normal. But he considered it now. Because of what had happened at the park with Celeste when they'd seen Calder, and then again at Westcreek when their mothers had discovered him and Celeste together. It had previously not been that bad.

And now on this ship…he could feel the lightness in his chest that would turn into the grating tension as his blood ran too fast and his breathing outpaced his lungs. The thought of losing Calder made all of it worse.

Quinn shifted in the chair, resting his heavy head against his arm. He let the waves carry him away and drifted off on the hope and fear that a familiar shape would return tonight, and he did—but not the way he'd wanted.

The night that had changed Quinn was a night they'd planned to meet—at the Serpentine, in London. It was dark and after daylight faded, the park was supposed to be secured. They should have been alone—but they weren't. They should have known that if he and Calder had made their way into the park, others would do the same. How naive of them. They didn't see the men until it was much too late. It was the first time Quinn felt the rush of blood so heavy it threatened his consciousness.

What happened next chilled Quinn to the depths of his soul. He honestly thought he and Calder would be used and murdered in the middle of Hyde Park. It was the first time Quinn truly understood the fragility of life—something most people didn't understand until the blush of youth faded somewhat. He and Calder were still children on the cusp of adulthood, nowhere near the size and power of the men who had them surrounded.

What's this young sweet bit of rough we have here…

Quinn woke from the dream with a start, his clothing and the chair he sat in soaked from his sweat. It had been quite a long time since he'd thought about that night. Every time it tried to surface in his mind, he tamped it down. Secured it. Refused it. Because when he considered it, his heart raced and sweat slid down his neck and spine, sending chills through his body that resonated in his gut, turning his stomach just as it did now. The sickening precursor to something much, much worse. Quinn needed to walk, needed to expend some energy, needed to get away, but he stood too quickly and stumbled.

He made it to the bathroom before he cast up his accounts. His hand went to his impossibly fast heart as he threw one arm out to the wall to steady himself. He was cold. He turned the water on in the sink and rinsed his face, but it didn't help. He turned back to the main cabin.

Quinn remembered as though it had been only yesterday. He remembered the moment he'd become the Quinn Calder didn't want. He'd become the man who followed every rule. Quinn couldn't have saved Calder from those men that night. If the park keeper hadn't come upon them when he had…Quinn couldn't have saved either of them. Since then, Quinn had made himself as safe as he possibly could.

He didn't draw attention. He didn't take chances with Calder in public. He refused to allow Calder to take chances with himself. He didn't tell his family how he felt—he told no one until…until Lulu and Warrick, who'd already known, as had—it seemed—most of the family already known.

He closed his eyes and remembered. That was the day Lulu had named this thing he had. She'd called it a panic attack, then she'd forced his attention to other things. Quinn leaned against the wall and looked around the moonlit cabin.

The blue velvet chair he'd been sleeping in—stained wet from his body.

The small table next to it with the blue inlaid tiles.

The dirty tea set they hadn't taken because he'd refused to open the door.

The soft blue rug on the wood floor beneath his bare feet.

He listened for the waves of the blue ocean slapping the hull of his ship.

The hum of the motors churning so far below deck.

He took a deep breath and smelled the sweat of his body covering him and felt the chill from his damp clothes.

His heart slowly steadied.

That night at the Serpentine had been the beginning, and every time he had to walk away from Calder, it had become worse. Quinn closed his eyes and let his body sink into the sway of his ship, and eventually he was steady enough to make his way to the bedroom, strip off, and try to sleep, once again.

Calder

alder woke the next morning with the heat of the sun beating though his open window, warming his sheets and his bones. He'd told himself he'd come to India to find out what Madoc wanted from his cousin Grayson, the current Duke of Warrick. Gray had enough to deal with. Returning to London in a position—as a third son— he'd never expected nor did he want and, on top of it, forced to marry a woman promised to his brother. Though that last part had worked out for the better, he knew Gray was still trying to figure out his…proclivities and how to manage something so private in a world that was now, for him, quite public. He and Gray both had very specific places in their family and in society, balanced at the knife edge of destruction.

Though Calder would never speak on it, he and Gray had shared an experience in Jodhpur several years ago when Calder had been searching for respite from a public life and Grayson had been in his self-induced exile. Well, not entirely self-induced. His father and brothers had been the cause of the exile. Gray had merely embraced it. Grayson had never shamed Calder for what he'd learned that night, never ruined him in the eyes of his family or society, and Calder figured he owed him for that. So when he'd found the unopened missive from Gray's dead brother—not quite as dead as they'd imagined—there was no way he'd allow Madoc to wreak havoc on Gray's precariously balanced position.

So here he was. Lying in bed staring out the lattice-shuttered window at the sun. Not moving. No plan. No idea what he'd do next because—he told himself—he'd come to India solely to protect Grayson. It had naught to do with the fact that he and Quinn would never be together.

He needed to find Madoc before Madoc sent someone less amiable than the Mary-Ann he'd hired for him last night. Not to mention the shower or bath he'd forgone the night before. He stood and pulled his trousers on then went out to the main room. Rakshan was sitting at the small table in the center of the room, staring at him.

Calder paused. Something wasn't quite right. He took another step, and Rakshan shook his head, just a twitch to one side, so he stopped. Then Rakshan cut a glance to the balcony outside the room, the doors wide open to the haveli. A breeze swept the curtains in and brought with it deep and ominous laughter.

Calder turned back to Rakshan, once again this time truly inspecting him. His hands were in his lap, tied at the wrist, his ankles bound to the chair. Calder closed his eyes once more and when he opened them, the ghost of someone he'd never truly thought to see again moved into the room. "Madoc," he said. He looked like Gray, except that half of his face was missing.

"You can either come quietly, or I can do some terrible things to Grayson's favorite valet," he said, nodding toward Rakshan.

"Do you mind if I get a shirt?" Calder asked, trying to find the other men who had to be hiding around the rooms to make the threat valid.

"I do mind," Madoc replied. "You won't be needing it."

Calder saw Rakshan's eyes widen and started to duck, but it wasn't fast enough. The hit came from behind his bedroom door, and his hands met the rug at his feet. He didn't have to open his eyes to know he was in trouble as the sharp threads of pain lanced through his brain. After that, his consciousness waxed and waned until he gave himself up to it against the struggle of sharp ropes and a blindfold to control him.

C

When next he woke, he was chained to a wall, his arms stretched above his head.

"Welcome to Ashoka's Hell."

Calder looked across the room through the heavy bars that cut across the wide opening, a swinging gate of a door chained shut. Light spilled from an entry in the ceiling, and Calder watched the figure of a man disappear up those stairs as if to the heavens, taking all the light with him when the door was closed—leaving Calder in a darkness so heavy he didn't have to close his eyes for respite.

Mr. Sargent wouldn't allow her to see the portrait in progress. It made her nervous, as though he didn't think it beautiful enough or that *she* wasn't beautiful enough or she needed more work or…something. She was quite disarmed. She didn't feel worthy of this honor. The paintings he had in his studio were magnificent. Bigger than life, so full of emotion and power and passion and just…the people seemed so alive it was like they were moments from stepping out to say hello and look down their noses at her as they surrounded her.

She wasn't sure why she felt that way; she'd felt nothing but welcome since arriving in Paris, most likely due to the amount of money her husband was allowing her to spend. *Allowing.* She shook her head. She shouldn't think of Quinn in such a manner. That wasn't how it was, not truly. Certainly it was his money, but he'd made it perfectly clear she could have whatever she wished, no questions asked, no permission needing to be given.

"There," he said suddenly, and she looked up. "Who were you thinking of just then?"

She turned back to him. She hadn't realized she'd looked away. "My husband," she said. "Quinn." She said his name and couldn't help but smile, her hand coming to her lips.

"That's who I want you to think of when I'm painting you."

Celeste tilted her head as she considered him. "Why is that?"

"Because the joy on your face is evident, the sensuality tinged with the slightest bit of mischief."

Celeste laughed, and he picked up another tool, dipping it and swinging it furiously over the canvas.

"I believe that's enough for today," Mr. Sargent said a few minutes later as he made some final scrapes across the canvas with a sharp silver blade.

Celeste stood and shook out her skirts. Since he'd been focused on her face, he had her sitting much closer than before when he'd been working on the full-length portrait. She didn't even need to wear the rose dress draped in silk georgette that was featured. She missed it because it was so very decadent and she felt alive and powerful wandering the streets of Paris in such a delicate and masterful creation.

"Thank you," she said quietly with a quick dip.

"Would you like for me to see you back to the hotel?" he asked, but she shook her head. She intended to go to the opera again today to watch the dancers. She went every few days, sneaking into the balconies to watch as they practiced. Lilly and Perry needed time without her, and she felt perfectly safe doing it.

"Thank you, though. I do appreciate it, Mr. Sargent."

"Please," he said, "you really may call me John. I don't mind at all."

Celeste smiled, then dipped her head one last time and left the studio, walking down to the street level and turning for the opera house. She wondered if Quinn had any idea how much he'd done for her. How free and amazing she felt being here, being in control of her own life, not having to worry about what anyone thought of her, how she'd be so very disappointing to her mother today.

A man stepped in her path and handed her a lily, and she lifted it and inhaled deeply as he smiled. "*Pour vous*," he said with a grin. She reached for her coin purse, but he put his palm out to her, "*Votre sourir est suffisant.*" *Your smile is enough.* He turned and went back into the little flower shop.

She stopped at a small street cafe and ordered a cup of tea. Paris was simply magical, and part of her never wanted to leave to return home—wherever home would be. Perhaps she could convince Quinn and Calder that they should live here. Except that Calder certainly couldn't, not with his duty to the Crown. Perhaps Quinn could buy her a flat here where they could visit often. Or she could live here on her own if that was what it came down to.

She sipped at her tea and considered it. There was no way for her to guess at the future, and it unsettled her. Until Quinn and Calder returned, there was no figuring out anything. It was incredibly disarming to think of them so far away from her, particularly now. She felt hopelessly lost without this man who'd only just become so very important to her. She wouldn't change any of it for the world, she couldn't regardless, and she refused to be regretful considering where she was now.

All she could do was hope for their safe return. Soon.

Calder

alder's muscles ached from the weight of his body against the shackles. With his arms pinned above his head, he'd tried to remain standing, but eventually his legs had given out from exhaustion and his arms bore the weight of him because they had no choice. It was an act of repetition he'd become familiar with if he was here for long.

Calder should have seen it coming. Perhaps he had; perhaps he'd allowed himself to be taken. He'd welcomed death that first night in Jodhpur. He shouldn't be surprised that death had answered. Faced with it now, though, Calder wasn't entirely certain he wished to proceed.

He wondered again where here was. No chance this was actually Ashoka's Hell—the torture palace had been destroyed and the specific location was lost to time, even as the archaeologists dug for it. They'd never find it. But it did make Madoc's intent rather clear. Apparently being dead had destroyed the man's mind.

Calder figured they were still close to Jodhpur. Since no light made its way into this dungeon other than what Madoc brought with him, he'd have no way to keep time. He wondered how soon Rakshan, or someone, might come for him. Calder knew this wasn't going to be easy, but he had no idea yet what Madoc wanted—beyond revenge. This was what Madoc had planned for his own brother, and Calder was here to accept it in his stead.

He wandered through his memory, trying to figure out where he'd gone wrong. Quinn. Quinn was where he'd gone wrong. Quinn was always where he went wrong. When he thought of Quinn, nothing else mattered and he lost sight of what he was supposed to be doing. He'd told everyone he'd come here looking for one man, but the truth was that he'd come here to escape another.

Calder brought his feet back beneath his body once again because if he didn't stand up now, he'd lose feeling in his arms. It was time for his legs to bear his weight. The tendons in his shoulders and elbows screamed from being stretched and he cried out, his voice rough and unrecognizable—and it couldn't have even been more than two days yet.

"Are you aware that you talk to yourself when you're spent?" The sound got Calder's attention, but he tried his best to not react. The voice came from outside the bars of the cell, deep in the darkness, and Calder wondered what he'd said aloud. "I'm not certain why you're so stubborn, Calder. There's no place for that here."

"Stubborn? I'm not certain I follow. How stubborn can one be while chained to a wall?"

"Quite stubborn, apparently."

Calder heard him pacing, in the shift of the dirt at their feet. It must be night because he'd managed to come in without much light, and Calder could only barely make out the exit high above his head. Or perhaps that was but a blind mirage. "I know our family never truly appreciated me. But they will soon enough."

"Will they? Are you including myself and Gray in that appreciation?" His mouth was dry, the muscles of his jaw stiff.

"You and Gray above all."

"Leave him be," Calder managed.

"Grayson?" Madoc asked, then he laughed, deep and throaty. Evil enough to make Calder's skin crawl. "That pretender? Why should I? He doesn't deserve the title. He doesn't deserve any of the things he has. He's disgusting, abhorrent, deserving of nothing but death—I would say torture but he would like it too much, now, wouldn't he?"

"Warrick? I believe if you know him well enough to know that—and judge him for it—it only says something about you, not him. Not to mention the chains you have me in. So sorry to have thwarted your plans," Calder said.

"Not to worry, I'll make some new plans. I suppose it's good that you came, because I can have some fun this way. I'll find another way to bring that horrible thief to justice when I'm through with you."

"Horrible? You speak of yourself, Georgie, not Warrick."

"I am The Warrick!" he yelled, and Calder looked up when he heard the crash against the bars as Madoc moved through the darkness, shaking the gate. The padlock tumbled, the heavy chain slipped away to thud against the dirt floor, and the cell gate swung open…and then, in the deafening silence, he was truly terrified. Calder searched the dark for any indication of movement, stared at the hint of light in the ceiling, and tried to make out the shift of a body in front of it. He knew Madoc approached him by the change in the air more than the dirt at his feet, knew Madoc was trying to throw his senses off.

He heard the match strike, his eye drawn immediately to the light as it flared between them, dancing inches from Madoc's fingers at the end of a long shank. Madoc was much too close, and the flame singed the soft skin of his belly, the hair crackling as it burned, the smell burning his nose.

Madoc lifted the match between them, leaving a red streak up his center before he held it close enough to be able to see his eyes. Calder tempered his breathing to prevent blowing it out and being trapped this close to Madoc in the dark, even as he wanted the relief from the heat.

At this distance, Calder could see in detail what had happened to Madoc, if not how. Madoc's face was scarred and angry, he assumed from the carriage accident that was to have taken his life. The accident he'd apparently survived. The long red cut down the side started in the hair above his temple, dragged the edge of his eye down, distorted his mouth into a partial grin—or grimace—then traveled back up, disappearing below his ear into the hair at his nape as though his face had been peeled away, then replaced.

It hadn't healed well, most likely from lack of medical attention, or perhaps simple severity. The similarity of his features to Gray's, however, was quite astonishing and the only reason Calder knew who he was for certain. When Madoc turned away and that scar disappeared, Calder would swear he was looking at Warrick and not his elder brother—the brother who was supposed to be dead just as his father and other brother, Lysander, were.

"The Queen of England says differently," Calder said, trying desperately to control his racing heart. "Her Royal Highness says that Gray is The Warrick…*Georgie*."

"I answer to Madoc," he growled.

Calder took a deep breath, forcing his fear down now that he had a visible target. Though he wasn't sure he preferred visibility over proximity and a chained gate. "You answer to nothing, George Madoc James Danforth. Because George Madoc James Danforth, previous heir to the Warrick Dukedom, is dead. You are dead."

"I am George Madoc James Danforth, eighth Duke of Warrick. I am not dead. I am the rightful heir. I outrank you. You will follow my requests as made of you." His voice was suddenly calm and collected as he reached for a lantern on the wall and lit the wick. It sent a chill through Calder, made him think twice about goading him further.

"You were never Duke of anything, Georgie, and you never will be. You, sir, are dead to the world. As the name on your tombstone reads. Dead. Here lies Georgie."

"But I'm not. As you can see, I'm right here." But his voice wavered and Calder knew he was getting under his skin with the childhood nickname.

"Yes, right here, in some dungeon in India, acting on some perceived wrong done you by Gray—Warrick. But he never did anything to you, you lackwit, and if you'd returned for the damned title, he would have handed it to you gladly."

"No, he wouldn't. Once you taste power—"

"No, Georgie." Calder shook his head and almost laughed. "Not for him. He's not like you and he never would wish to be. He's had control since the three of you died, died, years ago. You are dead. He's in control because Her Royal Highness says he must be, because it's his duty to the Crown, and he's nothing if not honorable. You know he never wanted for any title, particularly your father's. He already has plans to train up his heir to take over so he can abdicate. So go back, claim it for yourself. Stop prattling on about the title and do it," Calder yelled.

"There's no going back now," Madoc mumbled as he turned back to Calder, the long shank of the match burning slowly down but not put out. Calder couldn't pull his gaze from the flame.

"Then why the bloody hell are you doing this?" Calder asked. He felt perfectly insane. This entire conversation was nothing but a loop of insanity. "What reason do you have? You want to be acknowledged yet refuse to go back. You want the title but won't claim it. You want Grayson but you imprison me. Make up your goddamned mind, *Georgie*."

"That abomination doesn't deserve the title I was born to."

"You call Gray an abomination—what, exactly, does that make you? What he does hurts no one but himself—but you…" Calder jerked his arms, rattling the chains stiffly above his head to make his point. He let the words hang so as not to feign pity for himself, because he didn't pity himself. He didn't care if he was hurt or damaged as long as his family was safe. Grayson, Lulu, Roxleigh, Perry…Quinn. He closed his eyes. Don't think about him…

"What do you know of pain and hurt?" Madoc said as he walked slowly back to him.

Calder caught his gaze fully then, allowing his eyes to answer for him, because for fuck's sake, he was chained to a goddamned wall. What Calder currently knew of pain and hurt was quite a lot, in fact. "Fuck you," he said with another stiff rattle of his chains. Calder shifted on his feet, demanded more from his exhausted legs.

"And wouldn't you like that? Perhaps a bit too much, I fear." Madoc moved a bit closer, held the match between them again, an inch from the skin at the center of Calder's chest. He didn't move it closer, simply watched the flame as the heat of it sank into Calder's skin.

"You disgust me." Calder stilled his breath, spoke shallowly so his chest moved as little as possible, staying away from the flame, which had the secondary effect of not extinguishing it.

"I disgust you? That's interesting, considering. You should fear the things I know, the things I've learned while nobody saw me watching."

"You're the one who should be afraid," he mumbled. "But not of me."

"Is that so? And who is worthy of my fear?"

"Go back to London and find out for yourself," Calder said. Perhaps he could get him to return. Then he could be brought up on charges. There had to be something he could be charged with—wrongful imprisonment, torture, pure folly, insanity, the list grew in his mind. He looked into Madoc's eyes and saw nothing but madness—like his father. He closed his eyes against it, and the heat at the center of his chest bloomed as the match moved infinitely closer. "You bore me, Georgie," he choked out.

"Do I? My apologies. I'll leave you be," Madoc said, then he blew out the match, the flame licking his skin as it was snuffed. He dropped it to the floor, took the lantern and, after securing Calder in his cell, left.

Calder smelled the sulfur of the match on his skin as he collapsed against the chains. He needed to change his tack, needed to figure out what Madoc wanted beyond the title. The title was too easy, obviously. All he needed to do was claim it. Why didn't he?

Calder wondered for the first time in his life if he'd ever see his family again. His cousins had always been his life, not just Quinn, but the lot of them. Together they'd been unstoppable. If Roxleigh was power, Perry was wisdom and Quinn was innocence. Jerrod was intelligence, and Wilder was—he laughed to himself—Wilder was mischief, and Warrick…Warrick was pure menace. As for himself, he'd always been the negotiator in their little clan, the peacekeeper. When there was a disagreement, he was the one sent in to bring an accord. As for the women, simply categorizing them was dangerous. Even sweet little Poppy.

He would protect them all, *needed* to protect them all from whatever monster Madoc had become. Calder closed his eyes. He was here to protect his family from this man. Plain and simple. He needed to stay calm and figure out what Madoc wanted and then find a way to some amenable resolution. It was simple, so simple. He had only to do it while hanging from a wall, being terrorized.

Quinn

uinn found the telegraph office at the docks as soon as he disembarked in Bombay.

Tarak will find you

Use the British manned telegraph office in the east city upon arrival

Do not trust anyone

W

Quinn was already well on his way to not trusting anyone, including Warrick, but it would be rather difficult, considering he had to trust Tarak to get him where he needed to go. Warrick's telegram did little more than make him nervous. He knew this wasn't like visiting other countries. India was British occupied, but that didn't mean it was peaceful and friendly toward the British. There were those who believed the British to be interlopers, perhaps rightly so. It wasn't something he had any control over, and yet it put him in a precarious position, traveling alone in a strange country that didn't necessarily want him.

His only intention here was to find Calder and return to England.

He opened the next telegraph.

Headed to Westcreek soon

Keep going

Tell him everything

Trust him

I love you

Celeste

This brought a smile to his face, which he desperately needed at the moment, standing here outside the docks waiting for someone he'd never met to take him to Calder. Or at least closer to Calder.

"Lord Wyntor?"

Quinn turned. "Tarak?"

The man nodded. He wore a loose-fitting linen tunic with narrow leg trousers all in white with minor embellishments at every edge and a turban that the ladies in Britain so often tried to duplicate for fashion reasons. It was momentarily disarming to see. His dark skin shone in great contrast to the white of his clothing, and when Quinn smiled, the man returned it easily, the curls of his moustache canting up as he did so.

"This way, sir," Tarak said, and he turned and led Quinn into the crowd outside the Bombay docks. It was a bit like being swallowed whole by some great and colorful creature. Quinn's senses were overwhelmed by the colors, the scents, the textures. He felt a tug at his elbow and realized he'd stopped in the middle of the street, absorbing his surroundings, trying to take it all in. As if the air itself held spice, he could almost see and taste the color. Of course, the fact that the air was steady, not streaming constantly past his face, also added a bit to the experience.

"Apologies," he said, then motioned Tarak on. Quinn followed, engulfed entirely by his senses. He finally understood the draw of this incredible place.

<h1 style="text-align:center">Calder</h1>

alder had been hanging from the wall for long enough that the exchange of legs for arms had become second nature. Though he actually preferred the chains to what Madoc would do with fire when he opened the cell. Calder didn't think he could survive much more of that, even if the majority of the burns weren't too terribly bad. Madoc had taken too much pleasure in hurting Calder, and that alone made him nervous. He watched as Madoc came down the stairs once again, bringing the lantern with him. It was daylight this time, and Calder gathered his wits.

"Why didn't you come back? For the title," he said preemptively, catching Madoc off guard. "Once you survived the accident, why didn't you simply come back to London and claim your title?"

"The same reason you haven't done so," Madoc said as he wondered at him.

"The same—" Calder paused then and looked around the cell. The building was old, but the cell itself was not. It had been built into an alcove, probably made for drying herbs or something else rather innocuous. "You were held prisoner."

Madoc nodded.

"Here?"

He nodded again.

"What happened?" Calder asked, cutting his eyes to the scar on Madoc's face.

He shrugged. "They attempted to repair my face on the steamship from England, but without access to better doctors and more supplies, well—" His hand motioned to the ruined side of his face. "It's an awfully long voyage. I fought them as best I could, but I also had a broken leg, several broken ribs, certainly other injuries I'm not entirely aware of."

"But you survived, and still you didn't return."

"I couldn't then and I cannot yet. They're still out there. They'll—" He stopped suddenly, appraising him, and Calder thought his luck had run its course for the day.

"You remember the feel of these shackles?" he asked quietly, trying to sway the conversation once again.

Madoc's eyes went dark, and Calder regretted asking. "Quite well. This room became my new home as I recovered, and they…attempted to sway me—but it was all for naught, because the queen happened to know something none of us did—where Grayson was. He was right here in Jodhpur, and they'd had no idea."

"Ruined their plans, did she?"

"Interrupted them. No matter, I've my own plan now."

"You could share it. Perhaps I might be of some assistance."

Madoc shook his head and laughed then pulled a paper from his pocket. "I actually did come down here for a visit. I thought you'd appreciate this telegram from Gray," he said from the other side of the gate, as though they were having tea. "It arrived just this morning, and I wondered at it because Gray wouldn't send something so—simple. I think it must have another meaning." He unlocked the gate, and Calder went cold. Madoc hung the lantern on the hook closest to him, then tilted the paper to see the words.

Calder leaned back against the wall as far from Madoc as he could be, letting the earthen stones bite at his back, cooling the heat of the angry shoulders that supported him. "Stop baiting me, Georgie. I've no interest." Warrick's telegrams were much too carefully worded for Madoc to fully understand yet he seemed in a rare mood, jovial even, you might say. Frightening, you might also say.

"None at all?" His gaze met Calder's and he grinned. "Do you have another cousin in India that I'm yet unaware of? Besides me, of course. Certainly Gray doesn't yet know of me—that's why you came here, is it not? To deal with me? I wonder"—he tapped his chin with one finger—"just who might follow you to India and to what end."

Quinn. Calder shoved hard against the stones, flinging himself bodily against the chains before being jerked back to the wall, hitting it hard, then

hanging once again from the shackles as dirt rained down on his shoulders, and Madoc—just beyond his reach—leaned back and laughed. It couldn't be. Why would Quinn be here? Madoc had to be lying.

"Oh, Calder, I think you give yourself away."

Bloody fucking hell. Calder needed to work harder at staying calm. He shook his head. "Just let me die and leave them be. Take all of your anger out on me, kill me, torture me, whatever it is you've planned, but leave them be." He wrapped his hands around the chains attached to the shackles and pulled himself back to standing. He looked directly at Madoc. "Don't you have somewhere better to be?" Calder grumbled.

"Better than torturing you? No, not particularly."

"Is this torture? You should have been more specific. I'm certain I would have reacted much more gravely if I thought your intention was to *physically* hurt me."

"Physical, mental, what's the difference really?" Madoc said as he walked slowly toward Calder.

"See…it's this sort of thing that has me wondering, *Georgie*, why you and Warrick weren't better friends."

"What do you mean by that?" he asked, but the question stopped him and Calder realized again how much Madoc really didn't care to be compared to his brother.

Calder shook his head and looked away, then sagged on the chains for a minute. "Nothing…you know, brothers can just be so similar, hard to tell apart in action or looks."

"Nothing about my actions could be misconstrued for his."

"Oh, now that is absolutely true." Calder watched as Madoc bristled, growing angrier by the word. He decided to push. "Warrick has so much honor in him that he would die before allowing someone to be hurt either by his action or inaction. Good thing you have that lovely scar now, or nobody would know who you are. They would assume you—to be…The Warrick."

"I—*am*—The Warrick!" he yelled, spit flying from his mouth, his half-perfect face flushed red, nearly matching the ruined skin as the telegram crumpled in his fist then fell to the floor. Calder braced himself for an impact that never came.

So he pushed again. "Perhaps in your mind…but in England where it counts? You're nobody."

"I am The Warrick in God's eyes."

"The Letters Patent were forwarded to Grayson. The queen recognizes him as The Warrick, and there's naught that God can do about that. Don't you think if God wished for you to be The Warrick he would have interceded on your behalf by now?"

Madoc turned and slammed the gate behind himself, locking the chain then stomping up the stairs. His steps were quiet compared to the action since the stones were solid, which must have been quite unsatisfying.

Once Madoc was sufficiently out of sight, Calder set his mind to getting himself free. Calder studied the wall that held him and gave the chains a good yank. Dirt skittered down the wall to his shoulders telling him that last hard jerk of the chain had been enough to loosen them. Quinn may have just saved his life. Quinn. Was he truly here in India? He wasn't safe here, and regardless of what was, or was not, between them, Calder needed to find him and get him away from here. He searched the floor and found the telegram.

He needed to get to it.

He started working on the chains.

He turned and put his feet against the wall and pushed back. It took every ounce of strength he had left and then some, but after three tries, the chain came loose from the wall and clattered to the floor at his feet as he fell to his back. It was good to lie down, but it also hurt.

He dragged his hands over his face, the heavy chain scraping against his body as he did so, sending new fire through his skin. He had to deal with the shackles. He twisted and reached for the telegram as he peered at the bars between him and the stairwell at the far wall, hoping the sound had gone unnoticed. He had yet to deal with the chain on the gate, the locked door at the top of the stairs, whatever else beyond that he couldn't see. He straightened the paper.

I regret

Against advice

Our cousin followed

War

I regret… For Gray to say that, he must have known how disastrous his actions had been… Calder rolled to his stomach, wincing at the contact with his burned skin. He pillowed his head on his arm to lever his chest away from the floor. For the moment it was enough that he was no longer attached to the wall, but Calder had to find Quinn, he had to get him out of India, away from Madoc, he had to send word to London, to warn his family…

His organs settled and complained at his new position, his internals making audible adjustments as his muscles ached from the release of tension. He hadn't quite realized how painful that predicament would be once it was done. Certainly lying here was better than hanging from the wall, but not by much at the moment.

His stomach revolted against the pressure of the rest of his body, and Calder rolled to his side, only to wince from the pain in his shoulder and ribs from the stretched ligaments and pulled muscles. He had no idea how he was going to manage getting off the floor, much less making it the rest of the way to freedom, but the pain…he could handle this pain. He'd suffered much worse as of late.

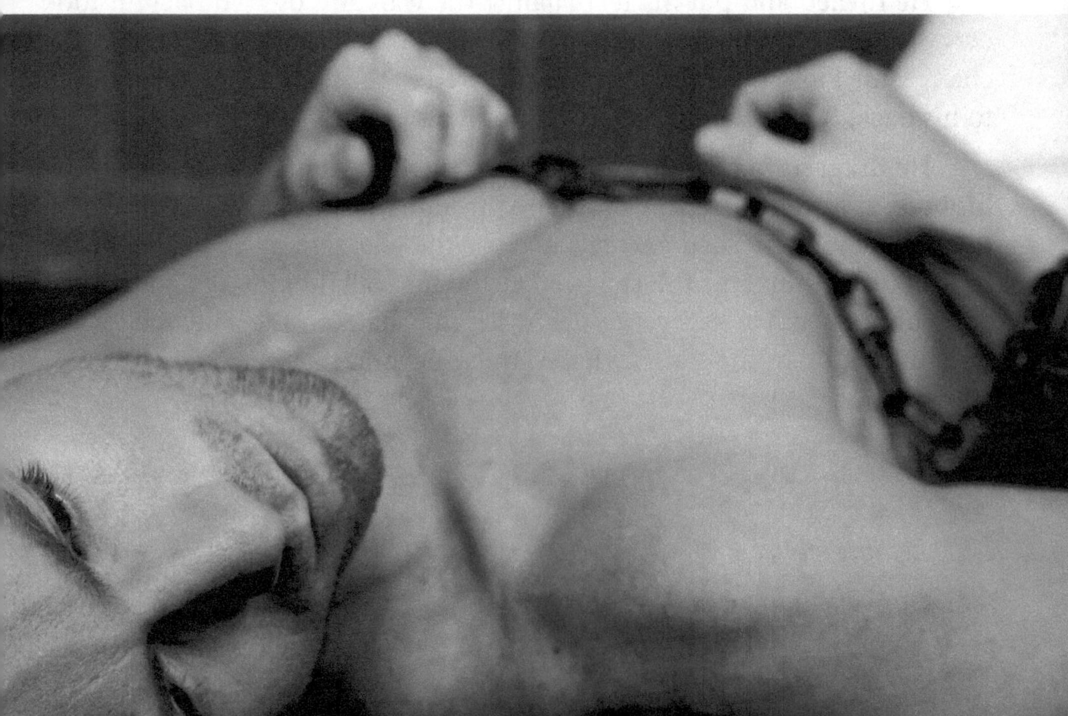

Celeste had convinced herself that she'd like the portrait when she saw the finished work. She practiced a skilled and steady smile so that when she saw it, she wouldn't insult Mr. Sargent, because he'd been so lovely and he was so very talented.

As it happened, she wasn't at all prepared for the feelings that swamped her as she stood before it in his flat.

She'd never seen herself in this way. She had this idea that she was beautiful, and Quinn had absolutely reinforced that—not merely with his words but in the way he looked at her with such heat and the way he touched her with such reverence. She imagined that what she gazed upon now was how Quinn pictured her—and it stole her breath.

She truly was stunning.

She shook her head as she brought one hand up to the pearls that wrapped her neck, the ones that belonged to the grandmother who wasn't hers, but who'd gifted her with this beauty—and it was a gift. Celeste understood that now for the first time. This gift, her skin, her eyes—she was beautiful. She couldn't deny it, standing before this portrait, examining the slope of her neck, the defiant tilt of her chin, the gentle curve of her hand at her waist, and the soulful gaze as she engaged the viewer and considered her husband and how wonderful he was. How lucky she was to have him. How blessed to have found someone who'd let her be who she was even as he didn't fully understand it himself. How blessed she was that he trusted her so implicitly that he gave her leave to simply be herself.

Her cheek warmed, and she reached up, surprised by the tear that streaked from her eye. Being told all her life how unwanted and ugly she was had made it more difficult to believe otherwise, even as strong and reasonable as she was. Being reminded daily how very much the people who were supposed to love her wished she were different—eventually part of her believed them to be correct, because they were her family.

Finally faced with a truth so perfectly opposite of that, a truth so powerfully inarguable…everything she knew shifted, and what she'd believed started to simply fade away like The Emperor's New Clothes, leaving behind only the truth and the inability to avoid it.

They were wrong. All of them. They were wrong, and they never deserved the right to shape her opinions to begin with.

Celeste felt a hand at her back and turned toward Mr. Sargent. "It's—" She stopped. "You've given me the greatest gift, and I'm overwhelmed. I had no idea…is this how most of your subjects feel?"

"Some of them, yes. There are those who are beautiful only on the outside and are rarely impressed with my work. But you, my lady, your beauty is both within and without, and this is what I've attempted to show." He paused, and they both gazed at the portrait for a moment before he spoke again. "You will forever be one of my most precious subjects, Celeste. Should I return to England, or you to Paris, I'd hope you would be amenable to sitting for me again."

"Yes," she said. "Yes, you may have all the access you desire. Only tell me when."

"Perhaps check with Lord Wyntor first?" he said.

"There's no need. He will agree." She turned to him. "Thank you again. I cannot express my gratitude for what you've given me. For how you've filled my soul with this work. For how you've changed the way in which I see my own world. Thank you." Celeste reached up and wrapped her arms around his shoulders, resting her cheek against his chest. His arms came around her, the warmth sinking through the layer of the fabric and comforting her. "I wish Quinn were here to see this. I know he'll be equally pleased." Celeste released him and stood back, turning once again to the portrait.

"How soon do you depart for England?"

"I have one final fitting with Mr. Worth at the end of the week, and then we're set to return."

"I'll have the painting prepared for shipment. Just send a note with your travel details, and I'll have her at the dock for you."

Celeste nodded, once again too overwhelmed with emotion for any words.

"I'll give you a moment? Take as long as you wish. If you need anything, I'll be in the parlor."

Celeste dipped her head, and he squeezed her elbow gently, his thumb sweeping the side of her arm. He released her as he turned, turning the electric lights on since the sun was fading, before he ducked through the heavy curtains from his studio to his parlor, leaving her alone with the portrait.

Celeste pulled a stool closer and perched on it so she could be level with her eyes. She sat for quite some time just staring at the beautiful woman she'd had no idea she was.

Calder

"I see you've finally managed to pull the chain down," Madoc said from somewhere over his head. "I honestly thought you'd have managed that sooner—a few days ago at the very least. I was beginning to think you weak."

Calder rolled to his back and covered his face with one arm, the chain dragging over his chest before he realized it would. He stopped it. He'd managed to crawl to the gate and had tried the chain, but it was solid enough to not allow any gap, and the bars were quite well secured in the walls, so Calder had returned to the floor to try to regain some of his strength.

"I imagine those chains must be quite uncomfortable yet," Madoc said.

"Why do you bother?" Calder asked. "What do you want? There's no point to this. You'll either kill me or let me go. If you let me go, you'll have to explain yourself to the queen or remain exiled. I see no end in which you triumph—none. Because either way you're a prisoner. One of your own making or one of England's."

"You ruined my plan," he said, and the banked anger resurrected in his voice sent a chill down Calder's spine. "I had done it perfectly. I'd collected those missives from the men you seek—just enough to make Grayson want more. Just enough to tempt him back to India and away from my wife."

Oh, hell and damn. One more thing Calder hadn't yet considered. That Gray was now married to the woman this man had been contracted to for years. "That's done. You can't have her."

"It isn't done, not if he's dead."

"But again, if he's dead, you cannot claim the title because you'll be thrown in prison. Explain to me how this all went in your head while you

were plotting, because it isn't making much sense to me here. It could be my exhaustion, lack of food and water, or the smell that is certainly myself, but I cannot figure out what the bloody hell you're trying to accomplish."

Madoc went silent, but Calder heard him pacing. Could see him move in the shift of the shadows above his head. "Those men need to be stopped," he said finally.

"So you attempted to lure Warrick to India, but to what end, Madoc? What exactly did you think would happen? You've been in hiding for years. Did you think that would all miraculously go away once Gray came here?"

"My intention was to return *as* The Warrick. You said yourself we look too much alike…save the—"

"Ruined face, yes. You do. So…you meant to take his place? His wife would notice."

"Cecilia is entirely too concerned with herself and her status to mind Grayson. I know her well. There's no reason she'd be familiar enough with Grayson at this point. She was trained for me."

"They've been married for weeks now, plenty of time—"

"Not Cecilia. She was cold and calculating. You think I was unfamiliar with my intended bride? She was very carefully selected and as such, she'd understand my actions should I tell her. She wants nothing more than money and status, both things I can give her. I can't imagine she's been cooperative with Grayson."

"Cooperative isn't quite the term I'd use, but I've a feeling you'll be terribly disappointed should you return and try to remove Warrick from his wife. She's had a…change of heart."

"Impossible. You can't change someone like her, someone who's been trained all her life for one certainty. No one would ever know that Grayson left and I returned."

"But his wife…you see—they were forced together, and now I'm quite certain you'd not be able to separate the one from the other."

"I'm certain I could."

"There's no arguing with you if you won't listen. Her father already tried to get her to destroy Warrick, and she refused. These men you speak of—Soundringham, Exeter, Bentleigh—they're rapidly losing ground."

"I'm sick of them."

"Aren't we all. Turn them in and be done with it."

"No, I—"

"My head hurts," Calder said. And it was the truth. "I cannot do this with you. Leave me be or get me some water. But I've no interest in your stories anymore. None."

"Need I remind you that you're not in charge here?"

"No," Calder said, giving the chains a quick shake then immediately regretting it. "Quite obvious, really, but what you fail to understand is that I no longer care. There's nothing you can do to me. Nothing. And you're too much of a goddamn chicken shit to return to England and do something to my family. So here we are, you and I, getting nowhere rather quickly."

"They're my family too," Madoc reminded him.

"Not anymore, Madoc. The minute you hid yourself you were truly dead, and when you took me? You killed yourself all over again. You need to think this through. You honestly have no options whatsoever. If you want your life back, you have to deal with me. Because without me, your life is worthless. You think Rakshan hasn't sent word to someone?" Calder waited for his response but was met with a full, heavy silence, which reassured Calder that Madoc hadn't harmed Rakshan. Perhaps he'd find Quinn, warn the family.

"Rakshan is unavailable at the moment."

"Never mind, then. Be done with me and him, and Quinn, and Warrick as well…they all know I'm here in India. If I disappear, all of London will come searching."

"Perhaps." Calder was surprised when Madoc simply turned and left. No production, no more argument or yelling. Might he be getting through to him somehow? He doubted it.

Calder didn't have the energy to stand, hardly had the energy to roll over. But while he was thoroughly, physically exhausted, his mind refused to slow down.

Somehow he had to get to Quinn…all he wanted was to see him again. To hold him again. To apologize for everything that had happened. To make love to him one last time…except that Quinn was married and Calder couldn't come between a man and wife. All he could do was save Quinn—then let him go—so he could be happy with *her*.

It hurt to think about and he forced all thoughts from his mind. It wasn't bound to happen unless Madoc decided to let him go, which was madness. He couldn't keep his eyes open so he rolled to his side and let himself fade to sleep.

The scent of something delicious roused Calder from his fitfully painful sleep and he rolled over, his hand coming down on a bowl of steaming food. He pulled it closer and realized the shackles had been removed from his wrists. He smelled the contents of the bowl—rice, meat, a curry of some sort. It was much different from the dry bread and small cups of water he'd subsisted on until now. It turned his stomach in knots he was so hungry.

He pinched a small amount and placed it in his mouth. He let it sit there a moment and soak onto his tongue. It was the most delicious food he'd had in the entirety of his life. He closed his eyes and smelled of it, let it wake his body and mind. Then he took another small pinch and did the same thing again.

When he thought his stomach might be able to manage it, he turned back to the bowl and took handfuls of it. Shoving it in his mouth, wincing when it stung his parched lips. Eating as quickly but carefully as he possibly could.

He had a hard time swallowing with such a dry mouth and looked around to find a glass of tea not far from him. He reached out and took it, the cup shaking in his unsteady hands. He smelled the spices, the cardamom and cinnamon, inhaled them, and decided it actually was the best thing in the world. Grayson was right. He took a small sip.

"Better?" Madoc asked.

"Mmm," Calder mumbled. "Was it poisoned? That's fine. I can die now happily."

"I rather thought you'd appreciate living."

"Don't be a tease," Calder said, waggling his finger at the ceiling as he lay on his back to let his stomach settle. "Have you figured out what the hell it is you intend to do with me?"

"I never had any intentions for you."

"That much is patently obvious, and yet here I am. So now what do you intend for me?" He closed his eyes as he concentrated on keeping the food in his stomach even as his gut began to cramp.

"I want Grayson."

"For what, Madoc? What will you do with him? You can't kill him and survive. You can't have his wife—the Church of England frowns on that these days. But you could return to England and take up the title. You could return to your life, to society."

"And my family?"

"You abandoned your family long ago. You were never one of us to begin with, and you know it. You were a Danforth, not a Trumbull. But if you think they'll welcome you after this? Well, I suppose we've already established that you're delusional," Calder said.

"Finish your meal."

"I'm afraid I cannot do that just now—starving and all. I have to let it settle a bit or I'll end up retching." And then it was quiet again. It had become obvious that Madoc hadn't actually planned for any of what had happened, and now he seemed to be stalling until he could figure out what to do next since there was no turning back.

Calder drifted off to try to sleep through the worst of the pain in his gut. He should have tried to get to the rice without the curry.

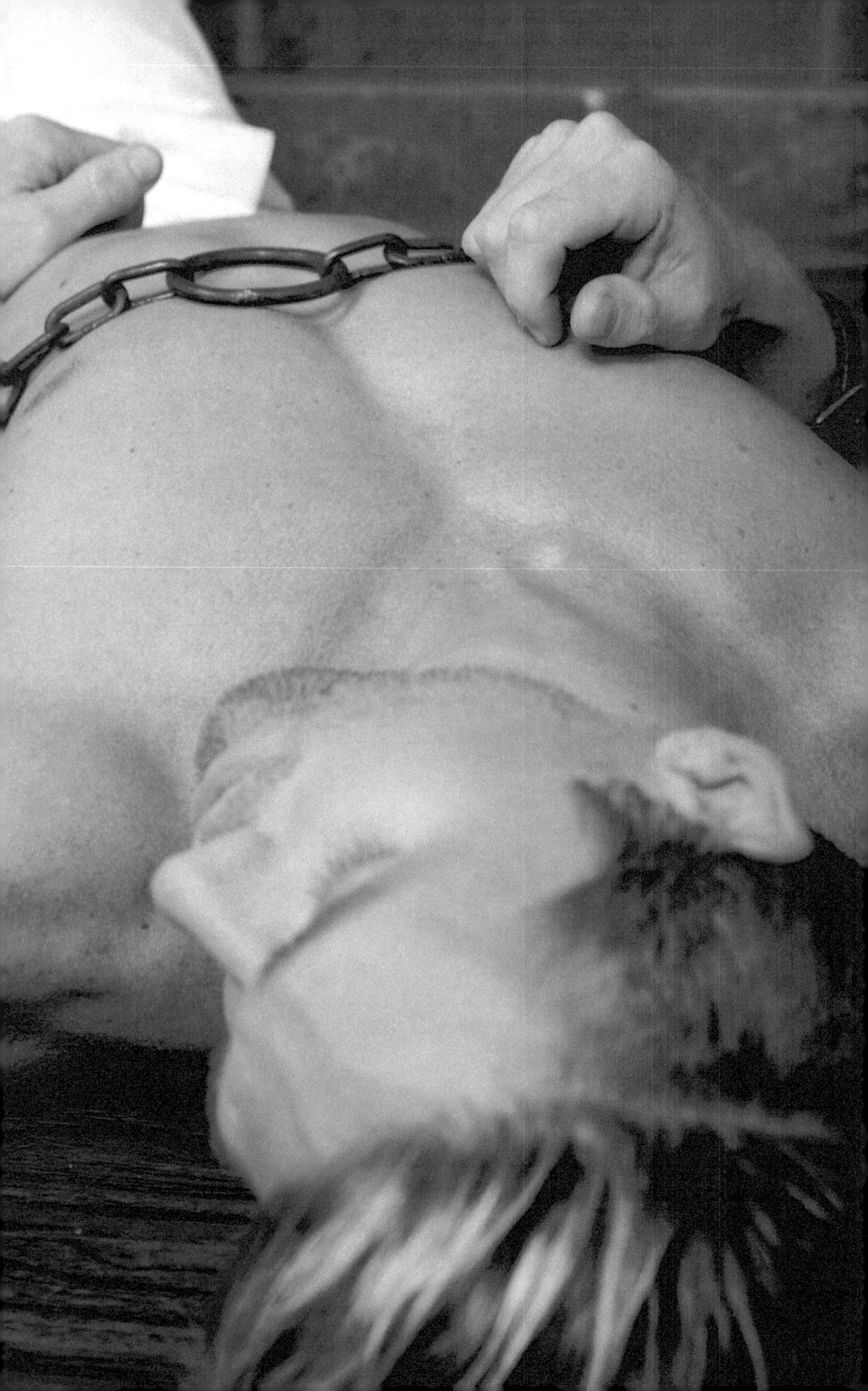

illy hugged Celeste again as she boarded the train behind Gray and Lulu. "I'll miss you! Be sure to write and give everyone my love," Lilly said with a wave as she stepped back. Celeste was too choked up to answer her, but she lifted a hand as the whistle blew and the train pulled out of the station.

Celeste was off on yet another adventure, and she'd only just unpacked from the last. When they'd returned home without Quinn, Celeste had been so terribly lost she'd sent a telegram to Francine—her now cousin by law and the only person who had some idea of what she was going through. Lilly understood, somewhat—after all, she was in Paris while Quinn was chasing Calder to India. But Lilly didn't understand everything.

Lulu had said she and Gray were going to Eildon for a visit, so Lilly had recommended she go with them to visit with Francine, and here she was. She thought perhaps Lilly wanted her husband to herself for a while, as well. They'd shared a suite at the hotel in Paris and were constantly bumping into one another, being underfoot. It was fine for a visit, but everyone needed a bit of room.

Boarding a train with two relative strangers to cross nearly all of England for a home she'd never seen that belonged to a woman with whom she had a strong connection was a bit daunting, but Celeste had never had any adventures growing up and she figured she was due.

Celeste went up the last couple of stairs and entered the rather large private train car. It was magnificent. A massive four-post bed loomed before her, facing out the windows that curved around the back of the car, watching like a sentry as the world disappeared behind her. Well, if that wasn't a statement, she wasn't sure what would be. She experienced an entirely new sort of anxiety at the thought of that bed, which was made so majestically for but a single purpose. It wasn't at all practical for a train and didn't speak to function.

The private car belonged to Perry and Lilly and was designed, built, and decorated to Perry's exacting standards. It was meant to always be hitched at the end of the train, for privacy. She walked around one side of the bed, keeping it in her peripheral vision as though it intended to harm her. There was a seating area, a dining area, fireplace. The furniture secured to the floor, pockets in the chair, ruffles stuffed with books, and large curtained windows.

She walked to the settee behind the bed and sat across from Lulu and Warrick. He was well pressed and dressed and a bit stiff, except for the hand that played quietly with Lulu's knee through the bright green silk of her traveling dress. Celeste had the feeling that he wasn't conscious of the movement, because he was always so very formal and kept any sort of emotion very well under his control.

Celeste pulled her eyes from his hand and smiled at Lulu. "I appreciate you letting me come with you."

Lulu smiled back, warm and welcoming. She pulled the long pin from her hat and tossed both the pin and hat aside as she let her long, strawberry-blonde hair loose. "I'm glad you're here. I've wanted to get to know you a little better. The last couple of times we spoke were a bit short."

Celeste nodded, but she was a bit fragile for any sort of deep conversation at the moment. "Well, I'm told this is an overnight journey. I'm assuming I have a berth somewhere close by? So the two of you can have some privacy here?"

"We do have use of a second private car. It's not quite as well-appointed, because it isn't privately owned. But it's just ahead of us. We thought we'd take that car and let you have Perry's so you can enjoy the trip," Lulu said.

"That's not necessary, really. That bed is…not built for someone like me."

Lulu's laugh filled the railcar, her heart, and Warrick's gaze with sunshine. "That bed really does make a statement, right? Sometimes I wonder about Perry. He seems a lot more interesting than he lets on."

"I'm interested in all the books stashed in the pockets of the chairs," Celeste said with a swift change of subject.

"I think Lilly must be quite the bookworm," Lulu said with a grin. "We should see what books she has around here."

Celeste agreed.

"Dinner is in an hour. If you take it in the other car, it'll be easier on staff," Warrick interjected. He was so difficult to get a read on. Lulu squeezed his knee, and his gaze dropped, and he turned away as though to hide any reaction that may have been unrestrained. She did see his mouth twitch in a slight grin, however.

"I think that would be lovely, Gray," Lulu said, and he turned back to her.

"I'll see to it." Warrick stood and left them.

Celeste reached down and pulled three books from the pocket of the settee she was on. "This really is a lovely way to keep your books safe," she said offhandedly as she perused the titles. They were all fiction—novels she hadn't heard of.

Lulu reached down and pulled a couple of books from the skirts on her settee as well. "Of course there would be a copy of Alice here," she said with a grin.

"Alice? Do you mean *Through the Looking-Glass, and What Alice Found There?*" Celeste asked as she turned a small red leather-bound book over in her hands.

"Let me see that," Lulu asked, and Celeste handed her the book. "Oh, Lilly, a woman after my own heart. She has two copies of *Looking-Glass,*" she said as she opened the book and handed the other back. "Look here, this one is a gift from Francine. How sweet."

Celeste opened hers. "This is a gift from Perry—oh." She closed the book and put it back in the skirt. "That inscription wasn't meant for anyone but Lilly," she said quietly.

Lulu pulled another book from the pocket. "Here's *Alice in Wonderland.*"

"I've read *Alice,* but not *Looking-Glass,*" Celeste said.

"You should. *Looking-Glass* has the Jabberwocky in it." She passed the first book to her, and Celeste stared at it then flipped through it, pausing on the illustrations until she reached the monster.

"*'Twas brillig…*" She shook her head and read the poem. "I have read this. My mother…she read it to me. We read this book together." Celeste

ran her hands over the pages as she tried hard to remember more about her mother. Her true mother.

"Francine and I talked about how I felt like I'd gone down the rabbit hole. Finding touchstones like Alice, things I knew to be real, anchored me here. I suppose that probably makes no sense to you."

Celeste gazed up to her then. "Francine. That's actually…" Celeste turned away. Then she shook her head. When she looked back up, Lulu was watching her very carefully.

"Actually?" she questioned, and Lulu stood and moved to the settee next to Celeste, taking her hand. "It's okay. You don't have to say anything you don't want to. If it's scary for you, just wait."

Celeste thought back to the day in the park, the first day of her life here. To Quinn and Calder, to her new parents and those she'd lost. She'd spoken with Francine some before she'd left for France; it was why she wanted to see her again. But this memory, this one was new. "That's actually why I wanted to see Francine again. I'm not from here either," Celeste said, then she took a deep breath, and another, as though she couldn't get enough oxygen. Maybe it was the speed of the train, that same feeling of weightlessness she'd had in the park as a child, all the memories that had been flooding back—but she was suddenly overwhelmed. Lulu's fingers went to her back, loosening the ties of her dress and then the corset underneath, and Celeste could once again breathe. "Thank you," she said quietly. "That's a rather handy trick. I've never seen anyone manage a corset without removing the dress first."

"Well, your dress laces in the right place. It was simple, and I've had a bit of practice."

"All right, I feel…nervous. But I feel better."

"Why nervous?"

"I—when I got here, I spent quite a bit of time in a children's mental hospital."

"You came here as a child?" Lulu nearly shrieked the words then covered her mouth with her hand. "Oh God, I'm so…oh my God, I'm so very sorry." She gathered Celeste in her arms and held her tight, and Celeste, she melted right into her. Celeste hadn't really considered it much because it had just been her life—but hearing the horror in Lulu's voice seemed to cement in her mind just how difficult her transition here had been. How she'd been treated. She'd been but a child. She closed her eyes and fought the tears.

"Can I ask you a question?" Celeste said, desperately wanting to change the subject.

"Of course."

"More of a… I'm unsure what it is," she said finally.

"You can say whatever you like," Lulu replied.

"I met Quinn that day, and Calder…"

"The first person I saw was Gray," Lulu whispered, then they both fell silent. They stayed like that for a while, until Celeste heard the door to the car open, and she pulled away, pushing her finger to her nose. "Gray, can you give us—"

"No, please," Celeste cut in. "Don't go. Please stay. I think that's enough about it for now. I want to talk more, but—just not right this moment, if that's all right with you?" One step at a time. She now had two people she could talk to about her past, and it was easier, this time, to say something.

"Of course it is, Celeste. You tell your story however and whenever you wish to. I'll always be here to listen if you need me."

Warrick was still standing by the door, unsure if he should approach. Lulu stood and went to him. "Celeste isn't from around here," Lulu said, and Celeste felt Warrick's heavy gaze land on her. She squirmed under the weight of it then turned away. "That's all. Everything's fine," Lulu finished.

"Supper is ready," he replied and turned his attention to Lulu. She smiled over to her and held her hand out, and Celeste stood, putting her hand on her belly and stopping when she realized her clothes were a bit undone.

Lulu laughed and came over to her, cinched her enough to be proper, then took her arm in hers. "I'm famished and exhausted. We should eat then read then sleep. Doesn't that sound lovely?"

"Yes," Celeste answered. "Yes, it does."

Quinn

Tarak was friendly but didn't speak much English, or he did, but he pretended not to so he wouldn't have to carry on a conversation with Quinn. The language he did speak with the other men in their group, Quinn didn't understand. So the trip from Bombay to Jodhpur seemed much longer than it probably was. The last leg was by horse. There were four men who accompanied him, setting up camp on the last night with Jodhpur rising in the distance. Tarak said it was still several hours away, time they couldn't pass at night because of dangerous wild animals.

Once they made camp, Tarak pulled out a package of smoked meat and apologized that there was no more water, handing him a canteen of some strange, horrible liquor and telling him to drink. It tasted terrible—too strong and yet watered down at the same time.

Quinn didn't like it and drank only enough to swallow the meat because he'd been so hungry. He quickly grew much too tired to stay awake, so he disappeared inside his tent and fell asleep.

Q

Calder's cock sliding into his arse was the next thing Quinn became conscious of. He kept his eyes closed and savored the feel of his girth, sliding slowly in and out, in and out, butting up against that elusive point inside him that made him shake with want.

"Quinn," Calder said at the back of his neck then bit him, holding his flesh between his teeth as he continued to move, and Quinn cried out, the joy at being close to Calder again more than he could manage.

Calder's arm slid beneath his chest, wrapping around his shoulder and pulling him tight into his hips where Calder pulsed in time with the breaths that puffed against his sweaty back, sending chills across his skin.

"Devil, please, don't leave me. Don't leave me again," he said, and his breath hitched, the salt from his tears making their way to his mouth when he turned his head to the side. That blond head rested there against his back as they twisted together, so Quinn could lay his eyes on him. "I don't know why, I don't know how, but I've found you, and I'll never let you go."

"But you will, Quinn, I know you will."

"I won't. I told my family. I told them all."

"That matters not. You're married."

"In name alone. Please, Devil—"

But Calder silenced him with a rough thrust that sent Quinn's spine to straight, shutting his eyes as he breathed against the feel of Calder so deep inside him it was like he was part of him. And he was. The fingers wrapped around his shoulder squeezed, the blunt nails biting his skin, and Quinn pushed back, ground his pelvis against Calder's.

"You're married," Calder said again.

"In name alone, Devil. You need to meet her to understand her. You need to come home, come back to us—"

Calder stopped and lifted away, the cold rush of air against Quinn's back sending shivers down his spine. "Us," Calder said quietly.

"To me, Calder. She doesn't want me like this." Quinn motioned between them, begging, trying to keep him anchored.

"Why would you speak of her while I am so far inside you I can feel your belly trembling against the tip of my cock?"

Quinn closed his eyes against the anger in Calder's expression. "I'm sorry," he whispered.

"Is that why you've come? Because she rejected you?"

"No! It's always been you."

"I was never your first choice, was I?"

"You were my first. You know you were. You've always been my first," Quinn said desperately. "What are you…"

Calder slipped free, and Quinn rolled to his back as quickly as he could, grabbing him about the waist before he could leave. "You love her," Calder said quietly. "I can see it in your eyes when I look at you." Quinn looked away, then knew it had been a mistake. "I'm right, aren't I? You do, you love her." The sound of Calder's voice as it wrapped around those simple words tore a hole through Quinn's chest.

"You don't understand." Quinn closed his eyes and shook his head, trying to untangle his muddled thoughts. He shouldn't have let Calder see that. This wasn't what he'd intended. This wasn't what he'd wanted. This wasn't going well at all, but he couldn't lie to Calder. He never had been able to do that. "Yes," he said quietly, "but it's not as you think." Every one of Calder's muscles tensed on him, and he felt it acutely against his own body, but it was when Calder relaxed that Quinn knew he needed to talk faster, because it was like he was saying goodbye with every part of him. "She doesn't love me, not like that."

"This explanation isn't getting any better."

"Please just come home, please just come meet her. I cannot explain our relationship to you—"

"Have you fucked her?" Calder said bluntly and Quinn couldn't look away. He froze—no…he hadn't, but his memory was instantly saturated with images of Celeste, naked, coming off for him within arm's reach, and Quinn knew those memories shone clearly in his eyes.

"Well, then," Calder said, "I guess that's all there is."

"No, Calder, I haven't. I haven't—we haven't had sex…exactly."

Calder's gaze narrowed on him. "Exactly? What does that mean? It's sex or it's not. The way your heart picked up a beat when I said it, the way your eyes went dark, the way your cock stirred against mine…that tells me you've had sex with her, whether you're willing to admit it or not."

"It wasn't—" Quinn's head started to spin, the blood in his veins pounding inside his skull like protesters at the gate. "Calder, I wasn't—" The weight on his chest dissipated as Calder left and was replaced by a weight of an entirely different sort when his lungs constricted and he fought for air. "Devil!"

Quinn reached out but felt nothing as his hands snapped together violently, and his eyes popped open to find the shadow of a stranger standing above him. It had seemed so real. But it always seemed so real. He was fooled every time he fell asleep, and every time he woke up…

Quinn had no idea where he was. He remembered eating with Tarak then crawling into his tent to sleep, and then he woke here with an unrelenting headache and a stomach that wouldn't hold food.

At least he'd gotten familiar with the tone of his dreams, Calder being close, then being distant. His dreams had managed to teach him something. They'd taught him every possible way that Quinn should avoid talking to Calder when next he saw him—if he ever saw him again.

Quinn sat up on the bed and tried to pick the man's features out of the shadow of his face, to no avail. "Where am I?" he asked.

"Matters not," the man said.

Quinn tried to place the voice but couldn't. The room swam, and he lay back down.

"Food," the man said then, with a quick wave to the table at the end of the bed.

"I can't," Quinn groaned.

"At least drink the water before you get worse."

Quinn nodded. The food, he thought, was probably drugged. Because all he did was eat and sleep and retch. But there wasn't much else for him to do. He'd spent the first day here trying to pry his way from the room in between the eating and sleeping and being sick. That hadn't worked and only earned him a swift punch to the gut when someone had shown up and found him prying at the window. So sleep and retch it was. Quinn wasn't yet so brave. He wasn't going anywhere until someone came and got him.

What woke Calder next was a cold splash of water against his face. "Goddammit."

"Wake up," Madoc said.

"You could have opened with that, you know. It may have been less messy. And now you've made a clean spot that doesn't match the rest of me."

Madoc laughed.

Calder froze. It wasn't the evil laughter he'd become so familiar with. That menacing cackle. It was simply laughter. "What the bloody hell happened to you?"

"What do you mean?"

"What do I—" Calder lifted himself to sitting, then turned around to face Madoc. He stood across from him, leaning on the open cell door. "What the bloody hell do you think I mean?"

"Are you referring to the accident specifically? Or was that more of a general question as to my overall demeanor?"

Calder stared. It was as if he were a completely different person. "Start with the accident," he said, taking the opportunity.

Madoc dropped his gaze, crossing his arms over his chest and kicking the dirt with the toe of his boot. "It wasn't highwaymen. Well, it was, but not really. The men were hired by Soundringham. My father had gone a bit mad and eventually was beyond the control of those of us close to him. I first became aware of it when we nearly—when Gray was sent away. We managed it for quite some time, but he became much worse after that. We'd tried to hide my father's increasingly erratic behavior for more than a year to no avail, so we decided to take him to the country estate, to protect him. Since my father was no longer an asset, and I wasn't interested in being part of their little scheme. Soundringham was concerned for their plans. My father held the titles to several properties of consequence."

"What? What do you mean?"

"Which part?"

"The properties. Start with the properties."

"They're gone now, sold off. Grayson sold off as much as possible to get the title solvent once again. Apparently my father left it in a horrible state."

"And you—what part did you play in this?"

"I wasn't interested in playing any part in that. I made that clear when they approached me before we quit London. They wanted to start bringing women to London from India—not for marriage. There was a property on one of the upper-class squares. It was set up to be a high-class brothel, but the prostitutes were not of the willing sort."

"Are you attempting to paint yourself the hero?" Calder asked.

"You asked, I'm answering. I wasn't interested. Their intent—in sending the highwaymen—was to kill my father and I, to then let Lysander take the title because Xander was easily controlled. He did whatever the strongest man wished for him to do. That had been my father, and without him he would have followed me—" He shrugged. "But they killed the wrong two men, and when they realized what they'd done—and that Grayson would have the title if the queen could find him—they saved me and brought me here. They thought to convince me somehow to their machinations."

"Who was in the wreckage, then? They found three bodies."

"Three bodies burned beyond recognition. I suppose the third was one of the highwaymen. I was a bit preoccupied by the fact that I'd watched my father and brother burned alive after having my face sheared off to pay too much attention to details."

Calder stared at the ground.

"What is it?" Madoc asked.

"I'm having a difficult time reconciling this oddly genial conversation with the fact that you've had me hanging from a wall for the past fortnight," Calder said as he pinched the bridge of his nose.

"Don't be so very dramatic. It hasn't quite been that long."

"I'll be as dramatic as I wish to be, considering the circumstance," Calder bit out.

Madoc shrugged. "As you wish."

"You realize this isn't the way this should have gone. You do…realize that?"

"I don't—"

"You could have simply come forward."

"You misunderstand the situation if you think that's true."

"Apparently…and I fail to see what your objective is."

"My objective…" Madoc turned and faced Calder, coming to his full height. "I was born and raised to be The Warrick. I've always wanted to be The Warrick. That's all I've ever known, and without it… I grew up learning everything needed in order to do so. In order to take the title and create my legacy. That was all taken from me."

"Not by Grayson," Calder said. "So why are you angry with him?"

"This is his fault. He's the reason I realized my father wasn't the man I grew up admiring. Grayson is the reason they wanted me dead, because he's the reason I spoke out against the activities my father engaged in—the activities beyond the business of his title."

"Your father was one of them." Calder sat there for a moment. "We didn't know he was involved." He looked around and scooted himself back against the wall so he could rest. Madoc hated Gray because Gray had shown Madoc that his father was a horrible man. What logic. "Have you truly thought this through? You cannot lay blame at Warrick's feet alone."

"I've done nothing but think for years. I spent months in this cell convincing Soundringham that I was no threat to their activities. I knew that if they perceived me as such they'd simply kill me. I was already dead— it would mean nothing to them. But if I convinced them that I'd be a party to their schemes, that I could one day return and take back the title…"

"And they believed you?"

"Of course they believed me. I was quite convincing. My hatred for Grayson was—"

"Invalid? Inappropriate? Unfounded? Ridiculous? Unjustified? I could go on," Calder said.

"Please don't." Madoc stood there for a moment, contemplating, and Calder simply watched him.

"You discovered that your father was a dishonorable man because of whatever it was that happened between you and Grayson, so you chose to take that out on Grayson?" Calder asked.

"I would never have known. If we hadn't discovered…if Gray hadn't—I never would have known—my father never would have known. What we did to Grayson that day—" Madoc shook his head and turned away. "He's an abomination."

"He's the abomination? Oh, that's rich. From what I hear, the three of you nearly beat him to death, yet he's the abomination."

"He told you?"

"Not in so many words."

"My father forced—"

"Your father forced you to beat him, of course he did. And yet it's all Grayson's fault somehow. Goddamn, but sibling rivalry is patently ridiculous."

"It wasn't sibling rivalry!" Madoc yelled as he turned back toward Calder.

"No? Well, then, what exactly would you call it?"

"I don't—you're twisting everything I say. That's not what happened."

"Then tell me differently so I can understand. Because what I'm hearing is that Grayson makes you jealous because he holds your title and fucks your wife. Tell me something differently so I might understand it."

Madoc made a sound that chilled Calder, then he turned and walked away. The look on Madoc's face had been terrifying, and in hindsight, Calder should have perhaps been a touch more frightened by it. He should have attempted to keep the conversation going since Madoc had seemed amenable. But the reality was that Calder was entirely done with the situation. It was absolutely ridiculous.

He'd lost everything he'd ever wanted. Everything. And for what exactly? Because Gray and Madoc's father was insane and his business dealings had gone south. Calder had nothing to live for—he wasn't going to beg and plead and pretend things to be true that were false simply to save his own arse…which was apparently exactly what Madoc had done. Madoc had convinced himself that Gray was the enemy.

He couldn't quite blame him for that; it seemed he'd been met with his own impossible situation. But he could blame Madoc for what he did now. He glanced up at the stairs where Madoc had stormed off and realized there were no bars cutting across the view. He'd left the gate open. Calder stared at it for a moment, unsure what to do next. On the one hand—freedom. On the other—trap. No way had Madoc left it open purposely. Calder had simply riled him overmuch, and Madoc had stormed off without thinking, right? But if Madoc had done it with purpose…

Calder stood slowly, brushing some of the dirt and sand from his trousers then—examining his thoroughly wrecked countenance—he gave up. He moved carefully, both from concern and from the pain that radiated from each step. It would take at least a week to recover from being stretched, burned, and maltreated for so long. If this was what Madoc had endured for months on end—no, he refused to empathize with him.

Calder made it as far as the gate and reached out, leaning into his grip on the bar, gathering strength. He wondered how high those stairs went. He walked toward them, keeping his gait steady and silent.

There wasn't much light carried down to this dungeon—basement— whatever it was. It spilled through the horizontal doorway and down the stairs, fading quickly as it was swallowed by the dark. Madoc had said it was Ashoka's Hell, but Calder already knew that to be false. He took a look around the room, but there was nothing terribly frightening about this place beyond the fact that it was underground and devoid of natural light. Remove the bars and all that was left was an underground storage area.

Calder turned back to the stairs. They weren't against a wall, but open on both sides. He placed his hands on the stair at waist level and leaned into it as he started to crawl. There was nothing to hold on to, nothing to catch him should he fall, just the steep stones of the staircase beneath his hands and feet. He concentrated on each step, his arms stretched to the staircase in front of him, his hands balancing him as he ascended.

The exit was flat to the earth, and there was no building above him, only clear sky. Calder lifted his hands up to the edge as soon as it was within reach then poked his head out before continuing. It was the courtyard of a

haveli. The floor was mosaic tile surrounded by a sheltered walkway that led into what would be the living areas. There were men at each corner watching him. Another man moved in front of him at the top of the staircase.

"Take our guest to his room, let him clean himself up," Madoc said, and Calder swung toward the voice that came from the shadowed walkway, nearly losing his footing at the top of the stairs. A hand reached out and took his arm, pulling him out to the safety of solid ground. Well, not entirely solid, considering they stood above that room.

"What is this place?" he asked.

"My home," Madoc replied.

"Your home? Weren't you held hostage here?"

"At one time, yes. I considered this haveli a parting gift."

"Are we in Jodhpur?"

"Of course we are. You think I hauled your arse all the way to Patna? That's several days even when all the rail lines are running. Besides, the British archaeologists are still searching for the palace. They haven't found it yet. Never will."

"There's nothing to find."

"Even if it did still exist, a place like that should remain buried for eternity." Madoc glanced away for a moment then back to Calder. "You're free to go, or you may stay here. I'll not cause more harm to you."

Calder considered him. "Have your intentions changed?"

"I don't know. Have yours?"

Calder had returned to India with the intention of finding Madoc and getting the information he had so Grayson wouldn't have to. That was still his intention. "If I choose to leave?"

Madoc smiled, making Calder think it wasn't a choice at all. "If you leave, you get nothing from me."

Calder thought of Quinn. He might be here in India; he might not. Madoc might already have him; he might not. Rakshan as well—more than likely he had Rakshan, in fact. Calder had no way of knowing who else he held. "What of the others?"

Madoc considered him. "If you stay, no harm will come to them."

Just the threat of something happening to Quinn made Calder ill. The telegram from Warrick had been real. There was no possible way it wasn't. How could he even consider trusting this man? How could he not? He was too weak to do much of anything. The man who held him upright wasn't all that strong, wasn't all that large, and yet Calder's weakness made him so.

What Calder didn't understand was, if those men wanted the title to control properties held by The Warrick, properties Gray no longer held, why did they still have need of the title? Perhaps they'd return to Madoc, try to resurrect him once again somehow since Gray's wife had turned them away. But to what end? There was something more to do with the title, and Calder had to try to find out what it was or this would never end.

And, again, there was Quinn and Rakshan. He inspected the haveli. There were plenty of places Madoc could have secreted them away within this home. If he stayed, he could look for them. If he left, he'd have to… break back in?

Calder turned to the man who held his arm and motioned for him to lead the way.

Quinn

 e's coming around. I recommend you keep him calm, still, and quiet. Don't move him much." Quinn assumed this new man was a physician by the way he poked and prodded him.

"Thank you." That was the original man.

"Perhaps less…" The physician didn't finish the sentence, and the man didn't answer him, but the stillness of the room grew tense. Quinn tried to keep his breathing level as he listened to the conversation between the man and the physician, but it was entirely too difficult. They had to know he was listening. One of them left the room. The other stayed.

"Why have you come to India?" the man with the familiar voice asked.

"To find someone," he replied.

"What plans did you have once you arrived?"

"None."

"Who are you looking for?"

What could he say? If this man knew anything of him, he'd know Quinn had no business in India. He had no business in Jodhpur. He shouldn't be searching for Calder.

"Not to worry. I don't require an answer, particularly from you. I have a feeling Calder will do all the explaining I have need of."

"Where is he?" Quinn asked as he sat up, but the light from the door behind the man hurt his eyes. He closed them against the sting of the light and frustration. Then he lay back down. *I should have gone home.*

"Wake up!" the man yelled as he kicked the mattress of the bed he was lying on. "The physician said you're fine."

"The physician said you should stop poisoning me," Quinn said.

"The physician said no such thing. Besides, I'm not the one who poisoned you. You need to learn you can't trust anyone in India."

"Why is that?"

"Because you don't belong here."

"I suppose I should thank you." Quinn shook his head and lifted his arm a touch so he could get a glimpse of the man from beneath. He couldn't see his face at all since he kept his back to the bright light from the doorway. Certainly intentional. "I have nothing to tell you," Quinn said, and the bed shook when the man kicked it again, but he turned and left, pulling the door closed and locking it behind him.

Quinn had truly ruined everything. As if being married wasn't bad enough, now he was being held against his will somewhere in India. He'd intended to find Calder, and possibly he had, but he had no way of getting out of this room.

He closed his eyes and let his dreams take over as they had wont to do every time he slept. At least they offered some comfort before tearing his heart out—again and again.

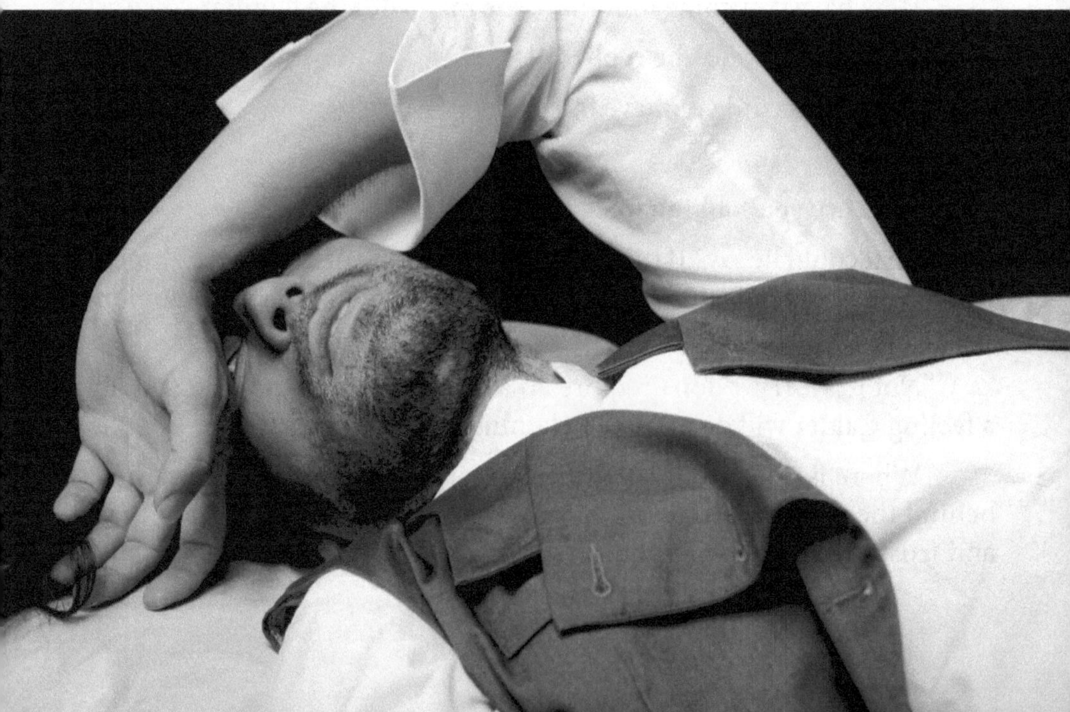

Celeste

eleste woke the next morning to the gentle lull of the train swaying along the tracks. She felt much like a babe in the arms of her mother, rocking to and fro to comfort her. It was lovely, really. Celeste closed her eyes and attempted to remember something of her mother, her true mother, before she'd come here. She couldn't. That hurt perhaps worse than the rest because she remembered being cared for, she knew she was loved before she came here, but that was all she knew, and it was distressing. Her journals filled in some of her life, but reading the journals of a child…the richness of emotion simply wasn't there. The only emotion she was familiar enough with to express had been anger.

She heard a quiet knock on the door, and a woman entered with a breakfast tray. "Sorry to disturb, ma'am. We've brought breakfast for yourself and your companions. I'll set it up on the butler here, shall I? Do you wish for me to wake the others?"

Celeste stood and waved her off. "No, thank you, I'll manage it."

The woman set out the plates on the table and left, pulling the door closed behind her. Celeste went to inspect the food. There were several covered serving dishes with eggs, bacon, sausages, fruits, breads, toast, a carafe with juice, and another with water, as well as two steaming pots, one with coffee and the other with tea.

It all smelled fantastic, and Celeste ran to the door at the opposite end of the car. She stepped out onto the little balcony that bordered the very rear of the car and across the gap to the balcony for Perry's car then knocked on their door.

The wind from the speed of the train whipped her nightrail and robe around her ankles as she waited. Lulu opened the door. "They've brought breakfast," Celeste said. Lulu motioned back to the other car, and Celeste bridged the gap once more and slipped through the door as Lulu followed.

Once the door was shut, Lulu spoke. "I want to let Gray sleep. He hasn't been sleeping well lately…" Her voice faded off, and Celeste turned toward her. Lulu took her hand, leading her over to the table. "Warrick's concerns are with Calder, who's been ignoring all of his communications."

"Why would Calder stop communicating with Warrick?"

"He made a terrible mistake. He told Calder you and Quinn are married."

Celeste pushed a fist to her rib cage at the sudden ache in her chest. "Oh no," was all she could say. She closed her eyes and shook her head. "No."

"Warrick has been a wreck trying to repair what he's done. He thought he was simply warning Calder before he heard in some other way. He meant no harm."

"No, certainly not, but after what happened between us in London, nothing could have been worse. Warrick couldn't have known that. Does Quinn know?"

"That Calder knows about the marriage? He does. Warrick had been trying to convince him to return. But once Warrick told him…Quinn stopped responding to him as well."

"I've done nothing but encourage him, send him off. But that's where he should be. They belong together. He needs to find Calder."

"And you? Where do you belong?" Lulu asked quietly as they removed the covers from the dishes.

"I belong wherever Quinn is. Unless that's an issue for Calder, and then I'll happily keep to myself."

"When you say you belong…"

"He's my dearest friend. If you're asking if we're lovers, we aren't, though we do…we do love each other."

"Don't you wish to find someone to spend your life with since you can't be with Quinn?" The look on Lulu's face reminded her of Quinn and the very conversation she'd had with him. She was so concerned and sincere—just as he'd been—and it opened her up in a way she hadn't expected with someone she knew so very little. "It's not like that. It's not… I truly don't want to be with anyone. I don't want anything more than a warm and caring relationship, the marital bed—" She shook her head and piled some eggs on her plate. "I'm not interested in partaking of that mess."

"Some people have no interest in sex. It doesn't mean anything other than exactly that. I imagine coming to terms with that in a world where women are chattel is somewhat difficult," Lulu said, and Celeste stopped what she was doing.

"Yes, I—Quinn helped, by virtue of patience and trust, but has yet to understand that I'm certain I don't wish for it."

"If you'd like me to explain it to him, I'd be happy to—"

Celeste shook her head; she'd not expected to be accepted so readily. Even Francine had had some questions. "No, I—no, thank you, but it isn't necessary. He'll get used to the idea. After all, it isn't like this marriage is anything but in name. He and Calder are to be considered the true marriage." Celeste twisted her hands in her lap. Lulu's hand rested on her shoulder, and Celeste turned back to find her gazing at her openly. Something she hadn't seen from anyone other than Quinn and Francine. It was so genuine she felt like crying, but she stifled it, pushing on her nose with the tip of her finger. "You're quite lovely," she said finally.

"Listen, you don't have to discuss this with anyone, and if you wish to discuss things, it can be with anyone of your choosing. Just so you're aware, I have quite a bit of experience with many different sexual orientations and beliefs and would be happy to help you navigate, or to simply listen and offer support. Whatever you need, I'll happily give. I understand how difficult this could be for you, particularly here."

Celeste did cry then, two hot tears streaking her cheeks as she nodded, and Lulu moved closer and wrapped her up in a hug.

"I'm assuming you're okay with hugging as we've done it before and you seem to be a bit of a melter, which tells me you're okay with it."

"Yes, yes, I'm okay with this. I need this. Thank you." Lulu held her like that, her hands running the length of her back and her arm, until Celeste straightened and she released her.

Lulu turned her gaze to the table. "Okay, I'm hungry. How about you?"

And just like that, they moved on. Celeste thought she'd feel awkward with Lulu until they arrived at Eildon, but what she felt was quite the opposite. It was almost overwhelming the amount of love and support she was receiving from this family of near strangers. It filled her, while at the same time it emptied her soul for want of having that from her own family. She vanquished it from her thoughts and uncovered another serving tray.

She could get used to this. To having friends, to having family, to not being judged for what she looked like or how she felt. To not having to actively hide and make herself smaller lest she draw the ire of those around her.

Celeste was beginning to feel strong and powerful. Frankly, she was starting to believe the people who'd passed her over, tried to get rid of her, or hated her for trivial things were truly missing out. She could easily see in the eyes of this family something Celeste had known all along, that she was beautiful, intelligent, and worthy of love and companionship.

Calder

alder sank into the tub again once the water was drained and refilled, this time to simply soak some of the soreness from his muscles. He was informed supper would be in two hours, then he was locked in this room, so Calder—after searching the room—ran a bath, finally, and then another. It wasn't possible for him to soak in the first bath, as filthy as he'd been, but the second was almost heavenly.

He should tell Madoc to upgrade his water closets to include showers.

He let his head fall back to the rim of the clawed tub as he thought of the last time Quinn had come to him and complained of the shower.

Devil, please, Quinn had said. It always made him tremble, that. Devil was a small simple word, but the meaning behind it was thick and full, because it contained every moment, from the first utterance to the last, in that one word, every single time. Because whenever Quinn said Devil, Calder heard I love you.

Calder closed his eyes and adjusted himself, Quinn's words from their last night together coming back to him.

It's not that simple…because it's you, Calder, it's you…

If you're hurt I want to talk to you, not be abused by you…

Hell, Calder thought as he sat up in the tub, his muscles regaining what tension he'd managed to lessen. He'd been the worst of men that night with Quinn. He'd let his pain and fear surface as anger and hate. But it hurt, physically hurt, to see Quinn with that woman. Celeste. His wife. No doubt they'd already consummated their marriage and were on their way to their first brood. Except Quinn had followed him to India. Why would he do that?

Calder stood from the bath a bit too fast as he stumbled toward the closest wall and held on. He reached out to take the towel that had been left for him on the rack. Goddammit all. What could Quinn possibly mean to do by coming here? His head spun as he stumbled from the bathing room into a room with a bed and two padded chairs. There was a wardrobe and window on one wall and a locked doorway across from it that led to the balcony over the courtyard of the haveli.

He needed to start paying better attention to everything around him. He managed to open the wardrobe to find several tunics and trousers. He pulled trousers on and a tunic over his head, keeping one hand anchored on the wall as much as he was able to prevent falling over. He slid his feet into the slippers just as the door opened and Madoc came into the room. "Do you have Quinn?" he asked before he could stop himself.

"Quinn? Ah, yes, our cousin. Concerned for him, are you?"

"Of course I am, considering your threats against my family," Calder replied.

"Our family, and I have no need for Quinn, do I?" he asked as he inspected Calder too closely for his liking, so he turned his face to the window, swaying on his feet. He heard Madoc laugh. "Come on, you need to eat more to regain your strength."

Calder turned back to him. "And what then? Are we friends now, Madoc? You kidnapped me and chained me to a wall for however long it was, and now that's all swept beneath the rug?" Calder leaned his shoulder against the wall.

"I'd never pretend to be that crass, Calder. I simply have no use for you—dead or alive—other than to bring certain men to justice so I can freely return to England for what is mine."

"I see. So you've had a good lie-down and dreamed up a new strategy, then?"

"Something of the sort. It'll do for now. Come on," he said with a weirdly playful shove to Calder's shoulder. "Let's dine."

Calder stared down at his shoulder for a moment, attempting to reconcile these friendly gestures with the man who had taken him hostage.

"Calder!" he yelled from the courtyard, and Calder finally leaned away from the wall and followed. What he wouldn't give for some insight into Madoc's behavior.

Calder left the room to find Madoc paused at the top of a staircase, patiently waiting for him. He cocked an eyebrow as he did so, and from that angle with the right side of his face turned away, Calder would swear he was looking at his cousin Gray—not Madoc. He didn't remember them being so similar when they were children, but then, he'd been preoccupied by other things.

Calder trailed behind him, descending the steps carefully, holding tight to the railing as he followed him into a dining room, which was open to the courtyard. Madoc motioned to a chair near the end of a table that would easily seat twenty, then took the seat at the

head of the table adjacent to him. Madoc lifted one finger from the table, and several servants stepped forward, presenting trays of food. Calder's mouth watered.

The colors, the textures, the smells, they flooded his system then as though it had been so very long forgotten. He took the food to his plate, this time avoiding the dishes he knew to be too spicy for his current digestion abilities. He tore at the bread, soaked up the sauces, and ate. It was easier this time—having had a bit of food earlier that day—and Calder's spirits rose.

He looked up to find Madoc staring at him instead of eating, and his eyebrows rose in question. "I was never much for the local cuisine," Madoc said.

Calder shook his head in disbelief. "You really must be mad," he said, instantly regretting it when he saw a shadow pass over Madoc's face, his eyes darkening before it all dissipated, and Calder was left wondering if he'd even seen it to begin with. "Sorry…about your father," he said quietly.

Madoc watched his hand as he spun a glass of water on the table in front of him. "Were I you, I'd be cautious in comparing me to my father."

Calder sat back to consider him. "So, what evidence have you to give the Crown of these machinations other than the letters you already sent to Warrick? That was not enough evidence."

Madoc groaned. "You could at least refrain from calling him that in my presence," he grumbled.

"You'll have to get used to it, you realize. Unless and until Her Royal Highness changes something, Grayson is The Warrick."

"Perhaps now, but not for long."

"So…evidence?" Calder asked, not wanting to rehash the fact that Madoc was mad at Gray for taking up the title.

"Paperwork including lists and leases, reports of missing women and children, photographs—" Madoc turned away. "Photographs—condemning photographs," he finished.

"All of them? Soundringham, Exeter, Bentleigh?" Calder asked.

"Yes, all of them, as well as Hepplewort and—my father, though they're already dead."

"That should be sufficient. Where is this evidence?"

"All in due time," Madoc replied.

"Oh, for fuck's sake, Madoc, what now?"

Madoc's gaze narrowed on him. "I'm in charge here, remember? I have to be sure you'll take me back to England a hero—for destroying this prostitution business."

"Ah…I'm sorry, did you say hero? Is that the new plan? You now wish for me to paint you a…hero? To whom, Her Royal Highness? To my family? Who exactly needs to be convinced that you are this hero?"

"Everyone," Madoc said with a smile.

"Following right in Daddy's footsteps, then," Calder mumbled to himself. "Can I at least finish my supper before all that?" he asked blithely.

Madoc laughed. "It's what will be done if you expect to leave here and carry on with your life as before. There's no other way. I have the evidence. No one else has what I have against these men."

"Why didn't you come forth before? Why all these… shenanigans?"

"I've told you already, my intention was to make Gray suffer, to take his place—"

"Ah, yes, the hard road. And I ruined your plans for revenge. Lucky me. Never one to take the shortcut, were you, Georgie?"

Madoc stood, and Calder shied for once in his life, but Madoc turned away and left him alone in the room as Calder simply stared after him. He had to be unhinged. Calder shook his head and finished his meal. He wasn't about to lose out because his cousin was losing his wits. No telling when he'd be allowed to eat again.

When he finished, he walked the perimeter of the room, peeking his head through the doorways to find out where they went, but they were dead-end chambers save the servants' entrance, which went to the kitchens. That could be useful. He had to search this haveli and get out of here tonight. He went out into the courtyard, intending to do what searching he could there as well.

Twilight cast the haveli in shades of deep blue as he stepped out to the mosaic tile. Madoc was sitting in a chair with his feet up, smoking from a glass hookah filled with brightly colored fruit and leaves of mint. Calder went and sat next to him, to try to get more from him.

"We didn't spend much time together when we were younger. You're, what, at least five years older than I am?" Calder asked.

"Something like that. I think Roxleigh is the only one older than I."

"Your father…he didn't allow much free time for you and Xander."

"No, he didn't," Madoc said.

"We could have been trained up together. At least Rox and I were in the same circles when we were young, but—"

"My father didn't believe the Trumbull line to be of good stock. Salvageable stock, yes. Good stock, no."

"Ah, I see. Miscreants and deviants, then, were we?"

"Yes."

"That must have been quite lonely. Did you have any friends at all?"

"Not particularly. Grayson was allowed friends because nobody much cared what he did. They assumed with myself and Xan there was no possibility of him taking the title…but they were wrong, the lot of them."

"Yes. Funny that."

"Fairly certain that if my father is laughing from heaven, it isn't because of that but because I'm yet alive."

"I imagine. Though imagining your father laughing is a stretch I can't quite manage. He was never the jovial sort, at least whenever I saw him."

"He wasn't the jovial sort. The family had the right of it. I'm not sure how he managed to sneak into your ranks, actually. Most of the Trumbull lines are so very carefully cultivated. My father simply didn't belong, my mother—"

"She's well, you know. She and Poppy are well. In case you wondered."

"I'm aware. I manage to keep abreast of all that happens regardless of my current situation. I'm aware they've come back to Grayson as if he's the prodigal son returned, as if I never existed, as if I am not the chosen one, as if I was never there."

"Madoc, they believe you and your brother dead. There's nobody left but Warrick."

Madoc exhaled heavily, blowing smoke in Calder's face as his eyes narrowed. He imagined Madoc was becoming tired of asking him to refrain from his use of the title, but Calder wouldn't. The man needed to get it through his thick skull that Gray was The Warrick.

"Perhaps that's it, or perhaps it's that my mother and Gray and Poppy always were Trumbulls, whereas Lysander and my father and I were most definitely Danforths."

"Is that a bad thing?" Calder asked.

"Not if you're a Trumbull. Likewise, not if you're a Danforth, but the two don't mix well, I think we've come to realize."

"No, not particularly well." Madoc took a particularly heavy drag of the hookah, then blew rings of smoke up to the sky. "At least you have a talent to fall back on, should this whole reclaiming-your-title not work out for you," Calder said, motioning toward the smoke rings as they dissipated above their heads.

Madoc's gaze snapped to his, then he smiled, and Calder saw something of Grayson once again. He really needed to start sitting on his right so the scar was always present in his line of sight to remind him that this wasn't Grayson. That this man had chained him to a wall. This man had plotted the kidnaping of Gray in order to take over the title as his brother. Calder would do well to remember all of that.

"I find it unfortunate that I believe we may have been friends under different circumstances, possibly in a different life," Calder said.

"I find it difficult to believe that you would believe that," Madoc replied. "What do you truly know of me?"

"Point taken."

Madoc bumped his wrist, offering the hookah to him.

He took it warily. He sniffed the end of the hose. "Did you poison it while I wasn't looking?"

"No, but I'll keep that in mind for future enemies."

Calder lifted the hose and inhaled. The smoke tasted sweet and spicy from the fruit and the mint. He rolled it around in his mouth for a moment too long before exhaling with a cough.

"It's a bit strong to hold to," Madoc said with a grin. Calder coughed again, residual smoke puffing out in front of his face as he offered the hose to Madoc, but he waved him off and Calder took another drag, this time gentler, with more air mixed in.

"It's an interesting blend," Calder said, and Madoc nodded then, this time taking the proffered hose.

"It helps me to relax, helps me to sleep."

"You have trouble sleeping, do you?"

"Dreams…they're not always welcoming."

"Perhaps try less kidnap and torture during daylight hours. I've heard it does wonders for restful sleep."

Madoc burst out with a laugh so hearty and genuine it was disarming, and Calder leaned away. It frightened him just how easy this had been. Just how simply he'd gone from captive to…what was he now? Captive acquaintance? He was still being held, not quite as much against his will, though he hadn't actually tested that. He had the feeling that if he'd chosen to leave, Madoc would have stopped him.

"That was brilliant. You're quite funny when I'm not so angry with you," Madoc said.

"Yes, well, so is a tiger friendly when it has eaten its fill of gazelle."

Madoc laughed again this time, more to himself. "Yes, well," he repeated, "we do what we must." And just like that, he was serious again.

Calder considered the room he assumed he'd be sleeping in if he couldn't find a way out. The wardrobe was much too heavy to move by himself to block the door, but one of the chairs might work, and if that failed, he could always balance a pane of glass taken from the window on the door handle so it would break should someone enter. Madoc might just be more terrifying now that he was off the wall than when he was on it.

"By the way," Madoc began quietly.

Calder regarded Madoc.

"I have a gift for you."

Calder raised his eyebrows in question, and one side of Madoc's mouth kicked up in a grin as his eyes turned cold, and Calder shuddered.

"Come," he said as he stood.

Calder followed him warily from the courtyard across to the opposite side of the haveli from the rooms he'd bathed in. They went up another set of stairs, and Madoc unlocked and opened the door to another room. Calder stood on the balcony that wrapped around over the courtyard, staring through the door into the darkness of the room—a chill rushed his spine. He wasn't sure if he should cross that threshold, or if he'd pushed his luck and he should turn tail and run. He contemplated Madoc, who motioned to the darkness in the room and watched, grinning. Calder was once again terrified that he was looking upon the next measure of his captivity.

"You're the worst," Calder said. Madoc laughed, and Calder stepped into the room.

"Please," Quinn begged when the door opened.

"Please what?" Calder asked.

"Please stop tormenting me." Quinn closed his eyes. If he didn't allow himself to see the man of his dreams, maybe he'd dissipate quickly to the recesses of his mind and leave him be to rest.

"You wish for me to leave?"

Quinn choked down the yes because he couldn't bring himself to lie. The truth was he wanted Calder to stay, but Calder never did. Not in the real world and not in his dreams, and Quinn didn't think he could deal with losing him over and over again for very much longer. "No…I don't ever want you to leave me again." He knew by now that it was simply another dream, but he couldn't help himself. How could he send Calder away? How could he not?

"I've naught to do with this torment. You bring it on yourself, Quinn, you know that."

"You do, because you're here." How was he supposed to control his dreams? He had to convince this Calder, the one who lived in his head, to stay away.

"But I'm not actually here, and somewhere in there you know it. You know this is another dream."

"But I'm not listening to myself either. The part of me that holds on to you is not listening. I can't take anymore. You've got to stop. I call you forth and I'm—I'm sending you away."

"A moment ago you didn't want me to leave."

"Because I don't! But this is pure torment, because you're not actually here." Quinn's chest constricted as a hand ran down the side of his arm from his shoulder to his elbow. It felt so real, then it dissipated with the sound of the door opening. Perhaps he'd won this time.

"Quinn?" The voice sounded strange, farther away than he'd judged. Quinn refused to open his eyes and allow his mind to trick him again. He listened to the footsteps move toward him, and the mattress dipped under his weight, making Quinn roll, their hips bumping.

"Please," Quinn begged.

"Please what?"

"Don't," he whispered. "Please don't make me beg. Not again."

"Quinn?"

The want to look at him was so strong that Quinn threw both of his arms over his face. "I'm sorry, I'm sorry for everything I've done, everything that's happened. I'm sorry you found out about us the way you did." His breath hitched and his voice caught. "I'm sorry I didn't stand up to my family sooner. I'm sorry, so sorry. For all of it I'm sorry, Devil. I love you, but please let me be—I can't take it anymore." His throat was dry, and the words hurt as he forced them out.

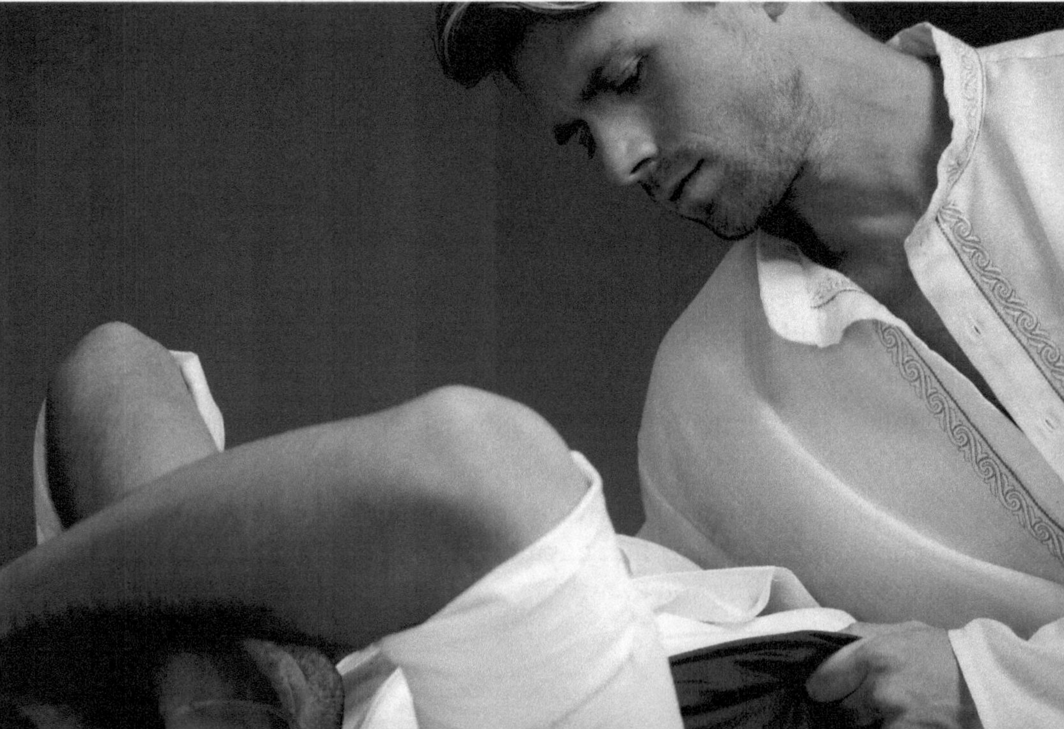

Calder's hands took his shoulders, tightening on them, giving him a quick shake. "Quinn, open your eyes."

"Devil, please, I can't."

"You can."

"I can't, not again. I can't look at you again only to see your body fade with the light. It's bad enough that I can feel you. It's bad enough to lose that much, but I can't…I can't see you fade from me again. Please go now, just… just go. Let me be."

"Quinn, I'm…I'm not going anywhere without you," Calder said against his cheek. The warmth of his breath sent a shudder through him, his body curling around Calder's as if to absorb his heat even though he knew it was bound to dissipate. Quinn took a deep breath, the scents foreign to him, but beneath the soap and the linen was his Devil. He tightened his eyes for fear they'd open too easily for want of seeing him.

"What the hell have you done to him?" Calder yelled, and Quinn froze.

"I haven't actually done anything but take him in and have him examined by a physician. The rest of this is his own doing," the man with the familiar voice said. That man wasn't part of his dreams.

Quinn reached for anything, any part of Calder he could touch. His fingers found the front of his shirt, curled around the opening, and knotted in the fabric as if he could physically anchor him here, then Quinn slowly opened his eyes. "Devil?"

The door shut, then locked. Calder's head dropped, then he turned back to Quinn.

"Devil?" he said again.

Calder nodded. He was gaunt. Smelled of mint and cardamom. His face was unshaved. He wore a tunic like the one Tarak had worn, but his was a blue color, or maybe it was just that the room was dark. His stomach clenched but had nothing more to give up. He broke out in a cold sweat.

Calder's hands tensed on his shoulders, and Quinn pulled at the tunic until they were within a breath of each other. "Devil?" he whispered this time. "You came for me?"

"God, Quinn, what the bloody damn hell are you doing here?"

Quinn pulled himself up to sit, his legs still stretched out on the bed, his hands still twisted in Calder's tunic. "I—I came for you. I came to explain."

"There's nothing to explain," Calder said.

"There's everything to explain. Celeste—"

"Your wife," Calder spat, and Quinn blinked at the ferocity with which he said it.

"My wife but—but not. Devil, it wasn't our fault. You must let me—"

"To what end, Quinn? You can explain it all you want, but the fact is that you're married. Married. You're…married." He said it as though he was allowing the knowledge to sink in. "Those whom God has joined together, let no man put asunder. How many times have I heard those words and feared them for this very reason? You have a responsibility to a wife. She will expect certain…" Calder closed his eyes, and his head shook as though he were trying to rid his mind of some horrible memory. "I cannot come between you."

"But she doesn't expect anything from me. She won't expect anything from me."

Calder's eyes snapped open, and Quinn took a sharp breath as the irises came to a sharp focus on him. "That's not possible."

"It is. She has no interest in me beyond friendship."

"So she says."

"And I believe her. If you speak with her, you'll believe her as well."

"Why would I?"

"She sent me here."

"For what?"

"For you."

Calder's breath stilled, and his eyes searched Quinn's face. Quinn refused to look away. He knew Calder would be able to see the truth of it. His dreams had taught him that much, at least. "And then what?" he said. "We return to England and all live happily ever after?"

Quinn swallowed against his dry throat, then saw how Calder's lower lip trembled.

"Regardless, none of that matters," Calder said with a shaky voice. "I've done enough in my life to draw the ire of God. I don't intend to come between a man and his wife. You—you…and your wife." Calder's voice bottomed out, as if he almost hadn't realized the words fully before they were carried away by his breath.

Calder's hands hadn't moved from Quinn's shoulders, and Quinn hadn't released his tunic. Quinn took a deep breath then reached, the distance between their lips disappearing as he closed his eyes.

He was a mere hairsbreadth away, but Calder pulled back.

"We can't," Calder said.

"No."

"No." Calder released his shoulders and searched his face. Quinn couldn't help but run his hands up his neck.

"You're truly here?" he asked.

"Sadly, yes. But nothing has changed, and we must get you back to London. You cannot be here, it's too—"

"Dangerous?" Quinn finished, and Calder nodded. "For whom?"

Calder stared into his eyes, dropped his gaze to his lips, his neck, to lower where their bodies were so tightly pressed together he could see nothing between them.

Calder's gaze came back, narrowed. "For both of us. But for different reasons."

"I love you," Quinn whispered. "I've given up everything—"

"In exchange for a wife. I'll not help you break those vows."

"But that's not—"

"I don't care what you have to say on the matter. How can I know the truth of any of it?"

"I've never—that is not my intent."

"And yet—"

"And yet?"

"You have no idea how this feels for me, do you? To see you with her? To see this intimacy the two of you have?" Calder took his hands and squeezed until Quinn relaxed, then pulled them from his tunic and leaned his back against the wall.

"I never meant to cause you any pain," Quinn said.

"And yet…just seeing you with her, Quinn." His voice quavered. Calder wiped his eyes, pinching the bridge of his nose, and Quinn sat up straight to truly study him.

"Devil," he said.

"I told you," he yelled, and Quinn shied from the power behind it. "I told you to stop calling me that."

Quinn stood and tucked what remained of his shirt into his trousers. He straightened his hair with his fingers, sweeping it out of his face. Then Quinn began to pace.

Quinn's eyes stung. His mind spun. His hands trembled. His stomach tightened. "Why? Why must I?" he asked. "That's us—*Devil*—that's part of us together. You've been pulling away from me this whole time. Ever since I met her, you've been leaving me. Why?"

"I just told you why."

"You promised me, Devil, you *promised* me."

"I promised I would always come back. But I intend to break that promise. You need to carry on with your life with her—without me. You'll be perfectly happy."

"Devil." Quinn couldn't catch his breath.

"Every—*goddamned*—time you call me that, it's like a knife through my heart, Quinn. What do you want me to say to you? We can't do this here. You have to get out of here. You have to go."

"I won't leave without you. I can't—"

"You can and you will. It's not safe. Madoc is probably just outside the bloody door listening to us as it is."

"Madoc?" Something shifted in his memory and tumbled into place like a lock. The man. He sounded like Warrick.

"Madoc," Calder said.

"Not—"

"Yes."

"But he's—"

"Apparently not."

The door swung open, and Madoc walked in like some sort of ridiculous punch line. "Is it time for the family reunion yet?"

"Oh, why the bloody hell not," Calder said as he stood and straightened the front of his crumpled tunic.

Madoc laughed.

Quinn shook his head. He pointed at him. "It's not… Wow, that's…a scar. I can't—you really look like Warrick," he said finally, and Madoc's jaw tensed, the muscles twitching below his ear, and Quinn backed up a pace.

"Quinn, allow me to catch you up. Madoc is angry because he's officially dead and Gray is The Warrick." He seemed to consider something for a moment. "Huh, I thought there was more, but that seems to cover it, doesn't it?" Calder asked Madoc.

Madoc frowned and twitched his head. Then he looked at Quinn. "Are you leaving or staying?"

"Staying."

"Leaving," Calder said at the same time. "He's leaving here. He has no part in this. I'm not even sure why he's here to begin with."

Madoc grinned. "Tarak brought him to me because he heard I was searching for a British man. He knows who I am and that I pay well. He thought he could get more money for him. Grayson has been gone from India too long, and my money is still good here while Grayson is no longer trusted. Tarak drugged him and delivered him."

"I meant in India, though. I appreciate… I have no idea what to say to any of that. Thanking you for taking Quinn hostage seems…"

Quinn sat back down on the bed and covered his eyes. He had no idea what was happening. Warrick had paid Tarak to bring him to Calder, but instead he'd sold him to Warrick's dead brother, who was now staring at him.

"You should rest more, drink more water. Eat something. Tarak gave you too much laudanum," Madoc said.

"He drugged me?"

"As I already said. Grayson told you not to trust anyone," Madoc said.

"How did you—"

"Listen, this is…endearing, really," Calder broke in. "I see you're already vying for that hero angle. But we need to leave. I need whatever information you have on those men so I can give it to the Crown to deal with. If you expect to be brought back to London in good stead, that's the first thing that needs to happen. That and you stop treating us like prisoners."

"I only locked the door so you would feel safe enough to talk. Because you know what the lock sounds like. Lends that feeling of security."

"How very thoughtful of you," Calder said derisively.

Madoc nodded, but his eyes narrowed.

"Madoc, I need the information."

"How do I know you won't turn on me?" Madoc asked.

"You don't. For once in your life you'll need to trust someone," Calder said.

Quinn looked back up at Calder, saw the shadows of his bones, the careful movements. The shortness of breath, the way the fabric hung from his shoulders. He stood and put an arm out to him. "Calder?"

"I'm fine, I just need to—"

"To what?"

"He needs to recover from what I did to him," Madoc said, cutting a glance at Quinn that sent him backing up again. A chill rushed his spine, and he scrubbed a hand through the hair at his nape to dissipate the feeling of it.

"Why would you involve him in that?" Calder asked, and blood rushed Quinn's head, thumping heavy in his skull.

"What did he do?" Quinn asked, but nobody was listening to him.

"Many reasons. They are my own," Madoc replied to Calder, and Quinn was lightheaded.

"You and your reasons, Madoc. Perhaps you should consider a new thought process, because whatever it is you're doing now to make decisions isn't the least bit rational." Madoc shrugged, and Calder turned his back on him. "This is pointless. I'm going to get some sleep. Wake me when you've made some reasonable decisions."

"I'll give you the information."

Calder turned back around, but Madoc wasn't looking at him, he was looking at Quinn, and Quinn didn't particularly like it. He held his breath as Madoc sized him up, and he tried to stand his ground.

"What do you mean, you'll give *him* the information?" Calder asked.

"I'll make the necessary arrangements to have the information released to Quinn. If you want it." He turned his gaze on Calder, and Quinn finally took a breath. "You return to London with him." Madoc stared at Calder as he pointed to Quinn, and his heart skipped like his finger had actually touched it.

Quinn watched Calder and thought the anger was truly going to get the best of the man. He looked quite prepared to beat someone to death, and Quinn was useless, like an accessory. He took stock of Calder. His bones were too evident, his shoulders curved as though he didn't want the fabric of his shirt touching his chest.

"Why are you doing this?" Calder asked, and Quinn simply watched Calder sway on his feet, like he'd been standing for much too long. He reached toward him, but Calder flinched and Quinn stopped.

"Because I want you away from me. I don't trust you here. And you have things to do that I've requested of you. It seems to me the best way to get those things done, and to be sure the both of you leave together, is to give Quinn the access to what you want. It makes perfect sense to me. Why aren't you following my logic?"

Calder's hands were shaking. "Your logic has taken entirely to many detours over the past fortnight. Why should it suddenly become simple?"

Madoc shrugged. "It has. Make your arrangements, Calder. You need to leave tomorrow. They're getting Rakshan now. I'd tell you to gather your things, but…I'm fairly certain you don't need the ruined trousers you wore here." Madoc laughed, then he turned and left the room.

Quinn stared at Calder. His blood ran cold. "What did he do to you?" he asked again as he reached for him, but Calder backed away.

"Nothing that concerns you," Calder replied.

"If it has to do with you, it concerns me."

Calder shook his head. "I have to find a way to stay here while you retrieve the information."

"If you don't return to London, he said he won't release it," Quinn said.

"Of course he did."

"I will not leave without you." He had to convince him to leave. He needed Calder with him, away from here.

"I can't leave Madoc here to his own devices. It would be irresponsible, considering…" Calder shook his head, and Quinn saw the moment he resigned himself to returning to London. With him.

"*What* did he do to you?" Quinn asked again.

"I didn't even have a moment's peace here," Calder said under his breath, fully ignoring the question, and Quinn was instantly guilty.

Calder collapsed to the bed, his head in his hands, and Quinn shifted toward him but heard yelling from the courtyard and moved to the balcony outside the room. "Rakshan is here," he said, and Calder pushed past him and headed to the stairs.

Celeste

She'd heard of Eildon Hill, but until she actually laid her eyes on it, Celeste had no idea the sheer grandeur of the place. "Rather large manor house and estate" was more than a bit of an understatement. The place was massive. The outlying structural buttresses, hidden as decoration over an exterior walkway around the house, only accentuated how truly large the manor itself was.

She walked into the foyer—it wasn't a foyer, it was…a small ballroom meant to greet people, with a massive stained-glass dome three or four stories above them, a staircase big enough for two hundred people, and an enormous round table that would hold more food than a local country fair.

She was overwhelmed. This wasn't a home; this was a palace.

"Celeste!" Francine ran down the stairs toward her, wearing buckskin breeches and a man's shirt and braces, and just like that the palace felt cozy and welcoming. She took her in her arms in a hug. "I've missed you. We have so much to catch up on," she said as she released her and leaned away.

"Look at you," Celeste said. "You're adorable."

Francine laughed as she hugged Lulu. "Well, I'm home and couldn't care less about society. I've had to get creative with the breeches, though, because my baby belly is getting too big!" She lifted the hem of her shirt between the braces and rubbed her round belly, and Celeste heard a masculine grunt behind her as Lulu laughed.

"I'll just go find Rox," Warrick said.

Francine and Celeste both laughed as well. He bowed over Francine's hand, then Celeste's, then kissed Lulu's cheek and moved swiftly through the entry toward the large double doors on the far side.

"Well. Enough talk of bellies. Now that we've done away with the men, would you ladies like to go for a ride? Or we could picnic in the labyrinth?" Francine asked.

"A ride? But you're—"

"Not a simpering miss, and I'm fully capable of riding for a little while longer, though it is becoming a bit uncomfortable astride. I never thought I'd appreciate a side saddle," Francine said.

"Since we just got off the train and out of a carriage, perhaps walking?"

"Perfect, I'll have Mrs. Weston send out a picnic. You guys want to change first? Of course you do. There's no need for this stuffy clothing here."

Stuffy clothing. Celeste was wearing her most comfortable traveling ensemble. It certainly didn't feel as comfortable as Francine looked in her riding trousers and man shirt, but it wasn't too terrible. She shrugged.

"Celeste, would you like to borrow some trousers, perhaps? I have some that would fit you," Francine asked.

She nodded before she lost her nerve. Francine took her hand and led them both up the massive staircase to their rooms, then brought clothes for each of them to wear. In no time they were wending their way through the hedgerow maze at the back of the house.

The fountain at the center was the true jewel. Next to it was a perfectly placed table and chairs with a tea service. "How did they get here first?" Celeste asked.

"There are several ways in and out of the labyrinth, some more expedient than others," Francine said with a wink. "I prefer the scenic route, while Mrs. Weston and the kitchen staff prefer the shortcuts."

Celeste filled her plate with finger sandwiches and small cakes. "I didn't realize I was actually hungry—breakfast on the train was rather large."

"It was, but it's also been a while," Lulu replied with a smile.

Celeste shifted in her chair, the trousers such an odd awareness between her thighs...and higher. She was used to wearing drawers, of course, but they were open for convenience, and Celeste hadn't ever realized that having fabric against her mons, rubbing between her legs, would cause such an odd sensation.

"Getting used to the trousers?" Francine said with a smile.

"Ah…yes, it's quite unfamiliar. I apologize if I'm—"

"Don't apologize. It's just us. So…how have you been? That's usually such a trite question, but I am asking honestly. The last I saw you was the wedding." Francine reached out and squeezed Celeste's hand. "I am so very sorry about what happened, truly."

"I'm doing well now, though I'm still quite concerned for Calder and Quinn, of course. I wish one of them would answer me."

"You haven't heard from Quinn?" Lulu asked.

"Not since he arrived in Bombay. Though he had to travel to Jodhpur. I'm unsure whether he's there yet. I just—" She shook her head. She'd already said everything she could.

"If Gray has any news, I'll let you know. He hadn't heard from Calder since Alexandria and Rakshan since they arrived in Jodhpur. But it's quite hit or miss when you're dealing with people so very far away. Not to mention there's still some issues with the British occupation. Telegrams go missing. If he missed Rakshan by minutes, he still won't get it until he returns—unless he has a reliable errand boy. At least that's what Gray said. It's all so crazy to me that the world isn't even wireless yet. Like, not even radio."

"Radio…" Celeste said quietly as her eyes lost focus. "I had a small clock radio with the loud click numbers when the time changed. They were on a loop, and the top half would flop down and the next number was visible. I remember recording…who was it?" She closed her eyes. "Prince on the late-night show, listening to 'Purple Rain' and 'When Doves Cry' over and over again. Oh…

radio," Celeste said. She remembered. All of these small things that seemed so foreign that she knew her family would have dismissed as lunacy were actual small pieces of her past. Just listening to Lulu and Francine talk about things brought back memories, like her mother reading "Jabberwocky," and random words like "radio" reminding her how much she'd loved music.

Francine watched her for a moment, then smiled. "I think my father had one of those weird clock radios with the flip numbers," she said. "It was funny that he didn't trust digital clocks yet, but his was plugged into the wall. How much more reliable was it when the power went out?"

"Right?" Lulu said. "Prince, I miss him. That music, he was raunchy and smart and amazing and gave no fucks about what people thought of him. It was a beautiful thing. I loved 'Gett Off' and '7.' Wow. God, I miss my iPhone all over again now."

"I don't remember those," Celeste said.

"I miss my iPod," Francine replied. "So much."

"What's an iPod?" Celeste asked, and they both looked at her.

"You left before the iPod? I'm sorry, really. They were life-changing," Lulu said.

"Definitely," Francine said. "Let's see, you were born in the seventies, so the Walkman? They were like that but didn't require tapes or CDs. They were tiny hard drives built to hold music, that's it."

Celeste shook her head. "Wow." She contemplated the fountain and considered how much of her life there she'd missed. Was it better to not remember certain things?

"You know, we should work on a timeline," Lulu said. "Birthdays, last days, that sort of thing. I wonder if we could manage sending a message? We'd talked about sending a message on the back of your portrait. Obviously, there are now three of us—it's possible there will be more of us."

"What would you say to them, or us?" Francine asked.

"I would tell you to find me," Lulu answered, and Celeste turned back to the conversation, watching the two of them volley thoughts between them as if it were the simplest thing in the world. She wanted that, she needed that carefree closeness to other women. To these women.

"But…I don't think we did, because wouldn't you know about it now?" Lulu said.

"Oh…now we're getting into Sheldon territory, chaos theory and time theory and all that craziness."

"Sheldon…" Francine cocked her head. "Cooper? Big Bang! Ha, he was such a nerd," she said.

Celeste shook her head; she had no idea who they were talking about.

"Perhaps we never know whether or not our message gets out, but shouldn't we try?" Lulu thought for a moment. "Okay, so you said you thought we switched bodies, because of the journals you found from Melisande, right?"

The journals. Celeste wanted to see them.

"Yes," Francine said. "She said she met someone who said they were from the past. But we're also talking about a woman who was unstable for reasons we can't pinpoint. We only assume it was because she was from the future and couldn't handle being thrown back in time."

Celeste's blood chilled in her veins. She knew what it was to be treated as insane. She knew it quite well, in fact.

Bring me that imbecile there…

Take that idiot back to her room…

"Well, yeah. The whole thing is crazy. So let's assume we can send a message to someone in the future. What do we say?" Lulu asked, bringing Celeste from her thoughts again.

"I would send Cecelia to help Madeleine, I think," Francine said. Then she turned to Celeste. "Celeste? Are you all right?" she asked as she reached out and took her hand.

Celeste hadn't shared much of her memories yet, but here in this clearing at the center of a labyrinth with these two women who knew so much, and were so confident…these two women she wanted as friends, wanted to trust. "My name was Grace. I left in April of 1988. I was ten," she said quietly.

Francine said, "My father wrote about a young girl named Grace. I thought it—" She seemed to choke and swallowed past a lump in her throat. "She was but a child. You, you were only a child? I knew you were born in the seventies, but I hadn't thought to ask…it was hard enough for me coming here as an adult."

Celeste looked away but couldn't stop the tears from falling so suddenly. Francine and Lulu both reached out to her, each taking one of her hands from her lap and squeezing, but it had the odd effect of leaving her open and feeling raw, her hands literally pulled out to her sides where she couldn't double in and guard herself. She dragged her hands away carefully, not wanting to insult but needing to shelter her body somehow, even as it was her emotions that were more in jeopardy than anything. "Do you think we told your father to find Grace?" Celeste asked quietly.

Francine shook her head. "I don't know. My father knew of her because he found her journal."

Celeste covered her mouth. Her eyes stung, but she couldn't staunch the tears as they came. "Did you…did you read her journals?" They were her journals, they weren't someone else's journals, but she couldn't reconcile it. Not yet. She pushed one finger against the tip of her nose to try to staunch the tears.

"I didn't," Francine said. "I'm sorry to say, I thought my father a bit crazy. I'd started to look into his research, but that was only recently. Just before I came here. When I graduated from college and got my own place, I finally opened the boxes of what was left from my real parents, and there were things, the portrait, his papers, some leather-bound journals."

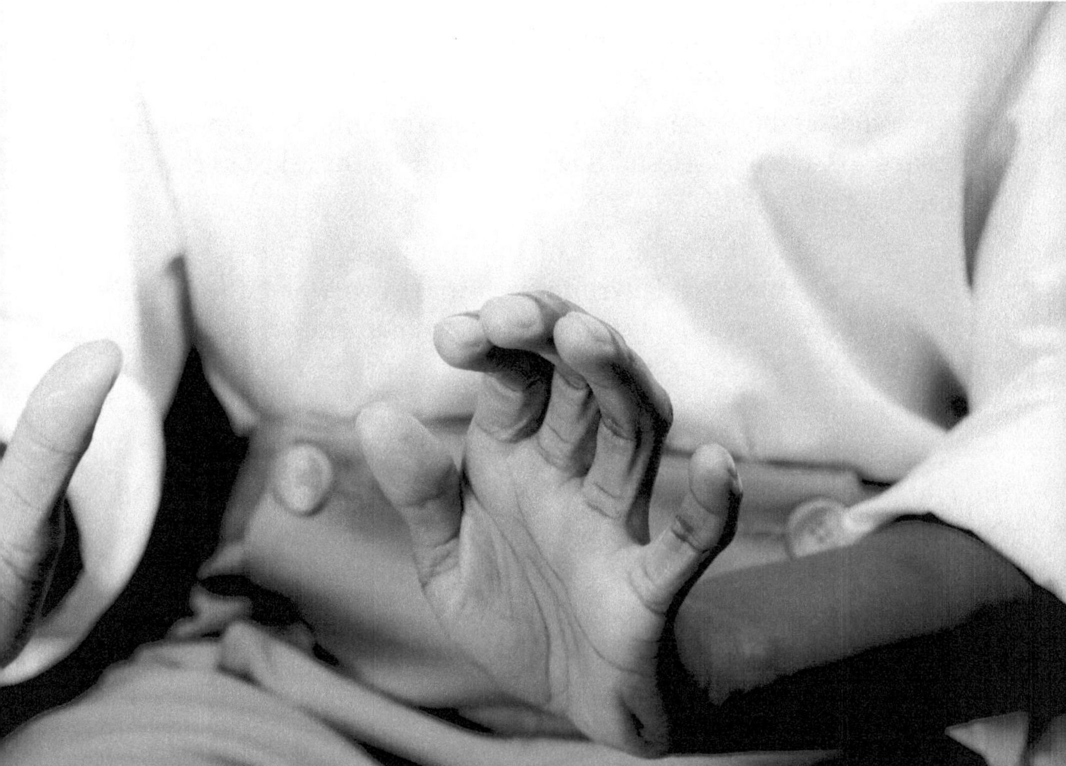

"My journals," Celeste said, "survive me."

"I believe they might. I believe it's possible you said something in those journals. It's possible that Melisande's journal is one that survives as well, but I hadn't looked close enough at all of them to recognize it now," Francine said.

"Would you like to be called Grace?" Lulu asked.

"No, I—" She stopped. She didn't feel like Grace. "For now, no. I've had Grace so very much trained out of me I don't think I would hear it, but perhaps in the future. Or not, I don't…" She shook her head. Some man in the future had her private journals. He read them. He knew her deepest secrets.

"It's okay, Celeste, you can change your mind about anything at any time," Lulu said. "I've only been here for a few months. It's a crazy ride, and I can't imagine navigating it as a child."

Francine spoke up. "That's why I want to send someone to Madeleine. I don't think she speaks English. If she does, it's very little. She must be terrified, or she will be terrified, whatever it is. If she had someone who understands, it may be easier for her."

"But you're the catalyst, Francine. Only you have access to the journals and the portrait."

"Not necessarily. My father had access to them. He read them." Francine became quiet.

"What is it?" Lulu asked.

"I could warn him…I could save their lives," Francine said.

"Who?" Celeste asked.

"My parents. I remember the date, the moment they died. I could warn him."

Lulu shook her head. "I'm not sure that's something we should even consider. Perhaps we should rethink all of this."

"It's not like we don't have plenty of time to consider," Francine said.

"Do you think we told him to find Grace?" Celeste asked quietly.

Francine shook her head. "We can't know. The only women we can warn are those who are already here."

"Except, wherever the journals are now…someone has them. Don't they?" Celeste said.

"Yes, Madeleine, if they collected my things from the taxi and took them to the hospital with me—her. If they didn't…those could be lost forever, but there are more in storage."

"My camera survives," Lulu said. "The camera Gray gave me…it's the same one. I'm certain it's my camera because of a flaw in the wood."

They sat in silence for a while, simply considering, until Celeste spoke up. "I want to thank you both for being so very welcoming. For being so warm and lovely. Even when I was just a normal girl, a perfect stranger. You had no reason to help me or to be so welcoming. I very much appreciate that."

Francine smiled. "I know your family was quite different from ours. I'm so very glad you've joined us."

"I agree," said Lulu. "I could use a few more smart women to hang around. I love Gray, I really do. But ladies, I need me some girl time." Lulu smacked her leg when she said it, and Celeste laughed. "Seriously," Lulu continued. "We need to have a sleepover, like Grease-style with the toenail polish and pillow fights. God, Francine, does Gideon ever think you're crazy?"

"Of course he does, but he says it's part of my charm."

"Well, yes. Gray and I—we're still getting used to each other. It's difficult to be myself fully with him because I'm still scared I'm going to frighten him. He has enough to deal with. He doesn't need his wife acting like a lunatic. Though I certainly wouldn't mind if he treated me for a wandering uterus."

Celeste choked on the sip of tea she'd just taken, spitting it across her plate.

"Did you—Lulu!" Francine said.

"I'm sorry! I just find it hysterical that…wait. Hysterical and hysteria… okay, so hysteria is wandering uterus and both are 'cured,'" she said, using air quotes, "by giving the woman an orgasm. Wow, this world and the things we've done to women in the name of medicine."

"Well, curing hysteria by uterus relocation isn't so bad when compared to some of the things they do. I mean, if you refuse to do the dishes and your husband isn't of a mind to keep you, he can have you committed. Pretty sure there are no wandering-uterus treatments in Bedlam," Francine said.

"No, I imagine not. Something else I want to help change. I mean, I'm here, so I have to do something. I can't sit idly by and let the world happen around me because I'm not from here."

"No, I feel the same. I've been working in smaller ways, though. The orphanages, education for women, suffrage…" Francine said.

Lulu nodded.

Celeste basked in the brilliance contained in these two women. "I wish…" she started. They both looked her way and waited. "I wish I'd been older, knew more of the world before I came here. But I do know I want to do something for the children who are sent to that asylum."

"I think that's a perfect thing to work for," Francine said.

"I can't imagine what you've been through, Celeste. I imagine you're lucky to even be here with us now," Lulu added.

"I am," Celeste admitted bluntly. It was absolutely true. "It's because I gave in and accepted the things they were telling me—but not before…not before I was treated for insanity. I can't—"

"Nope, and you don't have to. Just remember we're here if you ever wish to," Lulu said.

"Yes, if you need us," Francine added.

Celeste couldn't help but smile then. "Lulu, you…you said you're different even from Francine. How so? If you don't mind me asking."

"Oh, we're putting it all out there today, then? All right. Well, I know Francine is hetero and vanilla," Lulu started, but Celeste shook her head and Francine raised an eyebrow at her. Lulu laughed. "But I…um—I enjoy BDSM." Lulu smiled.

Francine gasped, her hand coming up to her mouth. "Really?"

"I don't…I don't know what that means." Celeste said, and she found herself biting her thumbnail, so she dropped her hands to her lap and twisted them together.

"It means I appreciate power play and other things. I won't go into too much detail because it's my bedroom and that's personal. However, I'm happy enough to share that much of my life with the two of you, and should you have any generalized questions, I'm happy to answer those as well."

"I still don't understand what that means," Celeste said.

"BDSM, bondage and discipline, sadism and masochism, domination and submission. It's a blanket term for all sorts of different sexual proclivities that focus on power."

"Sexual…proclivities?" Celeste asked. "These are things people enjoy sexually?"

"I think sex is mostly about some sort of power play no matter how vanilla a couple is. Man on top, woman on top, that's all inherent power structure. Some of us just like a more defined and more aggressive or powerful demonstration of those things."

Celeste blinked when her eyes unfocused as she thought back to Quinn and his inherent power over her. Without his commanding presence, she never would have started in that room. True, she'd shut the door and stayed, but if he'd turned away or told her to go, she would have. But then…he had tried to approach her and she'd refused. Perhaps that was the power play, that they were so balanced, that give-and-take between them. She shook her thoughts off and looked up to find Lulu and Francine still discussing it.

"That's so cool. So in your former life you also…" Francine waved her hand in the air as if to say the words.

"In my former life I was a professional dominatrix. I helped people discover themselves," Lulu said.

"That is so…cool!" Francine said again. "I can't even imagine. I mean, I'm not interested personally, but…huh. That seems like it would be pretty fulfilling as a job, helping people discover who they are sexually."

Celeste dropped her gaze, not wanting to give her thoughts away. Those stolen moments with Quinn were exactly what had helped her find her way. She'd had an idea before, but it hadn't been until she was faced with Quinn and Calder, then herself, and then Quinn, that she'd really embraced who she was.

"It was quite fulfilling," Lulu said. "My clients, most of them, were incredible people. Some of them I miss quite a lot," she said, her voice trailing off.

"I'm so sorry," Celeste said quietly. "It must be difficult to have such a close relationship and then to have it taken away so suddenly." Like Quinn. She knew that pain keenly as a small something twisted beneath her heart as though to remind her it was still there.

"Suddenly, yes. I was in the middle of a scene when I came here," Lulu said then.

"Whaaaaat?" Francine said. "How come you never said anything before now?"

"I was nervous…you know, it's hard to tell who will be open to certain things, and I'm perfectly all right with people not being accepting of who I am, but with you…you were my only connection to my life. I couldn't lose you." Lulu sobbed suddenly, and Francine came around the table and sat in her lap, wrapping her arms around her.

"Don't cry, my dear sweet Lulu. I love you no matter what," she said as Lulu's arms wrapped about Francine's expanding waist. They stayed there for a moment, just chatting about where they'd come from—a flaming crinoline incident and a carriage accident—and Celeste was content to listen. She thought, though, as she had already several times this day, that she had to be the luckiest woman in all of England to have been sent to live here and to be part of a family like this. She was suddenly overwhelmed, and before she knew it, she sniffled as well.

"Oh, Celeste, are we leaving you out?" Francine asked, and she stood and swiveled until she was on Celeste's lap, wrapping her up in her arms and rocking her back and forth as Lulu stood and bundled them both in a big hug.

"What is this, then?" The deep voice filled the clearing, and Celeste froze, as did Lulu and Francine.

"Rox, you frightened us," Francine said.

Celeste looked up to find Warrick standing behind Lulu, his hands on her shoulders, her hands dancing along his bare forearms. Roxleigh came and picked Francine up as if she were a bird with hollow bones, cradling her in his arms because he clearly believed her the most treasured woman in all of England.

Celeste twisted her hands in her lap, sad for the loss of heat from Lulu and Francine. Witnessing such great love filled her in a different way, though. It wasn't the same as seeing Calder and Quinn together, but it was such a deep feeling of love and trust that it filled her with a certain warmth.

Francine kissed Roxleigh's cheek then patted his shoulder and twisted out of his arms. "We were just having tea. Would you like to join us?"

"No, but thank you. We only stopped by to let you know we're going for a ride, but we'll return by supper."

"All right, then. You boys behave," Francine said.

"Boys?" Roxleigh said as he backed her up until her hips hit the edge of the fountain wall in the center of the clearing. "I promise you, madame—I am no boy," he said and took her in such a sweeping, searching kiss that Celeste closed her eyes and turned her head, but still she heard Francine whisper.

"Certainly not," she said.

When Celeste peeked to see if it was over, she realized Lulu and Gray had disappeared into one of the lanes of the hedgerows. What they were doing…well.

Roxleigh stood and straightened his waistcoat as Francine rolled his sleeves down and pulled his cufflinks from the pocket of the waistcoat to put them in his cuffs. It was such a normal, endearing thing to do. The woman knew what he did with his cufflinks when he took them off. "I left your gloves in the stables. Don't forget them. I don't want any new scratches I don't put there," she said quietly, and Celeste couldn't help but giggle.

"I knew you were fierce!" Lulu yelled from somewhere in the bushes.

"I never said I was vanilla," Francine replied with a crooked grin and a wink at Celeste.

Overwhelmed. Celeste was overwhelmed. They spoke on personal things so easily, so openly, so boldly.

Roxleigh laughed off a confused expression and shook his head. "We're off. We'll see you in a couple of hours."

Francine pecked his cheek and pushed him away.

"Warrick!" he yelled, and Warrick tripped from behind a hedge and followed behind as Lulu came out, straightening her shirt and trousers.

Celeste tried to smile at Warrick. His expression was cold, always so very serious.

"Well, that was a fun little interlude," Lulu said, and Francine laughed.

"I want to live with you all forever," Celeste said. "This place is big enough. Can't we all just live here?"

"That would be fun. We do have several house parties, and no doubt you'll join us for plenty of visits. You'll find it does get tedious having others around all the time, and I'm certain your husband would object to your absence," Francine said.

Quinn would object, but Calder…she was fairly certain he'd be happy for her to take up residence far from them. "I suppose…I've just been alone for so long. I love watching you be a family. I love watching—" Heat flushed her skin. She covered her face and looked away.

"Celeste?" Lulu said. "Are you okay?"

"Yes," she mumbled. But she wasn't. Tears streaked her cheeks and filled her palms as they cupped her face. She felt hands on her shoulders, soothing her arms.

"No, you're not. What can we do? Anything?"

"No, I…" She wiped the tears from her face stiffly, then dropped her hands. "That reminded me of the first time—well, when I saw Calder and Quinn together. I just…it was a powerful memory, I guess. I was overwhelmed, but I'm all right. I simply wish I could… I don't know what I wish."

"Together?" Lulu asked, and Celeste flushed again, covering her face. "Okay, hey, let's talk about something else—I know you miss Quinn. I don't want to bring you down today."

"Not today," she said quietly. "Thank you."

Francine and Lulu took their chairs, and Francine poured herself a little more tea then pulled a flask from the basket under the table. "Look. I can't have any of this French brandy, but it doesn't mean you ladies can't," she said, and Lulu laughed.

"I will if you will," Lulu said to her, and Celeste gave one quick nod. Why the hell not?

Calder

It certainly wasn't the best of the ships sailing from Bombay, but at least it was comfortable. Rakshan had managed to secure larger private quarters for he and Quinn—but not independent quarters. They'd have to make due.

Calder lay on the bed staring out the porthole at nothing but sky. He was trying to be amenable for Quinn's sake, but just being around him was a knife to the gut every time they shared a glance, and Quinn didn't seem to understand.

He kept insisting that Calder would understand once they returned home. But Quinn wasn't listening to what Calder was saying. It didn't matter. None of it mattered. It mattered that he was married, and that was it. Calder couldn't help him break his vows. They'd been taken in a church, before God. He wouldn't. He and God had enough disagreements as it was.

He turned away from the porthole to stare across the small cabin at the berth Quinn used. He was currently in the shower, the one amenity they did have on this ship, even if the water went cold much too fast. He should leave before Quinn was finished and came out. Just go on deck and wander, or go to the gymnasium. Perhaps he could spar with some stranger. He wished Rakshan had come with them; they could spar. There was no way he could spar with Quinn—one of them would end up dead, or very nearly so, most likely Calder since he was still so weak and he simply couldn't seem to rein his emotions in, a feeling he was wholly unfamiliar with.

Calder thought perhaps Rakshan had forced these close quarters, but Quinn had spoken with the crew; there were no other accommodations available. The ship was full. Rakshan could not have possibly arranged for all that, could he? No. Of course he couldn't. Calder wished he could have stayed behind in Jodhpur with Rakshan. Not here. Not close to Quinn. Not sharing this space with him.

The shower cut off, and Calder rolled over toward the wall, covering his eyes with his arm to feign sleep. He was too tired to try to get dressed and out of the room fast enough. The door opened, and every muscle in his body tensed as the breath left his lungs in a rush. The steam from the shower floated in and enveloped him, waking his senses as though to attempt to soften his resolve, but Calder pricked at the very thought of it.

"Would you like to join me in the dining room for luncheon?" Quinn asked.

Calder shook his head. "I think it would be better if we simply endured this trip as best we can without spending any amount of time together. I've notified the captain that I would prefer an independent berth if one should become available for any reason—"

"Are you hoping for someone to fall overboard?" Quinn asked.

"Nothing so morbid as that. People die…naturally."

"Oh, certainly, hoping for a natural death, that's not at all morbid," Quinn replied.

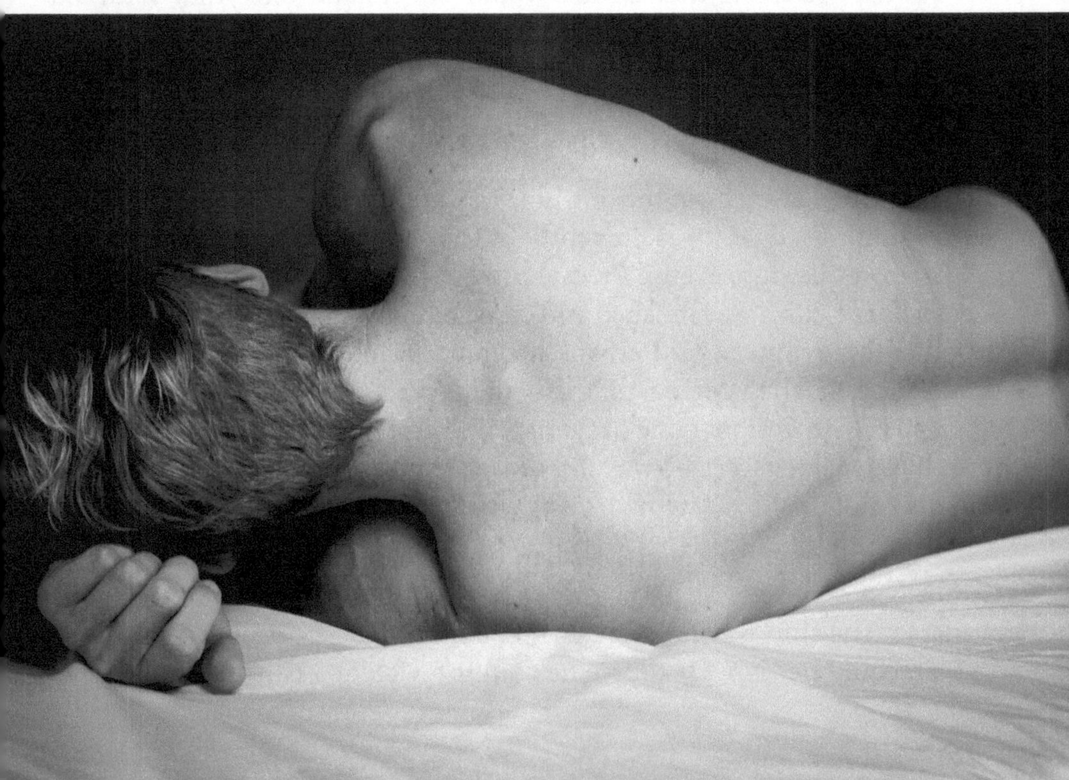

"Stop being friendly, Quinn. We are not friends, you and I."

"No, we aren't friends, Devil, and I don't suppose we ever have been. Don't you think it is about time we tried?"

Calder bristled at his use of the familiar. Every one of his muscles tensed then tried to jerk free. "What for?"

"We, at the very least, are cousins who will need to spend some modicum of time together whether we wish to or not. I would prefer it done cordially," Quinn begged quietly.

Calder refused to turn and look at him. He knew what he'd see—a face that could convince him of anything. "Cordial? I can be cordial. Just you wait and see how cordial I can be."

"I've seen your version of forced cordiality, Devil. It's quite frightening," Quinn said with a quick laugh, but he stopped when Calder lifted his arm and turned, catching his gaze.

"You want some sort of bastardized version of a friendship?" Calder asked through clenched teeth. "Rule number one, you don't get to call me that—ever…again." He nearly choked on the words. "Quit forcing me to remind you." The pain at the feeling of never hearing that name on Quinn's lips paled in comparison to the dagger that accompanied it every time he heard it now.

Quinn said reverently, "I will…I will endeavor to remember your wishes." Quinn swallowed, his throat moving against the collar of his new shirt. Then Quinn shuttered his gaze and tried to smile. It wavered. "In honor of this new accord, perhaps we could attempt friendship?" he started quietly, hopefully, his voice breaking, his eyes searching the room for somewhere to rest.

Calder stood and pulled his trousers on, then a shirt and his shoes. "Not today, Quinn. Try again some other time," he said, and he left the cabin a fully unkempt mess. He would shock the misses and the matrons. He didn't give a damn. He found the stairs to the upper decks and ran them two at a time, finally breathing when the humid air caught him full in the face, stifling his breath. At least, he told himself it was the air.

He walked to the back of the ship and scanned the water. Since they were on an older ship, unlike Quinn's new steamer, this one was driven by a large paddle at the back. He watched it spin, churning the water as it plowed toward the canal. He told himself Quinn would be fine. He didn't need to watch over him as Rakshan had told him to. Quinn was in the cabin; if the man wasn't well, he'd simply stay there. Quinn knew when to stay put. Calder felt guilty for leaving him there, effectively trapping him if he wasn't well enough to explore. He'd attempt to be more diplomatic on the crossing, give him time to go out if he wished to.

Quinn hadn't always been like this. At one point Quinn had been the one to push Calder, to bring him to heel. Calder missed that man, the power he'd wielded so easily and effectively over him.

They had a little over two weeks before they'd be in Alexandria—as long as the machinery remained in good form. Calder was hopeful, watching the paddle. It appeared sturdy and well assembled, not too much wear even as it wasn't terribly new.

He took a deep breath. Quinn was right about them being cordial. Eventually he'd need to reconcile that they'd be in the same places at the same times and he'd have to see Quinn with his wife. It wasn't as simple as avoiding society balls. They were family—a close-knit family. But friendship, that was beyond his comprehension at the moment.

The thought of seeing him with her…it still stopped his heart when he considered it. When he thought about Quinn taking her maidenhead and making her his and only his, it was like being opened balls to brains and letting her play in his entrails. She'd certainly been a maid when they'd married. She'd been well trained yet skittish. Quinn was absolutely the only man to ever breach that gate, and it would bind them in an irreversible way. Calder knew because Quinn had been his first as well—and there was no way to turn back and change how he felt.

Then there was the woman herself. Calder would have need to rub elbows with Celeste whether Quinn was present or not. Would it be better or worse seeing her without him? That bit seemed a bit more difficult for him to accept. He hadn't actually accepted any of it yet, but accepting her… he didn't know if there was enough cordiality in the world, which was exactly why he wanted to be in India and not returning to London.

Damn them all. Damn Madoc most of all. That bastard of a ghost should have stayed dead.

Calder turned to find a chair where he could rest, still recovering from that whole ordeal. And what was he supposed to do when Madoc finally returned? How was he supposed to tell Warrick about him? How would he tell his family?

He had no idea; the entire thing was beyond him at the moment. It was a perfectly horrible situation. Untenable. He leaned back in the chaise and closed his eyes and attempted to get some rest. He wasn't getting any sleep being in the cabin with Quinn so close at hand. All he wanted to do was touch him—but if he touched him…he didn't think he could ever stop. His restraint was exhausting him, but he didn't see how he'd be getting much sleep in there at all. Perhaps he could convince Quinn to sleep at night and leave him the cabin during the day.

Wishing for respite, Calder persuaded his mind to stop working and drifted off.

"They will arrive in London in roughly one month. I've verified they're on the ship's register," Warrick said.

Celeste stared, certainly for much too long. She'd never held this man's direct gaze for so long because he unsettled her. But now…she tried to see åcountenance of his. She felt a hand at her shoulder and turned slightly but still couldn't take her gaze from him.

He reached up and scratched at his jaw, glanced at whoever was standing next to her, then met her gaze again.

"Celeste," Lulu said, running her hand from her shoulder down to her hand and weaving their fingers together. "Come with me. Let's go for a walk in the gardens."

Celeste nodded but couldn't bring herself to move. Lulu's arm went around her shoulders, and she pulled her away. Celeste turned her head as she was led from the room, still watching him. Still hoping for something more. They reached the grand entry, and Lulu pulled the door closed behind them, and Celeste finally looked at her as they walked.

"Have you ever felt like the entirety of your life changed in a single second? As if you were on a certain path, and then, for whatever reason, it was all different and would never be the same again?"

"Something like that, yes," Lulu said.

"Of course—of course you do... I don't know what it is, but I feel as though…I'm terrified, truth be told. And I'm not entirely certain why. I can't put a pin in it. It happened when Warrick told me they were returning, the both of them. But there was nothing in that information or his tone that should have frightened me."

"He tends to have that effect on people," Lulu said as they stepped out the back doors from the ballroom to the large patio.

"It wasn't merely that, it was something more. There was…" She shook her head. "I don't know." Her hand came up and skimmed the pearls around her neck. "I don't know."

"I understand that somewhat as well, you know. There's something about these men we're drawn to. I feel as though I could tell you where Warrick is at any given moment."

"Yes, is that…is that part of this? Was I brought here for Quinn as you were for Warrick and Francine to Roxleigh? Warrick said Quinn was returning, and I knew it to be true. As simply as I know my own name, I knew. Is that part of it?"

"We think so."

"That's not…that's a terribly cruel trick. Quinn is in love with Calder, and I believe he always has been. As for me…I don't want anything from him, from either of them, beyond friendship."

"You really don't feel anything in particular for Quinn or Calder?"

"I do. I have this connection to Quinn. I feel that tether, like a slipknot on a rope that won't let go. I can see it, I can tug at it, and yet…" Celeste let go of Lulu and walked to a bench at the edge of the labyrinth and sat down. Lulu followed, sitting next to her. It took Celeste a while to decide how she wanted to say what she wanted to say. "I don't want that sort of intimate relationship with anyone. I wish to be part of Quinn and Calder's relationship in a peripheral way and nothing more. If they will allow me some small part of themselves."

"You don't want—"

Celeste shook her head. "I realize this is strange, but…I just don't want it. I think the very idea of it, the physicality of it…" She closed her eyes and thought immediately of Quinn and Calder and that night. Her breath shuddered through her, and she turned away from Lulu, attempting a small bit of privacy. "I think that's the best I can explain. I do feel something, but I don't want to touch or be touched. Any intimacy I want with them…is emotional, not physical."

"That's a reasonable request, and considering Quinn and Calder's relationship, I don't see why the three of you can't work something out."

"He hates me. Calder, he really, truly hates me."

"Calder? He's…he's such a lovely person. He is the nicest, funniest man. I can't…"

"Trust me, after what happened, he hates me. He blames me for ruining everything, and I did. He's right about that. I ruined it all, and Calder left, and then Quinn was forced to marry me. I have truly injured Calder by my actions. I don't blame him for his dislike, not a single bit. I deserve it." Her stomach tightened and her hands shook. She was angry with herself. She knew she couldn't change it, she knew she had no way of knowing what would happen, she knew it was irrational…but if she'd perhaps thought beyond what she wanted in that moment, things would be different. But she didn't want them different, so she added guilt to her list of shame. Her shoulders drooped.

"I don't know, Celeste. It seems to me it would take an awful lot for Calder to have such strong feelings for someone, and you…"

She shook her head. "I have Quinn. Imagine, for a moment, that it's Warrick."

Lulu stopped, and Celeste saw the realization sink into her. "God." Lulu stared across the lawns as Celeste considered.

"The Calder I saw socially, the funny, lighthearted man, was not at all the man I met that night when I followed Quinn."

"You followed him."

"Ah, yes, I…I followed him. I'd hoped to catch him with a mistress. I was hoping that I could persuade him to keep her on after we married—should we marry. But I didn't catch him with a mistress."

"You found him with Calder."

"Yes." She shook her head quickly; just the thought of them together started a slow drip down the center of her chest, thumping steadily against her mons. "God," she said as she turned away again, rubbing an arm across her chest to try to dissipate the visceral reaction she had to the memory.

"I think…" Lulu started, and Celeste closed her eyes. "Did you enjoy watching them, Celeste? Did that arouse you?"

Celeste dropped her face into her hands and curled over against her knees. Then she sat up straight and looked Lulu dead in the eye. "Yes. It did. It was the first time I'd ever felt that sort of attraction, and just the thought of them together is enough to make me want to…well. There must be something so very wrong with me."

Lulu smiled. "Actually there's nothing wrong with you. In fact, there's everything right with you, Celeste. So much so that we have a name for what you're feeling."

"What do you mean?"

"What we called this was autochorissexuality. It's a subset of asexuality in which a person has a disconnect between themselves and the object of their desire. If there are enough people to have a name for it, then, Celeste, you are not alone and there's nothing wrong with you."

"Auto—"

"Auto—choris—sexuality."

"Autochorissexuality. I'm not sure if I feel better having a name for this. It seems a bit of a relief that I can't be the only person to feel this way if there's a specific name for it." She tangled her fingers together in her lap.

"That's why I'm telling you. You aren't alone, but I doubt you'll find others like you here who are willing to discuss their sexuality so openly. So just know that there are others like you and it's perfectly all right."

"If that's true, I…I find it interesting that I don't have any desire when I see you and Warrick being intimate or Francine and Roxleigh, or even Lilly and Perry—and we were together in Paris for nearly a month. They were very much…I mean, they didn't hide their affections around me. It was endearing, but none of it arousing."

"That's reasonable. I mean, Rox is hot, but he doesn't do it for me. Warrick does. Perry is pretty handsome as well, and Francine, whoa, she is…well. She would have been my type, but I just don't feel that with any of them, but then the thought of Warrick, touching me, even just looking at me with that serious gaze of his." Lulu shuddered. "Uh, yeah, that…that will do it." She grinned and twisted her hands together in her lap. "Arousal isn't necessarily about the action, but more the person giving the action."

"Francine?" she asked quietly.

"Yes, I've had girlfriends. I love women as much as men, but Warrick—he and he alone—is my forever."

"Quinn likes women as well as men, but Calder…I don't think he's the same."

"I think I agree with you there, and perhaps it's something between Quinn and Calder they have to work out. Being bisexual with a partner who isn't can be difficult for your partner and other people to understand. How are you feeling? Are you okay? This is a lot of information, I think."

"I'm better, but I also feel worse—I mean…I can't be part of their relationship. And I don't want a relationship with Quinn separately. And it's strange to think about them when I…you know—but I've never felt this way before. I don't know how I feel. I just feel off-kilter."

"Okay, think of it this way. I used to get off thinking about all sorts of people. Tom Hardy, Charlize Theron, Idris Elba…"

Celeste shook her head.

"Right…eighties. Hrm. Han Solo?"

Celeste smiled; she remembered Han Solo. "I love you," she said.

"I know," Lulu quoted back, and they both laughed.

"Wow," Celeste said. "That came out of nowhere. I'd forgotten about that movie."

Lulu smiled. "Okay, so I may think about all of those people—their personality, that fierceness…"

"Warrick is definitely fierce. Menacing, I would call him menacing," Celeste said.

Lulu laughed. "He does menace well, that's for sure. My point is…oh, what was my point? Oh, right, there's nothing wrong with what you do in the privacy of your room using whatever's already in your head. I mean, if fantasizing about people was illegal, we would all go to jail."

Celeste nodded.

Lulu dropped her voice, "I have to say…I've seen gay lovers, and there is something so beautiful and primal and powerful about two men having at each other. Yeah, it's enough to curl anyone's toes."

"You've seen two men together?"

"Yes, in my former life. I witnessed all sorts of things at the clubs I frequented and worked in. Lots of people watch, Celeste. I think in some respect everyone likes to watch. Otherwise there would be no porn industry. The main difference being that you have no interest in joining and being part of the scene."

"No, I don't. I definitely do not want that. Calder was completely naked when he grabbed me and put me in the chair where they'd…" She groaned and hid her face once more. "I can't—I can't even talk about it. He was much too close. All of his nakedness was much, much too close to me."

"I bet he's a beautiful man when he's naked."

"Oh, yes, they both are absolutely stunning…I—I'm sorry."

"Celeste, don't apologize. You can tell me anything. Believe me, you won't say a thing that will shock me. It's not offensive to speak in an endearing way about someone you love. It doesn't break some sort of trust to speak about your own feelings."

Celeste grinned then.

"Are you wanting to try?"

Celeste nodded. "This is about me…my feelings."

"All right, then, lay it on me."

"The night before…the night before they found Quinn and I…the reason we were in bed together. We hadn't had sex. He hadn't touched me, except for my foot…a bit of my ankle… He was sprawled on his bed, naked, and he—he came off for me. Then he wanted the same in return, so I—I was in this chair with one leg, the one that he was touching, on the floor and the other leg over the arm of the chair, and he—his face was about eye level with the seat of the chair. And he would take a deep breath and close his eyes and smile," Celeste said.

Lulu stared at her. "Okay, yeah, that's…that's pretty hot. I totally underestimated Quinn. He always seemed a bit timid. I'm not quite shocked, but—"

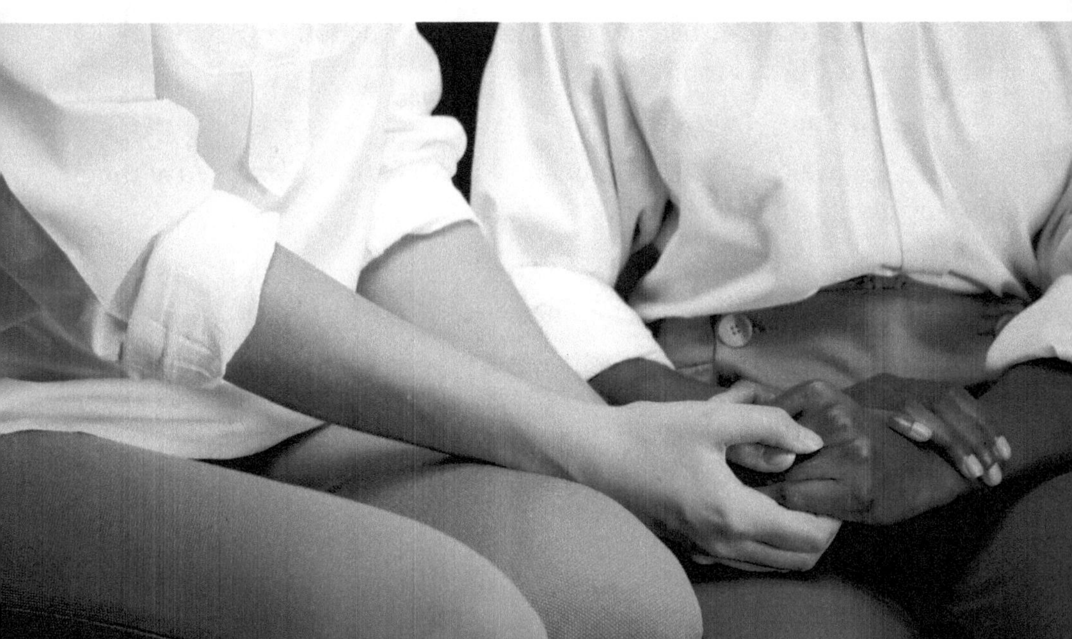

"And I'm not quite done… Lulu, he lifted his hand from my ankle and brought it to the chair between my thighs where a pool of my fluid gathered. He pushed two fingers into it then slid them into his mouth as though it was cake frosting." Celeste's skin was suddenly much too hot and much too cold. Her heart gave a stiff knock against her ribs, and she pressed her thighs together as tight as she could manage to stop the rush of blood.

"Fuck!" Lulu yelled, then glanced around to see if anyone was nearby. She leaned closer. "All right, that's…wow, that's probably one of the hottest things I've heard. He didn't even touch you?"

"No—and I think that was part of it, the fear that he might—but he didn't because he knew, so he took what he could get and…oh God, it was obscene, Lulu. Obscene. I came off for days on that memory alone once the shock of the wedding wore off."

"I bet, sheesh. Now I'm getting ideas of things to make Gray do." Lulu tapped a finger against her chin.

"You can't be serious!"

"What? Why not?"

"What are you all chatting about?" Francine said as she came out the back door and skipped across the patio and down the stairs.

The blood drained from her face, and Celeste turned away.

"Did you just skip?" Lulu asked her in a perfectly calm voice, as if they'd not just been discussing bedroom things.

"Of course I did. I've had my nap, and I'm feeling rather spry. Speaking of which, are the boys around?"

"In Rox's study," Lulu said.

"All right, well, I need him to help me run a bath." She winked at them and skipped off to find him.

"That's not what's happening, is it," Celeste said.

"Of course not. At least, not on her own."

"I thought society was much more proper than this—you're both duchesses."

"Yeah, well, we aren't their daddy's duchesses," Lulu said with a wave at the manor house. "And England isn't ready for either one of us," she finished with a wicked grin. "I bet if we went to the kitchens, we could convince Mrs. Weston to make tea and some of those little cakes."

"Oh, that would be lovely," Celeste said.

Lulu stood and took Celeste's hand and linked their arms, then pulled her across the garden and through the ballroom doors. This world she found herself in was so drastically different from anything she'd ever imagined. It seemed impossible. Strong, beautiful women who spoke their minds and shared secrets, wishes, hopes, and dreams? Being able to talk about her body and her emotions and the physicality of it all, the sex? This was not at all what Celeste had thought it was going to be like when she grew up.

Quinn

They would be in Alexandria on the morrow, and the best Quinn could hope for was a telegram from someone who wished for his company, because Calder avoided him at every turn. Quinn was lonely like he'd never been in his life.

Not being able to speak with Calder, to learn what had happened… it hurt. Having Calder so close but unable to touch him was the worst sort of discomfort, but he wouldn't give up. He'd stopped asking what had been done to him, but he didn't stop asking to try, because he was certain that eventually Calder would say yes. Calder never told Quinn to quit asking, and that gave him hope that something would change and he'd allow them to try to be friends.

Quinn would lie awake staring across the small cabin at Calder's back, and he knew Calder was aware of it by the cadence of his breath, the rise and fall of his shoulders, the way his legs moved and his hips shifted beneath the covers. He was equally discomfited by their proximity to each other. But calming that want was yet an impossibility.

Not knowing what had happened to him but knowing he was safe, not knowing where he'd been but knowing he was here now, not knowing why he'd been so weak but knowing he was getting stronger—it soothed and ached all at the same time.

Every morning Quinn would ask again if they could try, and Calder would inspect him as though he were measuring him, then simply say no and leave him be until it was too late to avoid going to bed…only to feign sleep. Neither of them was sleeping at night—he'd found Calder dozing on the deck one day, and he'd fallen asleep over luncheon leaning against the wall of the dining room until the butler came and shook his chair.

He closed his eyes, but sleep wasn't going to come tonight either. "Can we try now?" he said into the moonlit cabin.

"No," Calder said, and Quinn rolled over to the wall. Perhaps if he didn't stare at Calder's back all night, he could get some rest. He was very nearly there when Calder unexpectedly broke the silence. "I've had a lot of time to consider, and I've been thinking about something," Calder said quietly, and Quinn froze. "She's the girl, isn't she?"

"The girl?" Quinn blinked and rubbed his face. Had he fallen asleep? Did he miss something?

Calder fell silent.

Quinn turned over and sat up at the edge of his berth. Calder shook his head, as though he tried to erase an uncomfortable memory and move on.

"From the park, the girl from the park who was nearly trampled by horses. The one I couldn't pull you away from. That girl. Ten years ago in London after we…the day we kissed, in the forest—the first time."

Oh…God. Quinn hadn't even considered. He closed his eyes and hissed a breath between his teeth as his heart thumped against his ribs as though it knew better than he did. He shook his head. Could it be?

"She's one of them, isn't she? She was sent here for you. That's what it is. It was meant to be. This fated thing that is so prevalent in this damned family."

"One of… What are you talking about?" He needed to think, but his mind was simply not making all the connections he wished it would. "Do you truly think it's her?"

Calder sat up, stared out the porthole. Their knees were close enough that if Quinn leaned forward and reached out, he would be able to touch him. He didn't. "I think it's possible," Calder said. "I've thought on that day quite a bit. She came between us that day. You may not have felt it, but I did. She's always been there, this small wedge that kept you from giving everything to me."

"That wasn't her—that was me." It wasn't long after that day that a night in the same place had changed him forever.

"Same difference. Your surrender was much different after we met her."

"How could you think that? How could you—it wasn't her, it was something else."

"I felt it, I saw it. That day."

Quinn considered it; he'd experienced something unworldly that day, something completely foreign and unexplainable to him. But that wasn't what had changed him. "It wasn't her fault."

"So she is the girl."

"I think perhaps she is, though I hadn't…I hadn't remembered that day until you said—"

"It was that important to you, was it?" Calder said, cutting him off and contemplating him across the dark cabin.

The day we kissed in the forest—the first time.

"That's not what I meant. That day was important to me because of you. Not because of her, and she's not the reason—"

"The reason you faded?"

"Faded?"

"Like a photograph left in the sun too long. You were never again as vibrant as you had been that day."

"She's not the reason, Calder. You can't blame her for my difficulties. That I won't allow."

"You won't—then tell me what it was that changed you."

Quinn swallowed and stared off into the dark corner of the cabin. He closed his eyes as his heart gave a warning knock. They'd sworn to never speak on it, and perhaps Calder had filed away what had happened that night, much as he had. "It wasn't the day at Hyde Park that changed me, it was the night."

Calder straightened suddenly, and the air he took into his lungs was loud in the dark of the room. "We swore—"

"I'm sorry, but you mustn't blame her for how I changed. It wasn't her. She was nothing to me then." Quinn didn't want to talk about that night.

"That's not entirely true either," Calder said, and Quinn looked back to his gaze, heavy with discomfort.

"No, I suppose it isn't exactly true. There's always been something. But she isn't what held me back from you—if anything, she does nothing but push me toward you."

"Perhaps I—sometimes…I think…" He shook his head. "Perhaps she was always meant for you."

Quinn leaned forward on his knees, considering very carefully what he wanted to say. "I think if that's true, she is meant for both of us—not just for me, because there is no me without you."

"You're perfectly aware that I don't like women in the way you do," Calder said.

"That's not what I mean. She doesn't—" Quinn paused. "Calder, she doesn't like men."

"I've seen you together, Quinn. She's quite fond of you."

"Not like that. We're friends."

"You're quite a bit more than friends—don't attempt to diminish it for my sake. I can feel it, Quinn, I can see it on you when you speak of her. Don't pretend for one moment that I cannot feel exactly how you think of her."

Quinn considered again. "I'm sorry, I didn't mean to insult you. I meant that she doesn't want me—even if…even if at one time I wanted her. She doesn't want physical intimacy with me, or anyone. She wants to be left to herself."

"Marrying you is not the same as wanting to be left alone."

"No, it isn't. That was a mistake, and it wasn't our fault. My mother found us—"

"Found you…you compromised her before the wedding?"

"Not how you're thinking. I shouldn't have done what I did. She trusted me, and I allowed for something…"

"She trusted you?"

"Yes, I think she still trusts me. I haven't yet destroyed that."

"But my trust, you're perfectly comfortable destroying that."

"No, Calder, I'm not."

"But I don't…" He shook his head. "I don't trust you. How can I?" Calder said quietly.

"Please—" Quinn started.

"No," Calder answered, then he rolled back to face the wall, ending the only real conversation they'd had since leaving India.

Quinn stared at his back again and thought about Celeste. He did remember what he'd felt toward the girl that day. But he'd also seen how much it had bothered Calder when he'd spoken about finding her just to see how she was doing. So he'd forced the entire thing from his mind, if only to stop the obsession he'd seemed to have with her all of a sudden. And shortly thereafter he hadn't needed much help in forgetting—it was all he'd wanted to do.

Calder

Calder let the water rush his body and imagined that his aches and pains, inside and out, went with it. All of it, down the drain. Calder knew about Francine and Lulu out of necessity, but Quinn had never been told. It didn't come up, and there was no purpose to it really. Quinn didn't run with Rox and Gray; he spent some time with Perry, but Rox and Gray were much too bruising to Quinn's demeanor.

Calder needed to find out if Celeste remembered anything, if she was from another time, if she was like the others—then she really was here for Quinn. That was the theory they currently held, at any rate. Well, Lulu and Francine anyway, but Calder just thought it one of those mysteries of the world. They thought it was some sort of fated experience, because humans liked to have answers.

It was simply one more thing to keep Quinn from him. Perhaps God had sent her to prove a point that he wasn't doing as he should. He wasn't living his life as God wished for him to do. Calder rejected the thought. Why would He give him so much to take it all away?

He turned his face into the spray as it began to cool, but he wasn't ready to step out just yet. He needed Quinn to find his bravery and get out of the berth, because he couldn't face him just yet. Not after last night.

Calder remembered the night in Hyde, but he'd been so jealous of the fact that Quinn was drawn earlier to a girl that he hadn't considered what later that night had done to him. Calder didn't think much of it. They hadn't been hurt. Shamed certainly, terrified without doubt, but there had been no injury there. Calder had long since accepted that bad things would happen to him because of the way he was, but that had been Quinn's first experience with being mistreated by strangers, and it had been Calder's fault it had happened.

He should have known better. He did know better. But he hadn't known that Quinn had been suffering for it ever since.

Quinn

uinn sat on his berth and stared at the back of the door as he listened to the water from Calder's shower. The boat had weighed anchor a quarter of an hour past, but he couldn't force his hand to the door or his feet to move. He wanted Calder with him because he'd been on the edge for weeks now. He simply didn't feel safe at the moment out in the world. The shower cut off, and Quinn turned an ear toward the door that was closed between them. From outside the porthole he heard the horn for the first of the ferries that would take passengers to the dock.

Quinn grabbed the door handle and opened it, slamming the door behind him. He could do this. He would do this. He had to learn to survive without Calder somehow. He'd survived without Calder before; he used to be able to function without the fear of passing out. If he started to feel panic, he could do what he'd learned from Lulu, that paying-attention thing. Quinn knew, now, what had started all of it, and he understood why it had gotten worse as they'd gotten older. The fear of being discovered became more prevalent, more of a real threat.

When they were younger, they'd been careless. They'd had that youthful mind to them that didn't believe anything could go wrong in life, not truly… but the realization that something could go wrong became so tangible in his mind after the night in the park that Quinn had to stop himself from thinking about it or he would panic. And as the years went on, it only got to be more difficult to control.

Calder used to help him with it. And now…it was only exacerbated by thoughts of never seeing him again, which was unlikely. They were cousins and traveled the same circles. They would see each other regularly whether

they wished for it or not. But Quinn did wish for it; he wanted to see him, even as Calder wasn't interested in the same.

The clashing thoughts caught his breath, and Quinn closed his eyes for a moment as he steadied himself with a hand on the wall of the hallway. The paint was cold. He could do this, he had to do this, he had to just…change his mind. *Celeste*…hopefully he had a telegram from Celeste. That would make him happy. That would be lovely. He shook off his nervousness and hurried to the deck to disembark before his mind got caught up again.

Since he already knew where the office was, it was rather easy to navigate the crowds and make his way there before the majority of the other passengers. He stopped outside and took a deep breath as he remembered the last time he'd been here.

The last time he'd been here, in Alexandria, outside this office, was the last moment in which he'd felt hopeful about him and Calder. But Calder hadn't been here, and he'd lost all hope that day, even though he'd continued on.

Quinn stepped inside once again. There were no telegrams for him. He inquired if Calder had any and considered taking them for him, but finally decided against it. As much as Calder distrusted him at the moment, he thought better of it.

Quinn actually felt relatively good when he walked out to the street that led to the dock where he could get back to the ship. So he stopped and looked around. The telegraph office was situated on a corner, and the street adjacent led into Alexandria. Should he chance going into town? It seemed a terrible waste to come so far and not even see some of the world.

Quinn cautiously walked down the narrow street toward what looked like a busy thoroughfare. Carriages and pedestrians were everywhere. He stood at the end of the block and simply watched for a while. Alexandria wasn't so different from Bombay in structure, but it wasn't nearly as colorful, and the air wasn't thick with the spices. It was mostly just dusty.

He missed the smell of India—the close bazaars, the kitchens at the havelis where women cooked. He decided his wish for the smell of India had the side effect of making him terribly hungry, since he'd left without breakfast. So Quinn returned to the ship. Seemed odd that he liked the atmosphere of India, regardless he hadn't had a single good moment within her borders. Not even finding Calder had been a balm to his pain.

When he reached the dining room, it was almost empty, the majority of passengers having had breakfast early in order to disembark. He chose a table against the windows that overlooked the city and flagged a waiter. It didn't take much time for a plate of moderately hot food to be placed before him.

He should have at least had a telegram from Celeste. Quinn tapped a finger on the table as he considered it, then nodded to the waiter who handed him his coffee. He simply wanted an amiable voice in his ear, even if he had to conjure it from memory as he read her words. He hoped everything was well. He set the cup down but missed the edge of the table, and it went clattering to the floor.

Unfortunate, that, because the coffee had smelled divine. He gave the waiter a sheepish nod and waited patiently as he replaced the coffee with nary a sidelong glance. This time Quinn drank some of the coffee before settling into his breakfast. He demolished the plate of food in front of him and requested a second plate as well as two more cups of coffee.

Apparently he was feeling rather good today, as he hadn't had much of an appetite since…well. Since before he'd stepped foot in Alexandria the last time. He pushed the mess away and stared out the window toward the dock. The food in his belly saturated his blood, and his eyelids started to droop. He stood with the intention of finding a nap.

Calder

Calder watched Quinn from the upper deck as he walked the length of the dock toward the telegraph office then around the corner and into Alexandria. It seemed he was getting on just fine without him. Which was good. That was what Calder wanted—wasn't it? Quinn needed to be independent. He needed to be able to do things without the fear of one of his episodes. Calder thought perhaps if Quinn wasn't always skulking around for him, perhaps he'd settle, perhaps he'd return to the old Quinn, the fearless Quinn. With a woman at his side, he could be fearless. With Calder at his side…there was nothing but fear there.

Calder made his way to the boats to disembark and retrieve his telegrams. Turned out he had two, one from Rakshan and one from Celeste. He stopped just shy of tearing it to pieces in the street when he saw Quinn swing back around the corner in front of him, headed toward the gangway. He followed, stuffing the telegrams in his pocket as he went. He stayed to the back of the small ferry and followed Quinn as far as the dining room, then went to the top deck. When he got there, he settled into a deck chaise and pulled the telegrams from his pocket.

> *Mad is behaving*
> *War has been brought up to date*
> *You should try*
> *R*

Try? Calder imagined Rakshan was quite fond of telegrams in which he would always have the last word without argument. He tossed the paper over the rail and stared at the next. He unfolded the delicate paper and stared at the letters. They formed words and phrases that swam in his brain like unschooled fish.

Understand

What we have

Forced

The only one

Please explain

Too much love

Give up everything

Step aside

I will do nothing

Give up

You need

This telegram had cost a fortune. The only word that formed a solid connection in his mind was *why*. He assumed she'd send something to Quinn, but *why*—why would she even consider contacting him? He closed his eyes and leaned his head back, allowing the heat of the sun to turn his world red.

When his eyes began to sting, he leaned forward and tried to read the missive once again. The words danced for a moment as his eyes recovered from the sun.

Calder

I am sorry is not sufficient

No words ever will be

Please try to understand

What we have is not a true marriage

It was forced

You are the only one

Please give Q a chance to explain

There is too much love to ignore

I will give up everything in my life to see you happy

I will happily step aside

Whatever you wish of me it is yours only tell me

I will do nothing you do not ask of me

Do not give up on what you want just yet

Whatever you need

Please try

Celeste

He read it again. Had they orchestrated this? Had Rakshan and Warrick and his wife decided what should be done next? For some reason he didn't feel angry, he felt—defeated. Her words, as stilted as they necessarily were, had done something to soothe the anger he'd carried since the night they'd first truly met.

The night everything had gone wrong, that night, the night *his* world had changed forever. He'd been frustrated with Quinn before he'd discovered her on the balcony…

I hate the way you can't say no to people.

Tell them no.

Tell them you don't want to marry.

Tell them.

He'd yelled in Quinn's face—while still deep inside him—he'd yelled in the face of the man he loved, and he was only now shamed by it. Calder pushed a knuckle to his eye to stop the sting of it. Maybe he'd needed time to let that anger burn off. And yet…that was patently unfair to Quinn. What he'd done, how he'd treated him. The last words Calder had said to him…

So—we're done here, and you can see your way out.

Oh God, what had he done? He didn't deserve Quinn; he didn't deserve forgiveness. He didn't deserve any of it. It still hurt. What had happened? Remembering Quinn and Celeste, their gentle banter as they'd danced, the shared smiles. Something he and Quinn could never have, not ever. Never could they share something like that together. Their entire life was privately held and always would be. He could never declare his love for Quinn. He could never share it with others. He could never put a ring on Quinn's finger and claim him as his own before God and family and the world. *Never.*

Certainly Calder still had misgivings about Quinn's marriage; true or not, his vows had been taken before God, and the thing they all seemed to be dismissing was how important that was to Calder, as a person who'd never be able to take those vows and *mean* them.

He supposed part of him had always been jealous of Quinn because Quinn appreciated women in the same way he did men, which gave him that possibility. He could love someone and share that love and that happiness *with the world.* It was why the girl in the park—*Celeste*—had annoyed him so much. Quinn's attention, all of it, had been on her; she'd stolen Calder's moment from him. Taken it for herself, and she was still doing it.

Like a cloud had moved, the sun was blocked, and the telegram was cast into the shade. Calder looked up. Quinn stood there pinching the skin between his thumb and finger with the other hand—his nerves evident as he waited to be sent away.

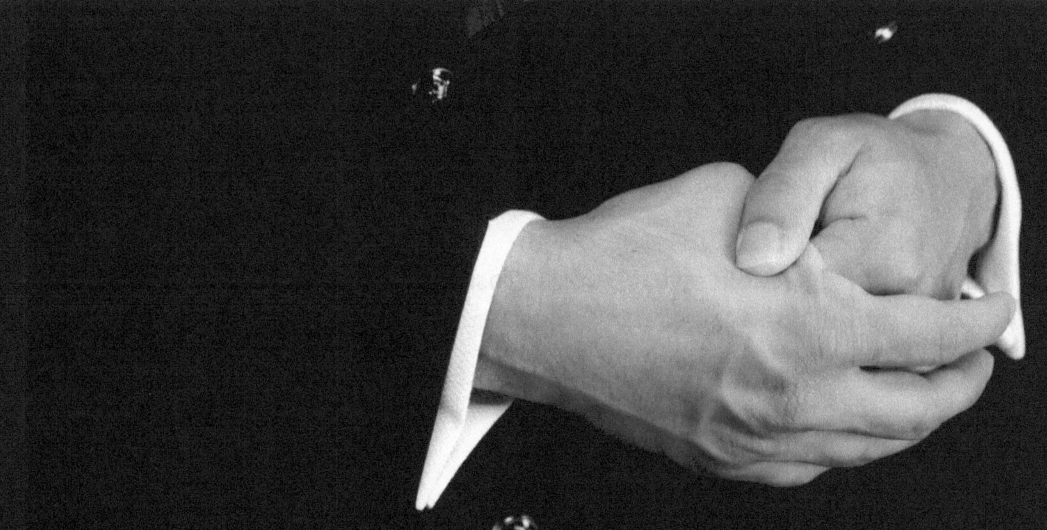

It hurt that he so patiently waited to be dismissed. Because that was what he'd reduced Quinn to—someone to be dismissed. So he didn't, but neither could he manage any words of comfort just yet. He remained silent. Calder reached out and separated Quinn's hands before he bruised himself. Then folded the telegram and put it away.

"I was headed back to the room, then thought you might be sleeping so I came up here. I saw you and thought…" Quinn shook his head. "I—" he started softly, then he moved from in front of the sun and took a seat in the chaise next to him, turned sideways, leaned on his knees as he debated his every word. Calder had to look away. Watching Quinn debate which words to use would break him. "Can we…can we try?" he asked.

For a moment Calder tensed at the word, wondering if Quinn had been party to whatever machinations had brought that word to him in two separate telegrams. He paused to consider before speaking—there was no possible way he could have known. He and Quinn hadn't been separated since Madoc's haveli. He hadn't sent any telegrams from Bombay. He'd deferred to Calder.

Calder closed his eyes and took a deep breath. "Not here." He stood and walked away but realized Quinn hadn't followed. He stopped and turned, looking over his shoulder and catching his gaze.

Quinn stood, straightening his trousers, pulling the edge of his coat back into place. Nervously checking himself. Calder raised his eyebrows, and Quinn's face lit for a mere second before he caught himself, then he moved to follow.

He let Quinn walk through the door to their cabin first, and Calder turned and pushed the door closed behind them. He couldn't make himself turn around and face him. He leaned his forehead against the heavy door and let the heat of his skin dissipate against the cool of the paint. After a few moments, he spoke. "I'm sorry," he whispered. "I'm so sorry."

Quinn was silent but for his movements. He heard him shift, then the berth complain as he sat.

Calder clenched his fist on the door handle, everything in him wanting to run. A cold sweat broke across his back and scalp, chilling him, and he shuddered against it. "I have been…I have behaved in a terribly ungentlemanly—"

"Calder, you don't—"

Calder waved his hand to stop him from finishing, because he did have to do this. He had to. But it was going to take him some time. He heard Quinn shift, settle in, and hoped it meant he understood. "My behavior toward you has been terribly ungentlemanly. The simple truth of it—it comes down to the fact that I am unbearably jealous. What you and Celeste—"

"Calder—"

"Don't," he warned again, and he clenched his hand in a fist against the door. "What you and Celeste have is a relationship I want for with every inch of my being. Every single part of me wants nothing more than to scream from the roof that you are mine, that I love you. I want to dance with you in the ballrooms. I want to carry you on my arm to society functions. I want everyone to know just how very precious you are to me." Calder heard his voice hitch, the words catching in his throat. Was thankful that Quinn didn't speak. He turned his cheek against the paint to cool it. Closed his eyes to concentrate. "The problem is…I never did let you know that. I didn't treat you in the manner to which you deserve."

Calder felt heat all along his back and pressed himself against the door to try to escape it, his hands unfolding against the cool of the painted wood. He hadn't heard Quinn move, he hadn't heard him shift from the bed, and the sudden warmth of him against his back was overwhelming to his senses.

"I'm sorry I never treated you as I should have. I never let you know what my true feelings were. I never—"

Quinn pushed against him, his hands coming to his waist, his mouth to the back of his neck. "I always knew. I didn't need the words from you."

"You deserve more than words, Quinn, you deserve every gentle touch I've kept, every smile I've ever hidden, every kiss I've stayed. You deserve someone who is much better than I."

"So do you. You deserve to be that man, but it isn't your fault that you cannot be. This is entirely beyond our control. That we have to keep hidden what we have isn't fair. Dealing with that hasn't been easy or simple for either of us, and I should have been more considerate in my public actions with Celeste—" Calder tensed at the mention of her name, and Quinn froze as though trying to figure out how to proceed.

"Don't," Calder said. "Please finish what you were saying. I need to become familiar with her name on your lips, as I must. It won't be effortless, mind you, and it won't be expedient. Just understand that I am attempting to do so." Quinn's nose ran across the uncovered skin at the nape of Calder's neck, just above the fabric of his cravat, and his knees nearly gave.

"Devil," he whispered.

Calder came undone. He turned toward Quinn, still pressed against the door, and with only a slight hesitation reached across the distance and grabbed his lapels, bringing Quinn's lips to his mouth. He was gentle. He savored the flavor of his coffee from this morning and the underlying taste that was nothing but Quinn. The most familiar and beautiful flavor in all the world to him.

Calder pulled Quinn's coat off his shoulders, undid his cravat and shirt, and flung them aside. Then he worshipped him with his mouth. He pushed Quinn until he was backed up against the wall. He kissed his way down Quinn's chest and torso, skimming his thumbs across his nipples, running his fingers across every muscle and through every furrow as he slowly came to his knees and undid his trousers, releasing his cock at his lips.

Quinn slid down the wall just a bit, his legs bracketing Calder's hips as he anchored himself there, and Calder took him deep into his throat, swallowing against the head of his cock and savoring the moan it brought forth, more from the barrel of Quinn's chest than from his mouth.

Calder worshipped Quinn as he should have done. He treated him now as he should have treated him always. Calder showed him with action how very much he cared for him.

Calder pushed against his belly with one hand to anchor him then slid one hand up the inside of Quinn's thigh and cupped his bollocks as they grew tighter against the shaft of his cock, one finger playing with the tight ring of his entry. Quinn's hands tangled in his hair, held him steady, wouldn't let him move.

Calder worshipped there as he should have been, on his knees before this man. He drew his head back and sucked the early seed from the tip of Quinn's cock as he swirled his tongue just inside his foreskin, letting his mouth slide it against the crown of his cock as Quinn shuddered into him.

"I'm…I'm going to fall, I can't—oh God, Devil, I…"

Calder drew back, his hands coming to his hips, his thumbs grazing those beautiful muscles, then he nuzzled past his cock to his soft lower abdomen, running his nose across the soft skin below his belly button. "Then take me to bed," he said. Calder looked up to find Quinn gazing down at him with an indefinable look of joy mixed with pain and hope and several other things Calder couldn't place. "Take me to bed," he said again. He stood in one swift move from his knees and took his mouth. He kissed him as though this were the last time he'd be allowed access to him. His hands held to the man's naked body like this was the first time he'd ever been given permission to touch him. He shook like a green boy.

Quinn's fingers worked on his cravat and shirt, pushing his clothes away before Calder had time to process his movements. Then Calder turned in his arms, but he didn't get far. Quinn wrapped his arms around him and pulled him tight against his frame, placing his cock in the seam of his arse. His fingers dug into Calder's skin as his teeth came down on his shoulder.

Quinn always was a biter. Even as he now preferred submission to domination, Quinn loved to mark Calder with his teeth. Calder returned the favor only occasionally because he knew Quinn liked to receive it as well, the marks something to be cherished between them. Quinn's jaw clenched enough to make the muscle of his shoulder jerk, but not enough to break the skin, and Calder flinched.

Then Quinn's hot breath was in his ear, the words heavy and thick and unrecognizable as they flowed from his mouth and bypassed his consciousness, resting deep in his soul as though no translation were necessary. Calder knew what he was saying; he didn't need to understand it.

They stumbled together to the bed, and Quinn turned him so he came down on his back, Quinn on top of him, his hips pressing his thighs wide as he bracketed Quinn's body protectively. Quinn then kissed his way down Calder's torso and back up again. "What's this?" he asked softly, licking the healed skin that ran down the center of his chest. "Does this hurt?"

Calder shivered; it no longer hurt, but the new skin was much more sensitive. "No, it doesn't hurt, just…try not to drag against it."

"I want to know," Quinn said as he came back up above him carefully, and Calder looked in his eyes.

"I will tell you, but not at this moment. Not…just yet."

Quinn dipped his head and kissed his chest, his gentle breath sending chills through his skin. Calder groaned, and Quinn rose above him, Calder

taking his mouth willingly, weaving his fingers into his hair. Quinn fumbled beneath the pillow and smiled when he came away with a small bottle of oil. Quinn sat back on his knees, and Calder draped his legs over them.

Quinn shrugged as he uncorked the small bottle. "Do you know how difficult it is to have nothing but unrealized sex dreams every time you sleep? I've had to do a bit of mitigation since you weren't amenable to managing it for me."

Calder shook his head. "Mitigation? Is that what we're calling it?"

"Absolutely," Quinn said.

"If it's me, I'm not very nice in your dreams."

"Of course it's you. There's not another soul in the world who would leave me so wanting." He filled his palm with oil and spread it thickly over his cock, and all thoughts of dreams fled. Calder's mouth watered just watching his movements. Quinn's thumb brushing over the tip of his own cock, the shift of his muscles across his abdomen. Calder pressed into the hardness of Quinn's thighs under his own knees, watched the tick in his jaw as he concentrated. Then Quinn sent a rill of oil sliding down the center of Calder's chest, and the whole of his body tightened against a shiver that went searching out from the center of him, finding the tips of his fingers, his ears, his toes. Quinn smoothed the trail left behind with a finger. "To protect," he said quietly, "against friction."

Calder tried to catch his breath but couldn't. His skin buzzed like an electric lantern. He leaned up and reached out, smoothing his hand below Quinn's cock. He rearranged Quinn's bollocks in that tight sac, savoring the sharp jerks of his hips punctuated by quiet gasps and grunts that Quinn couldn't restrain as Calder skimmed his hand teasingly along the seam of his cods that led to his arse.

Calder gathered a bit of oil from Quinn's cock and smoothed back again, pushing his finger past that taut barrier and massaging just far enough inside to make his cock jump and his arse clench around him.

Calder cried out when Quinn's hand found his cock, pushing his foreskin down as Quinn gathered the mettle and brought it to his mouth. "I've missed the taste of you," Quinn said.

Calder released him and fell back to the bed. "I'm yours," he said. "Do as you will."

Quinn

Quinn loved this man. More than he could say. More than was humanly allowable by any measure. It was unfair to the world how much love he took for himself and gave to this man. He oiled his fingers and played with Calder's arse as he set the bottle on the floor. Then he leaned down on one elbow, coming as close to him as possible while still being able to focus on his face.

The last time—the last few times—had been dreams, and he hadn't been able to hold on to Calder long enough to come off. Fucking his own hand had become the only outlet against his backed-up mettle. But now, here, with a willing man beneath him, offering himself, humbling himself before Quinn… The tightness in Quinn's chest eased as he concentrated on the feel of their skin together. The heat and the chill as they shifted. Their already sticky bodies adjusting to each other, their skin refusing to let go just as much as their hands.

He couldn't hold him enough, touch him enough, as though he needed the verification that this was truly Calder beneath him and not another goddamned dream. He needed to see it, needed to know Calder acknowledged what was happening, that he knew where he was and that they were together and that after this…there would be no turning back. Not ever.

"Watch me," Quinn said as he pushed that oiled finger against the tight ring of his arse until it gave and allowed him entry. Calder closed his eyes and drew in a harsh breath, but Quinn shook his head. "No, don't close your eyes. Watch me. I want this. I want to see you, to see in your eyes how my cock feels inside you." He slid closer, his arm beneath Calder's shoulder, his hand fisting in his hair to hold him still. "Look at me," he said, then he licked Calder's lips and pushed his tongue in his mouth as he slid his finger in his arse and waited.

Calder breathed, and breathed, and finally he opened his eyes and a tear streaked the side of his face. Quinn watched it go, watched it pool in the shell of his ear, sending a shiver back through Calder.

"What is this?" Quinn asked as he kissed the trail of the tear, then caught another with his lips before it could spill. Calder shook his head. "Tell me, please."

"You're married, Quinn. I—"

Calder's body shook beneath him, and Quinn kissed him again, bit his lip, then pulled his finger free as he lined up and pushed his hips slowly forward. "But let me remind you to whom I belong, to whom I've always belonged, Calder. I made a vow to you long before I ever met her. I'm yours, now, forever, and you're mine."

Calder's eyes focused, the rings of his irises expanding in the depth of the room, locking on Quinn's gaze. He lifted his legs, adjusting his hips. Quinn moved slowly, and Calder pulled his knees back with his hands, his ankles bracing Quinn's ribs. Then Quinn just relaxed and waited as their bodies came together until he was home. Home.

Calder calmed beneath him, his head falling back to the pillow, his vulnerable neck presented to him. His muscles shifted and melted, all the tension leaving his body as Quinn held himself still, just enjoying the heat and the pressure of Calder around him. He breathed, kissed his way down his jaw to his chin, then opened his mouth on it, sucked, and bit the edge of his jaw, feeling Calder groan through the vibration against his lips and his tongue.

Fucking Calder was an exercise in sensation, carnality, and power.

Quinn shifted, just slightly, pulling back only the smallest fraction, and a chill bloomed across his back, sending shudders racking his muscles. "Can you feel that? How I tremble? That's what you do to me. That's what you reduce me to, nothing but raw muscle and the vibration of tension. That's all I am when I'm inside you." He released Calder's hair and instead held his shoulder, keeping his body tight against his hips. He pushed, licked Calder's mouth open, watched as his gaze held his, refused to look away. "I love you, Devil, I always have. I always will. Just as there's nothing between

our bodies now, there will never be anything between us. Trust me. Just… trust me. Devil, you are my everything."

Quinn closed his eyes and tasted his mouth, slid his tongue against the back of Calder's teeth, sucked his lips into his mouth, opened his jaw wide with his heavy kisses until he thought they would both break from the patience and restraint. When he could no longer hold back, when it became more than just the feel of skin on skin, when it became two souls entwined, his heart freely given to Calder's keeping, he pushed, and he pushed, and he pushed.

Calder's hands flew up to protect them from hitting against the wall, and Quinn stroked in and out of Calder in earnest. Each draught pulled the early seed from his cock, each stroke soothing his ache just a bit more. They tangled together, and Quinn closed his eyes and just let his body have the moment as his mind quieted. Finally quieted. And all he was, was the stroke of his cock, the goose bumps of his flesh, the sweat from his skin, the tension of his muscles, and the breath of his lungs until he was nothing but the hot spurt of his mettle as he came off inside Devil.

Quinn collapsed and slipped slowly free. Then he slid down the bed to take Calder in his mouth, and as Calder's hands tangled in his hair and his grunts filled his ears, Quinn hummed and kissed and sucked until Calder screamed and tensed and bucked, and as Calder's seed hit the back of his throat, Quinn knew his world would never be the same.

There would be Quinn and Devil, or there would be nothing.

Calder

Quinn's legs slid down the bed as Calder lay there, his satisfied cock softening, his hands running though Quinn's hair as Quinn's head rested on Calder's belly. Quinn's arms were tangled with his legs, his breathing puffing across his skin, slow and contented in sleep. Quinn was so exhausted he hadn't even shifted in the bed before falling asleep.

Calder, on the other hand, couldn't sleep at the moment. He wasn't sure what came next, and frankly he was terrified because he was still so very apprehensive about his necessary interactions with Quinn.

Just as he and Quinn couldn't not be in the same circles, Quinn and his wife couldn't not be in the same circles as well. Society would take note. Which meant his jealously would be sorely taxed, and it would be entirely on him to control.

"Stop thinking," Quinn groaned, and Calder shuddered at the vibration of Quinn's voice across his no longer entirely soft cock. Quinn nestled his cheek into the crease at his abdomen, his nose nudging his cock as he did so.

"I can't help it," Calder replied breathlessly.

Quinn's hand came up to stroke him. "So I've not exhausted you enough? Let me help you with that." The sound that came from Calder's mouth was beyond his own comprehension, and Quinn laughed. "Much better," he said, planting a kiss at the tip of his cock against the softness of his foreskin. He played there gently, soft kisses and licks and lazy touches with his cold nose, all sending shivers through Calder's cock that went straight to his bollocks and up his spine, driving his heart wild.

"God, Quinn," he said, and they were the last discernible words Calder said for quite some time. Quinn made love to him with his mouth, slow and passionate, and Calder simply accepted it with grace and thanks. It was one of the most intense moments of his life. His concerns seemed to melt away in the fullness of their connection. Once again he allowed all of his fears to fade for a time in lieu of pleasure and a hopeful future with this man.

Calder awoke with a start, his heart racing as he attempted to discern what it was that had startled him. The heat of Quinn's body pressed the length of his back. The moonlight coming through the porthole lit the middle of the room but fell off too quickly to lend him any assistance in anchoring himself. Quinn's arms around him tensed, his fingers digging into his chest and leg almost painfully.

Calder held his hands, squeezed. "Quinn, relax, it's me."

"Don't go."

Calder's heart wrenched. "I'm here, I'm not going anywhere," he whispered, then he rolled in Quinn's arms, wincing as Quinn's grasp tightened and scratched at his skin. Calder's cheek came up against Quinn's

in the dark, wet with tears. "Quinn?" He slid one arm under his waist and wrapped the other around him, pulling him close as he kissed the tears away. "Quinn, are you awake?"

"I don't know anymore," he answered, his voice small and frightened.

"Wake up," Calder said into his mouth, kissing and licking his words into reality. "Come on, wake up for me. I'm right here."

Quinn's chest hitched and his arms tightened on Calder almost painfully, his fingers digging into the flesh of his shoulder and hip once again.

Calder did nothing but murmur assurances to him in the dark, tried to soothe him, tried to wake him. Nothing seemed to help, yet he didn't stop. Eventually Quinn's breathing quieted and his hands relaxed against him. Calder shifted to his back, pulling Quinn tight into his side as he stared up at the dark ceiling. Again, a certain guilt assaulted him. He should have known better. He should not have allowed his own jealousy to control his actions and hurt Quinn so deeply.

Even so, he was still torn when he considered everything that had happened. Tonight had brought a certain clarity with it. He was able to see past that seething anger and attempt to examine it all with a rational eye. A more rational eye—he certainly couldn't be completely impartial.

He felt now that he'd need to become much more familiar with Celeste in order to get past this, because if they were to somehow manage this, his relationship with Celeste would be of paramount importance, and right now all he knew of her was…nothing, really. He didn't know her at all.

"You're thinking again…instead of sleeping," Quinn grumbled against his chest, and Calder laughed, just a quick burst from surprise at how rapidly his mood would change.

"You're well?"

"I am," Quinn responded. "You expected different?"

"No, I…I think perhaps you had a bit of a bad dream."

"I've had quite a few of those recently," Quinn said, and he sat up in the bed, leaving Calder's skin bereft of his warmth. Quinn gave him his back.

"I am sorry," Calder said quietly, placing his hand against the large muscle that edged Quinn's spine.

"I know, but as I'm not in control of my dreams… if I were, they would have been done with long ago. I have no idea just how long these dreams may take to subside."

"They're bad," Calder said under his breath.

"They're bad, yes." Quinn took a deep breath against his hand, and they were both quiet for a moment. "Please don't—I know I don't have any place to ask for favors, but please don't leave like that again. Please talk to me. Even when I say something you don't like. Please, just don't ever leave like that, with so much discord between us," Quinn said.

"I promise."

"Don't…don't promise me anything either. Just…either do it or don't do it, but please don't make any more promises, because I just…I don't know that I—"

"Quinn, it's fine. No more promises, I—all right, no more promises. I will…endeavor to do as you wish in this from here on."

Quinn laughed softly. "That sounds like a promise," he said softly, and Calder smiled.

"I would appreciate a promise from you, however," Calder said.

"Is that so?"

"Yes. Can you promise me you'll give me time to become familiar with this new paradigm wherein you have—you have a wife? Promise me you'll be patient with me even as I don't deserve your patience, even as I don't deserve your understanding. I just—please try to be patient with me as I endeavor to fit myself to your new life."

"You are not fitting yourself into my life, Calder, you are my life."

"That's not how it feels at the moment," he said.

"I will…I promise to be patient with you. If I'm not, you will tell me."

"I will tell you. I will not run. I will tell you if I require patience. I can do this, for you."

Quinn turned his head as a sudden beam of light entered the porthole when the sun rose over the horizon, reflecting brightly off the water surrounding them, and Quinn glanced down to Calder as though he were shocked to see him still here. Calder simply watched him, took in his expression, the strong lift of his jaw with a day's growth of beard. The watery glow to his eyes that was entirely his fault. He smoothed his hand around Quinn's waist and pulled him back down to the small berth.

"Come back to me. It's still dark down here for a bit longer. Don't leave me quite yet," Calder said.

Quinn lay down, his head against Calder's chest as he shifted and burrowed into his side. Calder swept his hand up and down his side and his arm until Quinn's breath steadied and he fell into sleep once again. Calder wasn't sure about anything. He was frightened for the future in a way he never had been before, and his guilt at coveting this man…

When he knew for certain that Quinn was once again asleep, Calder said a prayer into the dark. "I'm sorry, but I simply cannot stay away from him. I tried. I left. But I love him with all my heart and my soul, everything that I am. If I believe in something, anything, it is that he is good and he is true and he deserves happiness more than anyone I know. Please help me to temper my jealousy as we work together, as we navigate this…this…life together. Please give me the grace to know right from wrong where they are concerned. I would have married him myself years ago if there had been the possibility. I am dedicated to him. I cannot walk away. If you find our being together breaks the covenant that binds their marriage…bring your offense to me and leave Quinn be. I am the one causing the offense, just as I always have been. I will happily bear your wrath upon myself until the end of days, if only to save him from your judgment." And with those words, he closed his eyes and drifted off.

"Do you think not sending a telegram to Quinn was the right thing to do?" Francine asked.

"I don't know. I can't know. But I need Quinn to rely on Calder, and I need Calder to know I'm entirely serious and will only do as he wishes where Quinn is concerned. If I sent Quinn a telegram as well, I think it would negate what I told Calder, because I told him I would not proceed in any way without his direction."

"We can go into town today and see if there are any more telegrams—if you wish."

"I thought Roxleigh had a messenger on retainer?"

"He does, and if a 'gram comes for him, he's notified as expediently as possible. But if you wish to get out of the house, we could just…happen to go there."

Celeste thought about it for a moment as she twisted her fingers together. "I don't think so. I think I need to give them room to do what they need to do, and that includes not looming over the telegraph office in hopes one of them sent something. I need to learn to be patient. It's never been my strong suit even though I've done nothing but wait my entire life. Once I find something I need I can't seem to leave it alone, which is precisely why I'm in this predicament to begin with."

"I'm not sure I could be so calm if Gideon were involved," Francine said.

"I imagine not, but then again, you and Roxleigh were meant to be together and he's your husband. While Quinn and I are married, he's actually meant to be with someone else. He and I are merely friends, confidants, something…but not truly married, not lovers certainly, nothing so intimate. That's for Calder and only Calder," Celeste said.

"Even so, I'm anxious as well. You have so much strength—I don't think you give yourself enough credit."

"Thank you. I don't feel particularly strong. I feel like I'm coming apart at the seams." She sipped her tea and took a cake from the tray as she leaned back in the chair and looked out over the lawn to where Roxleigh and Warrick were practicing with bows. Celeste heard the rattle of a carriage and stood, dropping her teacup to the rug on the ground when she was startled. "Oh, I'm so sorry Francine, I—"

Francine laughed gently. "It's all right, Celeste. Anything we bring outside is meant to get destroyed. It's merely china and a rug."

"Apparently I'm a bit more anxious than I was admitting to," Celeste said.

"Perhaps. Even so, the messenger rides a horse—so you can relax." Francine turned to find Roxleigh, and Lulu turned to watch the approaching carriage.

"Are you expecting anyone?" Lulu asked.

"No, but here comes Gideon. He and Warrick can deal with it," Francine said.

Francine and Lulu watched Roxleigh and Warrick cross the lawn. She could see the appreciation in their gazes and knew the feeling. It was odd to her that she could identify with certain parts of their relationships with their husbands, but others made no sense to her at all. Or they made sense…she just didn't feel that way. She very much appreciated the way Quinn looked and moved and behaved, especially when he didn't know she was paying attention. Calder as well, for that matter.

Her heart kicked at the thought of them and she sent up another small prayer that they were working things out. She remembered the telegrams from Rakshan that Warrick had shared with her. How they'd been found and what a disaster it had been. Celeste had ached for both of them. When Rakshan had told Warrick he'd intended to be sure they'd have to travel in the same cabin, and Warrick had told her he had no need to communicate with either Calder or Quinn at the moment, she'd decided she would. It had taken her almost the full two weeks to decide what to say to him. And all she could do now was wait and hope for something—

"Celeste, I think we should go inside," Francine said as she and Lulu both stood and walked to her side of the small table. "Come on, let's go."

"What, why? Who's here?" Celeste stood and looked around, but Lulu blocked her line of sight to the carriage, and Francine took her by the hand and wrapped an arm around her back to guide her around the side of the manor to the orangery. Lulu walked slightly behind, keeping Celeste from seeing the drive when she turned. But she heard voices rising, and they sounded none too happy.

"We shouldn't have turned them away," Celeste said quietly as the carriage disappeared down the drive.

"Did you wish to speak with them?" Roxleigh said from behind her. She hadn't realized he'd entered the parlor.

"Not necessarily," she said.

"I apologize if I acted hastily, but if someone is not allowed at my brother's home, neither are they allowed in my home, particularly when the person they've brought direct harm to is here. I only acted in what I considered to be your best interest."

Celeste dropped her gaze from the window and turned toward him. "I understand, and I very much appreciate that. My concern is more for you and your family. I don't want you caught in some scandal because of me."

Roxleigh laughed at that. Well, she thought it was a laugh; it was a quick, loud burst of noise. She shook her head. "If they believe they can rain scandal on my house, let them try and we'll see where that brings them," he said, and the force of his words resonated through the room and settled in her heart.

"Gideon, don't be harsh," Francine said, reaching out to him.

"No," Celeste said, "it wasn't harsh."

"I only mean to make it clear that my protection of innocent people will not be questioned by society. My protection for those under my purview—

which includes you as long as you're in my home, and of my family—comes at no cost to myself or to them. Perceived or otherwise."

A tear dropped to her hand, and she stared at it as though she was only just realizing it to be hers. She reached up and swiped the rest from her cheeks, and Lulu came to her. "Roxleigh."

"No, please, it's not what you think," Celeste said as Francine smacked his arm and he looked down at her, affronted. "It's not that I'm frightened or upset. I've never felt…I'm not familiar with such courtesy being extended to me. Perry was the first, and it was shocking then, and perhaps it's even more so now because it makes every word he said ring true. Not that I didn't believe what he said, or what Quinn told me about his family, but that…it's a difficult concept until you actually experience it, you see? I've no experience with this sort of care and consideration." Her voice hitched, and Francine rushed over as Lulu took her up in a hug, and then she was surrounded. There was really nothing more she could say.

She heard Roxleigh's voice break through the huddle, and she wiggled until she could see him.

"Believe what I've said, Celeste. You'll not come to harm as long as I can help it. I'll not see you injured further. I will also follow your wishes. To that end, if you would like to speak with your mother and mother-by-law, I will escort you to town tomorrow. They are staying at the inn at Roxleighshire for the night. They may not be allowed on my property, but I am not a monster."

Celeste launched herself at his neck before she could stop herself. His arms came around her, holding her solidly as she wept on his rather tall shoulder. "Thank you, Your Grace," she said. "Thank you." She slid down his front and back to her own feet as she released him and took a step back. "I apologize. I don't know what came over me," she said as she shifted uncomfortably, and Roxleigh smiled down on her.

"Well, Warrick and I were in the middle of a competition of sorts. So I believe I should get back to it. Let me know if you wish to go into town. I will make the innkeeper aware that we will be coming, ensuring he not allow them to leave."

Celeste nodded, and Roxleigh leaned down and placed a kiss on her cheek then turned for the door, Francine following close behind. He stopped at the doorway and spoke over his shoulder. "Celeste, you have my leave to address me as Gideon, or Rox, whichever you are more comfortable with. You're family." Then he left.

Celeste turned back to the front window, the carriage gone and the dust behind it already settling.

Lulu stood next to her and took her hand. "Whatever you need," she said quietly.

"These people are strange."

"Isn't it lovely?" Lulu replied.

Celeste nodded.

Quinn

It was nearly two in the afternoon before he and Calder were actually able to leave their cabin and make their way to the telegraphy office to send their replies. They'd been…occupied with each other. Quinn grinned to himself as he savored a morning in which nothing came between them for the first time, in quite a long time. Not the fear of the public, not the facts of their lives, not the circumstances of their travel. They simply quieted and enjoyed each other's bodies until they were starved for food and needed to leave the bed.

Calder bumped his hip against Quinn as they stood at the rail at the bow of the ferry. "You really must quit grinning like that," he said quietly. "It isn't merely that everyone is drawn to you but that it calls forth a rather obvious effect in me that I'm currently hard-pressed to manage."

"Hard…pressed," Quinn said as he leaned forward, his elbows on the rail next to Calder. He dipped his head between his arms as he glanced surreptitiously at Calder's rather obvious cockstand. He laughed when Calder shifted himself, pulling his coat closer, his waistcoat lower. "I cannot apologize," Quinn said as he rested his cheek on his arm and grinned up at him. "I haven't felt this in so very long…I simply cannot. You'll have to figure out some way to…hide your cock," he said, the word sharp at the back of his throat, and Calder shifted again uncomfortably. "I have an idea where you could hide it. If you're curious." Quinn turned toward Calder, who was attempting an air of menace to no avail. "Does that work? That face there?" Quinn waved toward him.

"Usually, yes."

But Quinn smiled again and stood tall when the edge of Calder's mouth turned up. "Terribly unfortunate, that." Quinn looked over the water to the approaching dock. "Who do you need to send telegrams to?"

"Gray, just to let him know we've arrived."

Quinn nodded. "I should—"

"Send one to Celeste, yes, you should," Calder said quietly.

"I'm sorry."

"Don't. She—" Quinn waited patiently, allowing Calder to find his own words. "She wrote me. Her words are one of the reasons I—we…"

"What do you mean, she wrote you?"

"She sent me a telegram."

"Why would she write to you and not to me?"

"She didn't send you anything? Nothing at all?"

"No." Quinn stared down at the water, unsure how he should feel about learning this. "Can I ask what she said?"

"You may read it if you wish," Calder said and pulled the folded paper from his inside coat pocket and held it out. Quinn wasn't sure if he should. He wanted desperately to read it, but…it wasn't for him.

"I don't know if I should," he finally said.

"I think, in this case, there is nothing she says that you cannot know. If there was something private, I would say so, but I think…I think she wouldn't mind. Somehow I believe she expected me to allow you to read it. She was very cautious in her words. I have a feeling that sending the telegram to me and none to you was in itself another message from her."

"How is that?"

"Read the letter," he said, then he took Quinn's hand with his large warm one and placed the telegram in it. Quinn stared at it for a minute then unfolded it.

Please try…

After he read it, Quinn folded the paper and handed it back to him. "She's quite special," Quinn said carefully. But his heart swelled in his chest as he considered what she'd managed to do with that simple telegram. Change Calder's mind. At least open his eyes and allow him to see the possibility. Calder's hand came up to his shoulder, and Quinn closed his eyes. "I've been trying to explain…"

"I wasn't listening." The gangway bumped against the ferry, and Quinn turned away from Calder toward the shore. "We'll talk more. Let's manage the missives. We'll have nothing but two weeks for us to talk about everything, Quinn. Everything you could possibly want to talk about, we will."

Quinn nodded but didn't turn back toward Calder; he simply wasn't strong enough to look at him just yet. And Celeste…she was a wonder. Whenever he thought he'd managed to know the depth of her compassion, she showed something more. She'd told Quinn to go, forced him to the boat, but he'd no idea she would attempt to contact Calder, not considering how frightened of him she was.

Quinn walked blindly, concentrating on the sound of Calder's short boots just behind him. When they reached the telegraph office, he pulled several sheets of paper and stood at the writing counter, staring at the quill and the inkpot. He heard the scratch of another quill as Calder wrote the words for his telegrams. "I don't know what to say to her," he said so only Calder could hear him.

"What do you want her to know, right now, that will hold her for the next two weeks?" Calder asked.

That I love her, Quinn thought. He watched Calder's profile as he concentrated, unsure what to do. Calder finished writing and put the quill down as he turned to Quinn.

"What are you afraid of?" Calder asked.

"The next two weeks."

"Tell her what you need to tell her. It will be fine."

"I'm not afraid of how she will react," Quinn said, quietly turning away.

Calder shifted next to him, his hand coming to his hip as he tapped his other leg with a fist. "You're concerned with how I will react?" he asked, his eyes shifting around the office. Quinn nodded. "Then don't tell me what it is you need to say."

"I cannot do that. I cannot lie to you, and I won't say something that will hurt you. I want to be able to explain, but I'm afraid—"

"No promises, right, Quinn? No promises. But I will listen."

Quinn turned toward Calder then raised his eyes to catch his gaze. "I need to thank her." Quinn waited for him to acknowledge him before he continued. "And I would really like to tell her…that I love her."

Calder

alder looked away and did his level best to control his reaction. But his best simply wasn't good enough. He could see the concern in Quinn's gaze out of the corner of his eye as his muscles tightened and his jaw ached from the clench. He breathed for a moment, considering his next words, then he turned back to Quinn. "Tell her…what you need to tell her," he said carefully.

Quinn shook his head, his eyes growing wider.

Calder couldn't unclench his jaw. "Yes, Quinn. Tell her what you need to tell her, and then you and I…we will talk. I'll be outside. Can you see this directed to Warrick at Eildon?" he asked, then he pushed his own telegraph to Quinn and turned without another word.

"Calder…" He heard the word and stopped shy of the door.

"I will be just outside," he said. "This I will promise you." Then he walked out.

Calder paced in the street. He'd convinced himself this would be easy, that she was giving way and had no interest in a true marriage with Quinn. He hadn't exactly considered the true depth of Quinn's feelings on the matter until just now. Calder stopped at the corner and looked down the street into Alexandria. He wanted to leave. Everything in him was screaming at him to run. His muscles twitched as his brain fought his heart, and he put a hand to the wall to hold on.

Quinn loved her. He knew Quinn liked her, was perfectly aware that Quinn was married to her, knew without a doubt that he may have wanted to fuck her, but he hadn't been aware that Quinn loved her.

"Calder?"

He turned to find Quinn standing just behind him, waiting patiently. "Not here," he said once again. Calder strode toward the gangway, thankful that the ferry hadn't yet filled with passengers and returned to the ship. He walked to the bow and stood next to the rail, his eyes on the cool blue water around him. He tried to let the thought of the cold water cool his blood and calm his heart, but it wasn't working.

Quinn brushed against his shoulder as the boat jerked, separating from the dock, and Calder pulled away before he could stop himself. He raised his hand in apology, but Quinn dropped his gaze, and Calder knew they needed to get to the room.

Once they did, Calder could not stop moving. He paced. He paced toward the porthole and back toward the entry where Quinn leaned against the closed door. Then he turned and stormed at the porthole once again. He was too hot; it was much too hot in this cabin. He jerked his coat off and threw it on his berth then yanked on his cravat, unwrapping it and tossing it aside as well.

He stared down at his hands, the hands that had only held Quinn this morning, and all of last night. Hands that had explored his lover's body. Been kissed by his lover's mouth. Supported his own body as he'd worshipped over Quinn's. He put his hands on the cold exterior wall and slid to his knees, leaning forward until his head also met the cool of the wall.

Calder closed his eyes as he let the heat of his anger dissipate somewhat. "I love you," he said. "I always have. I always will. It matters not what happens next. I will be in want of you for the balance of my days, there is no way about that. You think I don't care enough. I care too much. I can't manage in a world in which you are *within arm's reach* but beyond my touch. I cannot manage in a world in which you—I thought…I thought that when you said you loved me, it meant that you loved *only* me." The words hurt like knives as he said them. His gut tensed, and he slid farther, his hands coming to the floor.

Quinn sat on the berth next to him. Calder didn't look up, but he could see he'd removed his coat, his forearms now bare. Quinn reached out and took Calder's arm, lifting it to his lap as he removed the cufflink and slid it into his waistcoat pocket, then folded the sleeve to his elbow. Quinn tugged, and Calder turned toward him, raising his eyes to Quinn's, trying to figure out what he was thinking in his silence.

Quinn took his other arm and did the same, removing the cufflink and rolling his sleeve. He unbuttoned the collar of Calder's shirt to the edge of his waistcoat and released him.

"I love you, Calder. I've said it over and over. I don't know how many times I've told you I love you, and that will never change." He paused, and Calder knew the next part was going to hurt. "There is a part of me that loves her as well."

Calder's heart stalled then picked up its pace, and he dropped his gaze to the floor to try to catch his breath.

"Devil," he said, and Calder looked back up to him. "I love you in ways I cannot define, not even to myself. There's no comparison. There never will be. But I do love her. It isn't in the way a man loves a wife. It isn't in the way a brother loves a sister. There is no definition for the love I have for her either. She was there for me when—"

Quinn choked, and Calder realized he'd been staving off tears the entire time. He knew what Quinn was about to say. She was there when Calder wasn't. She'd replaced him in his heart—some small part of his heart had given up a bit of space for her because she had been there and he had not.

"Without her I would not have survived you leaving. She kept me grounded as she helped me to realize what I truly wanted, what I truly needed—you."

He shook his head. "Why?"

Quinn slid from the bed and sat cross-legged in front of Calder, their knees touching. "She loves me as well. She wants me to be happy, and she wants what's best for me."

"You're married. Why doesn't she believe that she's what's best for you?" he asked.

"Because she knows that what's best for me…is you."

"Can we…can we just be? For a moment, can we just—" He shook his head. He didn't know what it was he wanted or needed, but Quinn nodded and patted the space next to him as he leaned back against the bed, and Calder turned and sat next to him. Just one knee touching now, but it was enough. Quinn took his hand and brought it to his lap, running his fingers along the edge, tracing his lines. Soothing.

"The first night you left, I slept in your bed, did you know that? The next day, after I saw you at the inn, Warrick told me you were gone. That's how I found out you were gone—Warrick told me."

Calder closed his eyes, appreciating that Quinn's voice was so steady and without censure.

"I had nowhere to go. I couldn't go home. So I went to her…"

Calder listened as Quinn told him about those first days with her. How she'd helped him and how he'd found her. It wasn't easy to listen to, but he needed to hear their story. Calder knew the story of he and Quinn; he'd lived it. It was the most important story of his life. Now that she would be a part of this, it was important that he learn the story of her as well. So he listened quietly, patiently, and he tried to understand something about the woman who'd married his man.

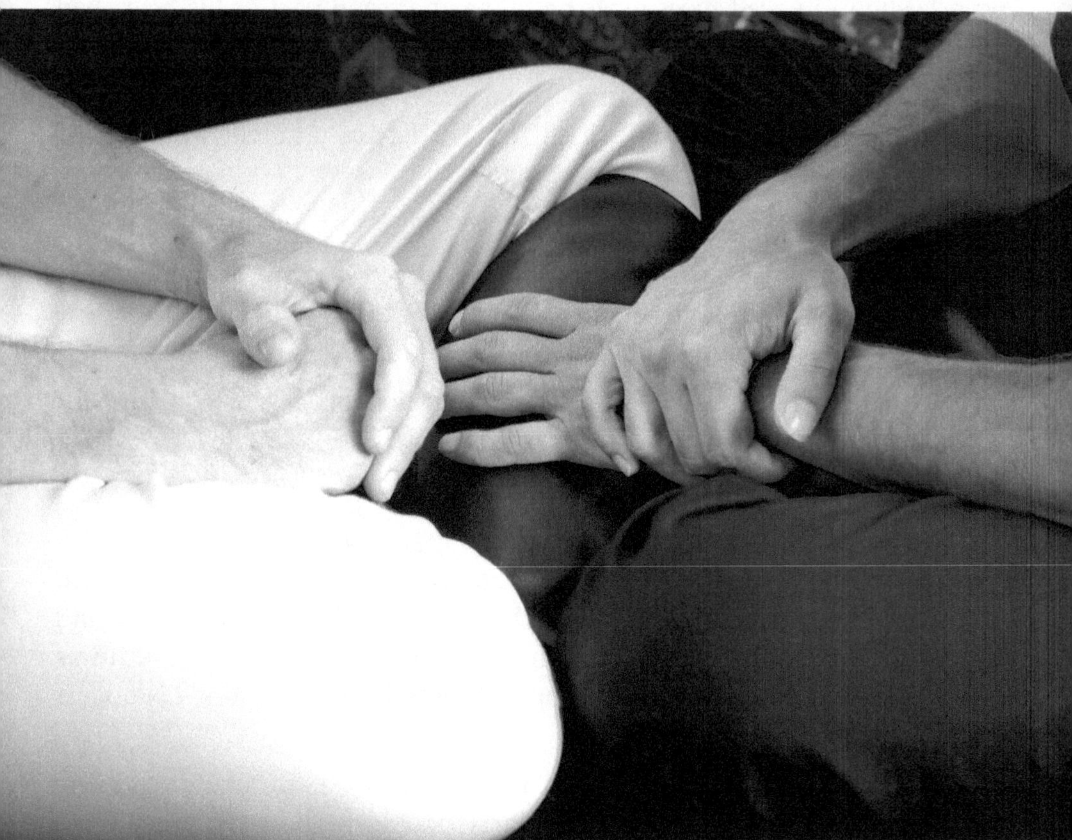

Celeste

Celeste

> *Celeste*
>
> *Thank you is not sufficient*
>
> *We leave Alexandria tonight*
>
> *Home soon*
>
> *I hope*
>
> *I love you*
>
> *Until Marseilles*
>
> *Quinn*

Celeste took a deep breath and looked out the window over the lawns. "Was there anything else?"

"Calder sent a note to say they were leaving Alexandria and they were still traveling together. That was all," Warrick said.

She turned toward the room. "I need to see his mother."

Roxleigh and Warrick exchanged glances, and Rox moved toward the entry. She heard him give instructions to the messenger who'd brought the telegrams to them, then the hooves as he returned down the drive.

"The carriage will be ready in half an hour. I will attend you," Roxleigh said as he returned to the parlor.

"I would like for Lulu to come with us as well, if that's acceptable to you both."

"Of course it is," Lulu said before Roxleigh even had a chance to answer.

It wasn't until they were underway that her nerves hit her. "I'm not feeling so well," she said quietly.

"Should we return?" Lulu asked.

Celeste shook her head. "No, I have to do this. I need to…I need to do this for Quinn and Calder."

"What is it you intend to do?"

"I intend to be sure our families can do no harm to them. To any of us, and I believe I know how to do it."

When she sat down with her mother and Quinn's mother in the back dining room, Celeste wasn't sure she'd be able to see it through, but when his mother reached out and patted her hand—as though nothing had happened, as though nothing at all had been between them, as though she hadn't intentionally trapped her son with a woman with whom he'd had no interest in marriage—Celeste found her calm.

"Where is Quinn?" his mother asked carefully.

"You know perfectly well where he is. Why have you come to see me here?"

"Celeste, my…my sweet, we just decided to visit the country for a few days and had heard that you were visiting your family here. We decided to stop for a visit, see how my son and new daughter are," she said.

"Lady Cheshire, I'm fairly certain you're aware of how we've been doing. I hardly believe you came here for that, or that you have no ulterior motive in coming here," Celeste said coldly.

"Dearest Celeste, you can still call me Adeleine—"

"No, I shan't. We are not that familiar, you and I." Lady Cheshire bristled and straightened her back, and Celeste looked to her own mother. "As for you, I truly have no idea why you would wish to make an appearance here."

"I wanted to inquire as to your condition."

"My…condition? Do you mean to ask if I'm breeding? How is that any concern of yours? You wanted nothing to do with me, and now you're interested in whether or not I carry his child? Are you hoping she will resemble you instead of me so you can pretend the doting grandmother?"

Lady Cheshire smiled and reached out to pat Celeste's knee but thought better of it when Celeste narrowed her eyes on her. "Of course we're interested in the grandchildren," she said. "Children are important to a marriage."

It was not lost on Celeste that the word "important" had been emphasized. Lulu tensed next to her. "Children are sometimes important to a marriage, sometimes not as much. After all, Quinn is but the spare, is he not? He's certainly not the heir. He has no titles to pass to his children."

"Not directly, no, but if something should happen, he would take the title and—"

"I see. So you're here about the title and the line."

"Children would legitimize your marriage," her mother said, and Celeste's gaze snapped to her.

"I thought you would be quite happy to have the color of my skin fade and die with me. What would happen, Mother, were my children to bear too much of a resemblance to me? What exactly would you do then?" Her mother's eyes widened as though she hadn't really considered it, and

Celeste nodded. "Let me explain something to you very clearly," she said as she looked to Quinn's mother. The air shifted, and she knew it was because Roxleigh had moved forward from his post at the door to stand at her shoulder. "If you think my husband did not make me aware of the telegram you sent him, you're mistaken. If you think you can speak to anyone I care about in such a dismissive and callous manner, then return as if nothing happened, you are mistaken."

Celeste took a deep breath as she tried to control her temper. "You are to leave here and not concern yourselves with our life in any way whatsoever. You are not to contact us or to speak with us unless we first contact you. At no time are you to approach my family or use any of our names to your benefit. At no time will you discuss the details of my marriage and whatever it is you may perceive it to be." Her mother and Lady Cheshire exchanged a glance, and Celeste smiled. "You see, I may have children, I may not. I may be with child as we speak, I may not. But you will never meet our children, and Quinn will never take the title if you so much as set a toe where you are not first invited. I certainly hope I've made myself perfectly clear.

"As to you, Mother," she said as she turned toward her, "I still fail to see what it is you're after by being here, but have no doubt that when I discover your ulterior motive, you will be dealt with accordingly. You seem to have misjudged the family you married me off to." Celeste stood and took Lulu's hand as they moved toward the door. She heard them quietly arguing and stopped, looking one last time to find Roxleigh behind her. He simply raised his eyebrows in question, and she nodded then walked out with a smile as he turned back to the women.

"Is everything Lady Wyntor said perfectly clear?" he asked.

Celeste didn't wait to hear any reply; his voice brooked no argument.

Quinn

The next two weeks were spent in a haze of sex, food, and talking late into the night. Quinn told Calder everything that had happened between him and Celeste. Moment by moment, everything he remembered. Calder forced himself to sit still through the stories until he couldn't, and then he'd make love to Quinn to quiet him until the next day and he would ask for more.

They would arrive in France this evening, much too late for the telegram office to be open surely, but perhaps not too late to go into Marseilles for some green air, solid ground, and fresh food.

"I can see some light," Calder said. They swayed on their feet when the paddle slowed their forward movement. It took another hour to get the ship into the harbor and for them to disembark. They found a small cafe that was nearing close, asked for whatever they had available if they could wrap it to take with them. They were given a small basket filled with cheese, bread, and two bottles of wine with the corks loosened. The perfect French picnic.

Quinn and Calder walked from the shop on Quai de la Fraternité and hopped on the passing cable car, taking it to the beach where hundreds of rowboats spent the night. They removed their shoes and stockings and rolled the ends of their trousers and walked on the sand until they were far enough from anyone that they could speak freely, all the world cast in shades of blue with the moon and stars reflecting off the surface of the water.

Calder found a broken hull and flipped it over against another boat, and they sat inside on the edge, their feet in the gentle waves, their hips and shoulders brushing together as they shifted. Quinn took a bottle of wine from the basket and pulled the loose cork out then took a long draught and handed it to Calder.

"So much class in you, sir, I'm overwhelmed," Calder said.

Quinn laughed. "Hand me that bread," he said as he put his hand back out. Calder searched for the loaf of bread, not bothering to lower the wine bottle as he did so. He shuffled through the basket then pulled out half of a baguette and handed it to Quinn, who took a bite. "Who's full of class now, my lord?" he said as Calder downed nearly half the bottle.

"Well," he said when he lowered it and handed it back to Quinn, taking the bread from him. "I knew if I left it to you, it would be gone before I got any. It was preemptive consumption."

Quinn chuckled. "Preemptive consumption, my arse. There's another bottle in there."

"Is that so?"

"That is so."

"Well, then." Calder quieted as he picked at the bread, and Quinn knew he had something on his mind and he was going to have to pull it from him.

"What is it?"

"You've told me all about what happened when I was gone, but you failed to tell me the most important parts," he said as he picked, tossing small bits out to the sand.

"What do you mean?"

"What you described was all quite mechanical, Quinn. I want to know how these things felt to you. I need to know how invested you are." Calder's voice was small, and Quinn knew this had been very difficult for him to ask.

"If you meet her for yourself under better circumstances, you'll understand."

"I don't think I will, Quinn. We are not the same—you and I—and I think perhaps you're lying to yourself where she is concerned."

"I'm not. I've told you that I love her, but that it's different from how I feel for you."

"But I need to understand it, and I don't. I cannot walk blindly into a home and see the two of you together. If we walk in and I see that look in your eye, the one that has always been mine alone, without understanding why it's there…I'm just trying to be honest, Quinn. You've told me a great deal about her. About the time you spent together—but it's all terribly superficial."

As Calder spoke, Quinn understood how nervous he was by the way he wouldn't turn to meet his eye. He considered what Calder said and realized he'd actually made a conscious effort to keep all emotion from the stories he'd told about Celeste to spare the man his feelings. He should have known Calder was smarter than all that. "What do you wish to know?" he asked nervously.

"You told me about that night, after Gray told you I was gone. You went to her house—tell me more about that. Tell me why."

"I…I had never felt so alone in my life as I did that night. I'd gone back to your townhome, but it was so dark…I couldn't make myself go inside again, and I certainly wasn't going back to my mother's house—she would have interrogated me to no end. I didn't have the will for that. I found myself at Celeste's house. I climbed her trellis."

Calder shook his head. "Any house I live in, I'm removing all exterior wall decorations."

Quinn laughed.

"What?" Calder asked.

"Celeste said the very same that next morning."

Calder stilled next to him. "You compare me to her?"

Quinn's smile faded. "Not…not by intention, only in this instance." Quinn reached for the cheese and cleared his throat, which was suddenly tight. "I got to her balcony and found her…managing herself—as she so eloquently put it." He tried but could not help the smile as her voice echoed in his memory. But he bit off a piece of cheese to try to cover it.

"And then?" Calder asked. "How did that make you feel?"

Quinn closed his eyes. What did that feel like that night? That night was magic, but Quinn wasn't sure he could say that, because this—what Calder was asking from him now—this felt like he was cheating on her. But he couldn't very well tell Calder that. He closed his eyes and conjured the sight of her there in her chair, spread wide before the mirror, his forehead pressed against the cold glass of the door as he watched her learn how to bring herself off.

"I hadn't known," Quinn started, and a flush traveled his chest and arms as he spoke, as he thought about her and that night. "I hadn't known then that she was so very chaste. I'd assumed her a virgin, but she didn't know anything about physical pleasure until she saw us together," he said, his gaze landing on Calder's mouth as he lowered the wine bottle and licked a red drop to his mouth where it stained his lip. Quinn closed his eyes. "She told me the next day—"

"Do not skip forward this time, Quinn. I want to know the rest."

His voice was low and guttural, the dregs of the wine caught in his throat. "It was easily one of the most beautiful moments of my life, Calder. Watching her take her own innocence. Watching her slip to the floor because she was so overwrought she couldn't manage to stand to get to her bed or to even stay in the chair. It was overwhelming. I cracked the door, and the smell of her sex hit me…" He groaned and shifted as his cock answered his sudden need with blood.

Calder pressed the wine bottle to Quinn's mouth, and he took it and tipped it back, draining the rest of the wine before pushing the neck into the sand next to the boat and opening the next.

"I went to her, I wrapped her in quilts, and I lifted her and put her to bed. Then I lay facing her, and I slept soundly for the first time in days. When I woke, she was watching me."

"What did she say?" Calder asked, sliding toward Quinn as he took the cheese from his hand and slid it in his own mouth. His strong mouth.

"She didn't…she—she was angry with me. I thought she was embarrassed, but she wasn't. Well, she was, but more than that she was angry with me for having watched her. She was so overwhelmed that she couldn't talk to me until I sat in the chair to put my shoes on and she spoke to my reflection."

"And she wanted more from you?"

"She didn't. That's what I keep trying to explain to you. She doesn't want more. She said she was aroused by watching us, but she didn't…" He shook his head and closed his eyes to keep Calder from seeing his own arousal in his gaze. "Could you imagine? Seeing something so erotic it could bring you off forever? For her, that was us." If Calder would just touch him. "She didn't want to join us, she didn't want to be with you or with me, she simply wanted to watch. Us. Together." Quinn opened his eyes and let Calder understand what that idea did to him. "She still wants to watch us, Calder. She hasn't said as much—she would never—but I know she does. She thinks she can remember that one night and come off for a lifetime on the memory, and perhaps she can…but I know she wants to be part of this, somehow. Not as a participant, but as an observer."

Calder's hand palmed Quinn's cock suddenly as he leaned farther and pushed him over to his back, crawling between his legs and hovering over his chest.

"Uh…God, Calder," Quinn groaned out.

"Just talking about that night has you this hard? Or is it the idea of me fucking you while she watches?" Calder was waiting for him to answer, but Quinn couldn't catch his breath; his mind filled with the sight and scent of her, his cock hard beneath Calder's hand— "Tell me about the other time. The time before they caught you. The time she watched you come off," he

said as he ground his hips against Quinn's. Calder's cock was just as hard as his, and Quinn closed his eyes and grunted against him.

Quinn took a deep breath, and then another, and as he caught his breath, he went on. "She sat in the chair again, different…a different chair. She wouldn't allow me to touch her. I'm fairly certain I would have if she'd allowed for it. I am sorry for that." Quinn opened his eyes, and he held Calder's gaze when he said it.

"How much did you want to touch her?" Calder asked.

"Very much," Quinn said breathlessly.

Calder leaned closer to his mouth. "Keep going."

Quinn could almost taste the wine on his breath. He licked his lower lip. "I'd gone to my room. She walked in while I happened to be…managing myself," he said with another short laugh. Calder's eyes went dark. "She came in and sat down and watched as I did so—for her."

"What, Quinn…what did you do?" Calder's hands skimmed down the front of his shirt between their bodies and released the buttons of Quinn's trousers, sliding his hand in and stroking him to fullness.

"That…" Quinn said on a gasp, allowing his head to fall back against the wood of the boat. "I did that."

"What else?" Calder asked, his mouth hot on his chin, his neck. Quinn didn't know what to do with his hands; they were flung out, just hanging there in the air. He wasn't sure he could touch Calder, knew he couldn't help him do—whatever it was he intended to do.

"I played with my cods," Quinn said, and Calder slipped past his cock to his tightly drawn-up bollocks. "Oh God." The touch was match to flame, and Quinn was terrified that Calder would stop any moment as a sort of revenge.

"What then, Quinn? What did you do next?"

Quinn pushed his hips into Calder's arm, his cock rubbing its length against his forearm as Calder massaged his bollocks. "I used both hands," he said. " I licked my finger, I used my own mettle…" He couldn't speak anymore as Calder rolled to his side, bringing Quinn with him by wrapping his leg around Quinn's, then he put his finger in Quinn's mouth.

"Like this? Is this how you wet yourself?"

"Yes," he said. Then Calder's finger left the curve of his tongue and swiped the seed pooling on his belly before he slid his hand past the hand on his bollocks and teased his arse.

"Is this what you did?" Calder asked. "Tell me how."

"No, not like that. From behind," Quinn said.

Calder pulled his hand away, slid his finger across the tip of Quinn's cock, and shoved past the band of his trousers. He skimmed down the crease of his arse then pushed inside in one swift motion.

"Yes, God, yes, this is what I did," Quinn said as he grunted a momentary complaint until Calder found that spot inside him.

"What did you do next?" Calder asked.

Quinn twisted his hands into Calder's shirtfront as he arched against him. "I came off for her, Devil. I came off so hard I could see the stars."

"Come off for me," he said against his neck. "Come off hard for me, Quinn. This one is mine," Calder demanded.

Quinn pulled Calder's shirt tail from his trousers, baring his belly as he worked toward his end. He wrapped his arms around him, grabbed his arse, and held him tight, and then he did as he was asked. As he bit down on Calder's shoulder, he came off for him, his cock pulsing heavily between their bellies against Calder's forearm, his mettle trapped there. Quinn collapsed against Calder as he dragged his hands free and rolled to his back, taking Quinn with him.

"Bloody hell," Calder said; he sounded surprised.

"Devil," Quinn said softly, "I love you."

"Yes," Calder said softly, his voice unsteady. "I think you do." Calder sounded shocked, and Quinn moved so he could see his face. Quinn wanted to reassure him, but at the same time he wanted to do it all again.

Calder

alder pulled the linen napkin from the basket and moved to clean himself off, but Quinn stopped his hand. "Don't you want the rest of the story?" he asked.

He did. He wanted to hear more. He wanted to understand why he was so aroused from bringing Quinn off like that. "Not here."

"You say that quite a lot," Quinn said, falling to his back next to Calder. Calder laughed and wiped the mettle from Quinn's belly and his own arm and belly as best he could then stood and put himself to rights. As right as he could be under the circumstance, anyway. He tucked the head of his cock between the buttons on the fall of his trousers so it wouldn't be quite so blatant on the walk back. He was confused. It wasn't because of what had happened between himself and Quinn—they were always like that. He was confused because it had all started with talk of Celeste.

Quinn had become aroused simply from remembering that night, watching her, and what's more, it had worked for him quite well. Calder didn't like the fairer sex. But he hadn't been thinking about her. He was thinking strictly of Quinn as he brought him off. Even the words, it was all what Quinn had done to himself. That he'd done it for her benefit mattered not in the moment. Watching Quinn become so aroused from that memory was powerful.

But he'd also said that if she'd allowed him, he would probably have fucked her as well, and that was…too far. That wasn't something he could live with, and he knew it. If they were together now—if they were doing this—then they were doing this. There would be no one else again as there had been in the past. Except for Celeste—but not like that, it couldn't be like that.

She needed to fit with them somehow. She would have to, but she couldn't have that. He reached down and yanked Quinn to his feet and tried to brush the sand off, giving up in favor of behaving more inebriated than they each were.

Calder picked up the second bottle of wine and downed a quarter of it before passing it back to Quinn and cleaning up what was left of the picnic so he could dispose of it.

"We could take the train to Paris and then to Le Havre," Quinn said suddenly. "The route runs daily. We could be in England sooner. If you wish it."

Calder stopped what he was doing and looked at Quinn. "Is that what you wish, to be back to her more quickly?"

"No, that's not what I was saying. I would like to be home, but not before you're ready. I won't lose you for my impatience."

"I'm not sure I'm ready for that. As much as I'm ready to be back in London, I'm really not at all prepared." He hadn't realized that until just then. Because once they were back in London, they had a wife to contend with. Or rather, he had a wife to contend with. Quinn was happy with his wife. "I'll consider it. The train will leave, what, eight or nine in the morning?"

Quinn dipped his head. "Whatever you feel is best, I will be happy with."

"So you're in no hurry to return?"

"I am, but again, I'll not rush back if you aren't ready. We could stay in Paris even, if you wished."

"While that's tempting, we have to return so you may retrieve the information from Madoc's solicitor and we can give it to the queen to deal with."

"Ah, yes, that, the whole purpose of the trip. Well—"

"Yes, well. Not the whole purpose," Calder said, allowing his annoyance to slip its tether.

"No," Quinn said, and Calder took his face between his hands, sank his fingers into the hair at his nape as he pulled Quinn toward him and kissed him. He savored the flavor of the wine on Quinn. When he pulled back, he leaned over to pick up the basket then smacked his arse on the way back up, just because he could.

"What the devil?" he said.

"Yes, I am, aren't I?"

Quinn glared at him, but it didn't last long, melting into a smile. "Come on, then," he said, and without thinking about it, Calder took Quinn's hand as they walked the length of the beach back toward the cable cars so they could return to the ship. When they reached the street, Quinn shook off his hold and they walked separately to the tracks, but too restless to wait, they started walking the street.

"That was…interesting," he said quietly.

"What was?"

"You, Devil. You bringing me off while I told you how it felt to take myself in hand for Celeste," Quinn said as he stopped and blocked Calder from moving on.

"Yes, it was…interesting. I'm not quite prepared to consider it, though, if you don't mind, and it is getting rather late tonight. We should get back to the ship." The streets seemed to be emptying rather quickly as the wind across the ocean picked up.

Quinn started walking again. "I was only saying that it was interesting, and I could be interested in doing something like that again, if you would be amenable."

"Not here, Quinn." Calder saw the grin spread across his face. "Sorry."

"Not to worry, I'm not all that fragile. Here's the car," he said as he pulled Calder back from the tracks and they turned to jump on board as it slowed for them. They made it back to the docks and to their room in no time, then argued over who would take the first shower. Seemed a silly thing to argue about, so they shared the shower, as small as it was.

As he crawled into bed that night with Quinn pulled tight against his side, his head resting in the same familiar place on Calder's chest, his breathing slowing into the heavy draught of sleep, Calder considered what they'd done on the beach. How bad would it be to have her there with them? If she truly didn't want anything but to watch…could he allow for something like that?

He wasn't entirely sure. He wasn't even sure if he'd be able to stand in the same room with her, let alone have a conversation or a fuck. He supposed that was just one of the myriad things they needed to figure out.

Quinn

In the end they took the train to Paris and stayed the extra time they would have spent on the ship. It was a lovely compromise. Their last full day in Paris they spent at a private home outside the city with John Singer Sargent and some of his acquaintances. Their time there was quiet and peaceful, and they were allowed to be themselves, together, just Quinn and Calder. Nobody knew them or said a thing about it, or bothered to care.

They lunched, swam in the stream that led to the pond on the property, rode horses, and simply enjoyed themselves and the company of the other men there.

"We could do this," Quinn said as Calder leaned back against him in front of the fire in the parlor. They were leaving to return to Paris soon and had a train and a ship to catch. The following day they'd be in London.

"How do you mean?" Calder asked.

"We could have a home, a private estate. We could live there, be ourselves there. We would of course have to attend society at times, but we could do this. If they can manage it here in France, why not in England?"

"You know why not in England. We're strangers here. None of these men knows us. We're a known quantity in England. Both of us," Calder replied.

"All right, but think about it. If we were careful, if we were far enough from London and bothered no one…"

Calder shrugged instead of arguing, which generally meant the discussion was over. Quinn only hoped that Calder would consider what

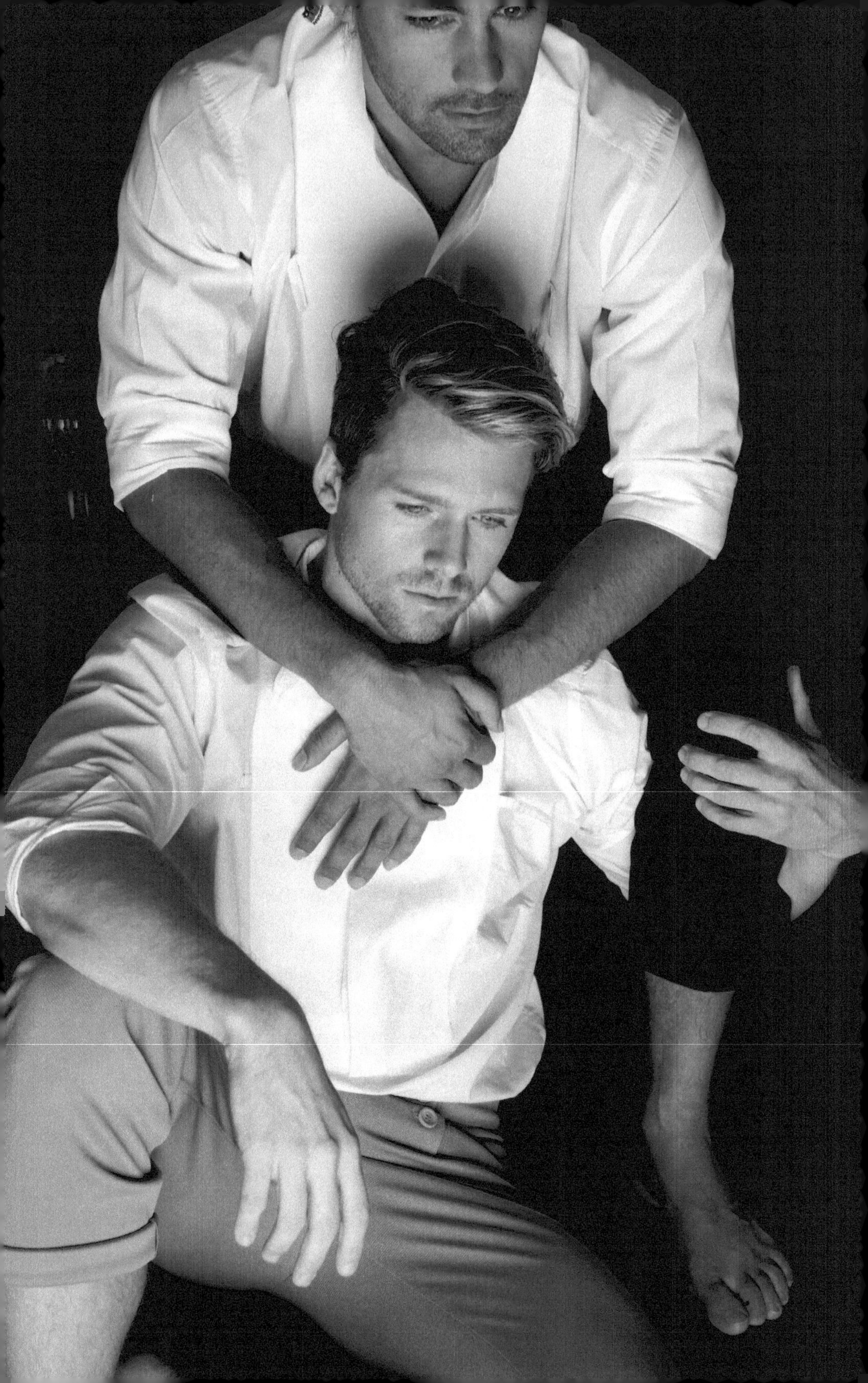

he'd said. What did London care what he and Calder did beyond their purview as long as they didn't flaunt it?

"You seem to forget I need heirs," Calder said quietly.

"I haven't forgotten that. I think about it constantly, in fact. It runs my veins like ice." Quinn leaned forward and wrapped his arms around Calder's shoulders, burying his face in the side of his neck.

"So do I, Quinn. But don't mistake me. I've considered a life like this. I've considered abdicating. I don't know that I can without calling more attention to myself, but I have considered it. I've considered it all."

"I didn't think you had," Quinn said quietly. "You never mentioned it."

"Of course not. Why should I get your hopes up for naught?" Calder said.

"Then why tell me now?"

"Because I told you I would be honest with you, Quinn, and I intend to see to that, if nothing else."

Quinn squeezed Calder as hard as he could, and his hands came up and held on to his arms as though he never wanted to let go. His head fell back against Quinn's shoulder, and his gaze rolled to meet Quinn's.

"Never mistake how much I love you, Quinn. If nothing else, know that. Know that I've tried," Calder said, and his voice was tender and raw as it shook, and it scraped along the outside of Quinn's heart, leaving a permanent mark there.

"So have I," Quinn said, more breath than words coming out. Then he kissed him, slow and gentle, like his lips were a trembling butterfly he was afraid would take flight. He slid a hand into Calder's shirt, letting his warm skin soothe his cold fingers.

"We must get back," Calder said.

Quinn nodded. He never wanted to leave this place, except that he did, because he needed to get back to Celeste. The door to the parlor opened slowly. "Gentlemen?" Sargent said quietly.

Calder stood and pulled Quinn up, but didn't immediately release him. It was so decadent, this allowance of touch with witnesses. He stared at their hands joined together, the heat of their bodies shifting so closely, more than was proper. He looked up to see John smiling at them, unconcerned, unfazed. Quinn suddenly understood Calder's jealousy and knew he would work hard with Celeste to mitigate it. He understood, standing here touching Calder with people watching and not at all minding, that he and Celeste had something Calder never would have in that, the ability to be true to each other in a very public way, regardless of how trivial.

Calder tugged, and Quinn followed him to the carriage.

Calder

The first thing they did when they returned to London was retrieve the information from Madoc's solicitor. Calder took it directly to Buckingham so Her Royal Highness could deal with the men involved. That was it—it was over and done, and he and his family were out of it. He thought he would be relieved, but he wasn't because they may have finished this bit, but they had yet to deal with Madoc himself.

Madoc had instructed Calder to tell the queen that he'd been instrumental in gathering the information—which he had been, there was no lie there. All the information Calder turned over had come directly from Madoc. However, he'd also instructed Calder that he wasn't to elaborate—to anyone—on any other information about him that might paint him badly, and he was to leave Madoc's return to London society and reintroduction to his family to Madoc himself. There was no way in all the land Calder was going to let that happen.

He managed to slip an idea to HRH about notifying the family so as not to blindside them when Madoc returned and, thankfully, she agreed. Madoc didn't get to outweigh the queen. It was that simple. No matter what he said or did, this one small piece was true. So Calder would inform Gray before he found out in some less appealing way.

As for the queen, she'd said nothing to Calder about reversion to Madoc. She would need to serve the Letters Patent to him for it to take effect—something she hadn't discussed or mentioned—and until then, the title would be held by Gray. Calder hoped she was as intelligent in this matter as he believed her to be in most things. Even if Gray didn't want the title to begin with, leaving it to his brother wasn't exactly a better option, but regardless, they may have no control of it.

They quit London hours after meeting with her in favor of Westcreek and now…now they waited.

And the waiting was going to kill him.

It was worse than reality because of the things he managed to conjure in his thoughts. His mind had always been infinitely worse—except where Celeste had been concerned. Nothing about the reality of her was less than what he considered, because it was all fully possible. He knew, now, just what she meant to Quinn, and while parts of it were better than he expected, there were things that he simply couldn't reconcile. Like Quinn's want of her—he'd said himself he would have fucked her—well, he'd said he would have touched her…but certainly in that instance, touching would have led to fucking. So in Calder's mind, fucking was what he'd heard.

Celeste, it seemed, held all the power in that relationship, and she'd ceded it to Calder. Which made him quite wary and uncomfortable, really. It was a great deal of responsibility. He still had too much jealousy to be able to think equitably about the situation. Not only that, but…where was Quinn's power? The Quinn he'd fallen in love with was determined, opinionated…powerful. Drawing that out of him had been such a beautiful thing. Turning the spare into something worthy of an heir. He needed to feel in control of something, some part of this.

Quinn hadn't seen her in weeks; that sort of longing after such an intensely intimate experience would only serve to compound his feelings for her. And Calder knew Quinn to be a good judge of character, but if Quinn were blinded by this woman's graces…the way Quinn spoke of her, she had no failings. She was graceful and gracious and true, and the trouble with grace was that if you were not true in purpose, you could easily hide mal intent behind it.

Calder knew all too well what it was to let love blind you. It was the reason they were in this predicament to begin with, because if he'd been able to think clearly, Calder would never have stayed to watch Quinn dance with her, he would never have obsessed over her, he would never have taken that jealousy out on Quinn that night, and with a clearer head…she may never have seen what she had. Except if none of that had happened, he and Quinn would be in that same horrid rut.

Calder realized too that it was entirely possible she thought very little of him from the minimal exposure she'd had to him. She'd had but one night with him—completely naked and threatening her, with his cock in her face. He dropped his head to his hand and rubbed his eyes. Not so very gentlemanly, that.

Calder looked out the window of his and Quinn's room at the Westcreek Park dowager house, knowing somewhere out there Celeste was making her way toward them. Toward Quinn. There really was nowhere else for this to take place other than Eildon, but Calder had refused to be so far from a possible escape—though he didn't say that. This was the perfect setup; Perry and Lilly had opened up the spare house on the property so Quinn and Calder could retreat here in privacy while they waited for Celeste to arrive.

And wait they did.

Quinn spent his time going through the papers on all the properties Perry had found that would be of interest. One in particular caught Calder's

eye. A small estate in Giggleswick. It had been a seat, but had fallen from entitlement and into disrepair, and so now the overrun estate was up for auction.

Calder appreciated that it was a mere half day by horse from the seat of his marquessate in Canford. He hadn't said as much, but Quinn had already made it a priority, even as it needed much more work than all the other properties. It was similar to Westcreek, though on a smaller scale, with a manor house and a small dowager cottage.

Quinn had also purchased a townhouse in London, taking over

a property near both Roxleigh and Perry, on Grosvenor. Pretty soon there would be nobody on the Square but Trumbulls. Perhaps they could wall it off like a private estate within London. Fancy that. Not that it could or would happen.

Calder heard the carriage at a distance, and his breath caught as a chill rushed his spine. It was time for him to leave. He had to meet Gray to tell him of his brother. At the same time, Celeste would be reunited with her husband—his Quinn. Calder had decided against being a witness to that. He'd decided it was in everyone's best interests if he simply stayed away from their reunion and perhaps came back from his visit with Gray once everything had calmed down some.

"Quinn, I'm headed to the house. Are you ready?" He turned from the window to find Quinn quite a bit panicked.

"I'm not—I'm not prepared. I want you here with me."

"I cannot do that for you. I think for all of our sakes this is better. You and she will be free to reunite—happily—outside my purview."

"I understand that, but I still…" He shook his head and pinched the skin between the fingers of one hand. "I'm frightened of what comes next."

"I am as well, but we've agreed to do certain things. We must do those things, and then we can move forward. I must speak with Warrick, and you—you must reacquaint yourself with your wife and I…I do not need to be here for that. I will see you after," he said quietly, doing his best to modulate his voice and not let any hint of the frustration and nervousness he felt get through. But he was nervous, and it wasn't because he had to tell Gray about Madoc. It was because he was giving Quinn the power and the opportunity to leave him for her. Quinn had sworn it wouldn't be like that—but again, how could Calder truly know anything?

"Both of us?" Quinn asked.

Calder turned back toward the window, watching as the carriage now pulled away from the main house. "Perhaps just you at first, can we? When I return, would you meet me alone? I think that would be best, easier. For me."

"Whatever you wish."

Calder turned away from the window and walked to him. He stopped just shy of touching him, stared into his eyes, and held his gaze for entirely too long. If this was the last time it was just them, what would he tell him?

Nothing. He'd told him enough; finally, Calder had told Quinn everything. Calder ran a thumb over the crest of Quinn's cheek, kissed him softly as his hands soothed, searched a bit, tried to make memories. Then he walked out without another word or glance to where his horse awaited him. It felt like goodbye, and his chest ached for it.

He mounted then held his horse—restless no doubt because of his own tension. He should have gone on to the stables behind the main house, but he didn't. He waited. As the carriage pulled up the drive, he stayed himself, even as every bit of him wished to bolt. He knew she was aware he was here. The curtain slid open at the door, and he saw her face in the shadows. Fear was lovely on her, but he imagined she was lovely no matter what expression she wore.

He looked back at the house to see Quinn standing in the window, then back to Celeste, but she was still watching him. Unmoving. He could do this. He closed his eyes and took a deep breath, then he opened them and stole her gaze, holding it. He nodded once, then he kicked his mount and they were off.

He found Gray in the parlor and asked for a moment alone. After everyone shuffled out, Calder turned to him. "We need to speak," Calder said quietly.

"You think me daft?" Gray asked as he motioned to the door everyone had just departed through.

Calder shook his head. "I have something important—"

"First, I want to apologize," Warrick said.

"There is no need. You did what you thought best at the time. I understand."

Warrick nodded.

"I have something quite difficult…that I must tell you."

"What more could there be? It's over. I'm summoned to Buckingham next week—I imagine to give my statement."

"She sent for you?" Calder hadn't known, and he wasn't sure what it meant; he was fairly certain it wasn't merely to get Gray's accounting of matters.

"She did."

"She didn't say anything else?"

Gray turned to him, the gaze in his eyes the one that made him feel naked and afraid. "What else would she have to say to me?"

"She may have questions or…need information on the manner in which we came about the information," Calder said.

"After several years of searching, you found a disgruntled member of their group. Is that not true?"

"Of sorts, yes, but this man is quite a bit more than just that." Calder was suddenly cold. He turned to the tantalus on the sideboard. "Whiskey?" he asked as he poured two tumblers and carried them to the chair before the fire. He handed one to Gray, who was eyeing him suspiciously. "Please," he said, motioning to the chairs.

"Carry on." Gray pointed for him to continue as he leaned back in the chair, palming the glass. Between the words and the glare in his eyes, Calder was chilled to the bone.

"Your brother—"

Emotion on Gray's face wasn't something one saw often, as he was so very much in control of his expressions that one had to truly know him to have any idea of what he was thinking, and even then, there were many times Calder was still struck dumb.

"Lysander?" he asked coldly.

Calder shook his head.

"Madoc." Gray said the name as he swirled the whiskey in the glass and stared at the fire, and Calder heard the shudder in the word.

"Madoc," Calder repeated. "He's alive."

The tumbler Gray held shattered in his hand, whiskey and glass spraying in all directions as he stood. "That's not possible!" he yelled.

Calder stood as well, out of simple self-preservation—fight or flight—as Lulu rushed into the parlor.

"What's happening? Oh Jesus, your hand!" She ran to Gray and pulled his hand from where it hung loosely at his side, dripping blood, whiskey, and pieces of glass to the floor. "Gray?" She examined his face then turned to Calder. "What is it?" she asked quietly when Gray didn't speak. "Calder, what?"

The blood drained from Gray's face, his gaze on the fire. He wasn't with them anymore; his mind was somewhere else altogether. "As it happens," he said quietly, "Warrick's eldest brother is not dead." He watched Gray as he said it, refusing to say his name again. Gray flinched nonetheless, and Calder watched as an expression like fear crossed his face, watched him slip to his knees in front of Lulu.

"Leave us," Lulu said quickly as Gray's hands wrapped around her skirts, leaving bloody handprints streaking the delicate fabric.

"But—"

"No—we can finish this conversation later, Calder. Leave, now!" she yelled, and he did. He pulled the door closed behind himself and waved the staff off then pulled Perry with him to his study to let him know what was happening.

"I can't believe it," Perry said.

"Neither could I, and yet here it is. He's ugly as a badly fucked Molly, but he survived the accident. He's alive."

"Oh God help us, he's The Warrick," Perry said quietly.

"Not quite yet. The queen is aware, but she has yet to issue the Letters."

"But she will, she must."

"Must she?"

"I don't—I don't know," Perry said finally. "Bloody hell."

"Exactly." They sat awhile in complete silence, then Calder spoke. "Listen. Gray cut his hand, and I don't know how bad it is. Lulu is with him and a good judge of injuries, of course, but you should perhaps get some salve and water and bandages ready. I wouldn't go into the parlor just yet, or at all, without permission."

Perry nodded and rang for the butler. "How are Quinn and Celeste?" he asked carefully as they waited.

"Goddammit all, but today is a disaster. I want nothing more than a warm bed and some sleep," he said quietly.

"Have you seen her?"

"Briefly, before I came here to speak with Gray." Calder pinched his lower lip between two fingers as he remembered the fear in her eyes.

"Will they stay the night?" Perry asked, changing the subject back to Gray and Lulu.

"I don't know. I would hope so. You should attempt to keep them here. He doesn't need to return to London just yet."

"If Gray wishes to leave, there's nothing I would be able to do to stop him," Perry said.

"I know. When I leave, I'll be sure they're putting the horses up. Tell the stable master to make excuses. That will help, at least. HRH has demanded an audience with Gray next week…while she can do as she will, I would hope this means she intends to speak with him before she does anything about the title, but the reality is—I have no idea where Madoc is at the moment, and that poses a very real problem."

"He hasn't mellowed with death and age?" Perry asked.

"If anything, he's become infinitely worse." Calder put one hand to the center of his chest, skimmed his thumb down the center line and thought of the chains and the wall, and he turned away. "But that is a conversation for another time."

"I'll keep an eye out for Gray and Lulu. You should go."

"Yes, I should," he said, but he didn't move.

"But?"

"Exactly. But…what awaits me at the dowager house…"

"She really is a lovely woman, Calder, and I'm sure you've heard this enough as it is, but perhaps from someone else? She's lovely. And she wants you and Quinn together more than anything else. I can see her dedication to that end without a doubt. That, I promise you."

"I appreciate those words," he said. He supposed he should go back, but his legs didn't seem to be cooperating at the moment. "I can't move," he said.

"Quinn is going to be concerned."

"I'm aware." He closed his eyes again; he really was exhausted. If for nothing else, he needed to return for Quinn's sake, to prove he could keep his word. He'd said he would return, and so he should. He stood. "Well, then," he said quietly. He drank the rest of the whiskey he'd forgotten he still held and set the tumbler on a side table. "I very much appreciate everything… and all that," he said as he waved a hand in the air to be cordial.

Perry stood and took his shoulders. "Calder, I don't know what will happen next, but I do know that there are not three better people in this world. You are all dedicated, and you are all loved." Calder nodded, and Perry pulled him in, slapping his back in a stiff hug. "Now get out of my house," he said with a push toward the door.

Calder laughed and stumbled for the door, but when he reached it, he turned back. "Thank you," he said, then he stepped out into the entry and finally out into the fading light. He may not have made any promises to Quinn, but he had a promise to keep nonetheless. He left the horse with the stable master and walked toward the dowager house and hoped—hoped they would come to some sort of understanding.

eleste waited for Calder to disappear into the main house, then she put her hand on the door to the carriage. Quinn was here. She'd waited for weeks, and finally, they were both here. She saw the curtains shift in the window and turned her gaze to the main entry. She could see the light from inside, watched as it darkened, and then he was there, standing at the top of the steps, waiting for her.

"Quinn," she said to herself, then she flung the door wide, picked up her skirts, and jumped down before the footman could even lower the step. She ran up the stairs and flung herself at him bodily and realized just why Calder wouldn't want to be here for this. She released Quinn and stepped back. "I'm sorry, I—I shouldn't have," she said and cut a glance back toward the main house, the waning light limning it in gold.

"Come," Quinn said and took her hand and pulled her into the house, through the entry, and into one of the parlors, shutting the door behind him. "I've missed you," he said quietly and took her in his arms, and finally, finally, Celeste could breathe. Though not very well as tightly as he held her.

She pulled her gloves off behind his back and dropped them to the floor, running her hands through his dark hair, ruffling it and smoothing it, and holding him tight. "I've missed you as well, so very much, my love," she said.

They clung to each other until the light shifted and the room was washed in gold as if it had dripped from the walls of the main house and down the hill to the dower house, coating everything in its path.

"Quinn," she said. "Quinn." All she could do was hold on to him. He pulled her toward the settee, and they fell together, him leaning back and her in his arms, and she did naught but gaze out the window at the warm light.

"You are the most incredible woman, Celeste. What you've managed…"

She closed her eyes and nodded against his chest and patted his belly where her hand rested, playing with the buttons of his waistcoat. "How long do we have?"

"I don't know. What he has to do right now…it won't be easy." Celeste sat up, studying his expression, trying to find more, but he just shook his head. "I cannot explain just yet," he said.

She straightened, putting some space between them so they could speak. She twisted her hands in her lap as he too straightened on the settee next to her. Then his warm hands covered hers, and she lifted her gaze to his and once again felt much more at ease.

"We're all frightened—all of us. We're all nervous. None of us knows what comes next, but that we all truly want to try to…understand what it is we're doing. It's all right. We'll be all right."

The flutters in her belly increased. She looked at him and considered, her eyes roving his form. "I…" She reached out and trailed a hand down his waistcoat, and his eyebrows came together. "I've had so much time to think, and now with you here, this close to me, being able to touch you again, I believe I truly know myself. I believe—I've never loved another soul as I love yours, Quinn. I've never felt for another person as I do for you. I believe in my heart that if I could be attracted to someone in the way you're convinced I should be, that it would be you. But looking at you now…I adore you, I want to be close to you, I want to touch and hold you and confide in you and be with you in every possible way but one. Quinn, I know now beyond doubt that I do not wish to touch you intimately, and I do not wish for you to touch me in that way either." She took a deep breath, then dropped her gaze, waiting for him to try, once again, to convince her.

His hand squeezed hers, then his other hand slid beneath and tangled their hands together in a knot of indefinable fingers. "I believe you," he said. "Celeste, look at me." She did, and he captured her gaze, and after a moment he smiled. "I believe you."

Something shifted, something locked, something solidified, and something else reached beyond them as if searching for their missing piece. For Calder. She experienced all of these things as if someone worked the loom of her soul, weaving and wafting all of her bits and pieces tightly together, and for the first time she was truly at peace in that knowledge. It was a weight lifted, and she untangled their hands, kissing his fingers as she did so. "How are the two of you?"

"Nervous," he said.

"What happens next?"

"He wants me to meet with him when he returns, then I will send for you. Is that acceptable?"

"Whatever you both need. It's not for me to say, honestly, Quinn."

"But it is, as you are a part of this as well."

"Not quite yet, I'm not. Calder must accept me first, and we aren't nearly there."

"But he will."

"You seem quite confident."

"Because I am. He and I… The past two weeks have been a revelation, really. I cannot thank you enough for being the catalyst that not only destroyed what we had become—a damaged and horrible thing—but also the catalyst that brought us back together. We are not the same people we were before he left. We will never be those people again, and this is a beautiful thing. I cannot express to you the change. So yes, I'm fearful, but I'm also more hopeful than I've ever been in my life. We'd put ourselves in this horrid rut wherein we did naught but injure each other. You've helped to change all of that, and now we can only be stronger."

Tears pricked her eyes. Celeste wasn't sure what to say to that. Only a couple of months ago she'd been considered worthless by her closest family, and now…she had this family who appreciated her, every bit of her. They easily saw her strengths, and they didn't try to break her down or take that from her. They built her up with every word they had for her. They rose above the fray, and they pulled her with them.

Celeste heard the footsteps on the gravel before Quinn and turned to the window. "Should I…what should I do?"

"Stay here until we're upstairs," he said. "I'll take him to our rooms, and we'll find you. You'll be fine?"

"I'm more than fine, Quinn."

"It may be some time."

"Whatever he needs," she replied as they stood and hugged quickly. Quinn placed a chaste kiss on her forehead before hurrying from the parlor and closing the door behind himself.

It seemed so quick, they hadn't even a moment to catch up meaningfully. She followed him to the door like a magnet, her hand coming up to the warm wood as it closed, her forehead leaning against it as she sent up a silent prayer for Calder, and then for Quinn, and finally for herself.

Quinn

Calder stood just inside the entry, haggard and worn. Quinn walked to him, then simply took his hand and pulled him through the foyer and up the stairs to their rooms. He set him on the bed, then ran a bath and returned to him. Quinn stood Calder up and slowly undressed him, led him to the tub, and helped him in, then he knelt beside it and took up a sea sponge and the only soap available—lilac—and began to wash his body. Every inch of him.

His rolled-up sleeves were wet, the front of his waistcoat and trousers soaked by the time he reached Calder's head and lathered his hair. Calder sank below the surface of the water, his knees poking up at the end of the claw-foot tub as Quinn smoothed the soap from his hair.

When Calder pushed out of the water, leaning back against the high end of the tub, he finally looked at Quinn. "That was one of the most difficult moments of my life, Quinn. I'm not sure I've ever experienced someone else's pain in such a visceral way. It shot through me like a knife. It was terrible, absolutely terrible."

Quinn reached up and wiped the liquid from Calder's cheek, fairly certain it wasn't just from the bath. Then he leaned across the tub and took his face in his hands, and he kissed him. He poured everything he had into that kiss. His heart, his soul, his hands, and his body. He gave it all and held nothing back.

Calder's hands came out of the water and pulled Quinn to him, refused to relent, holding and giving as much as Quinn did, until Quinn's shoes slipped on the slick, wet, tiled floor and Quinn splashed into the bath on top of Calder, the both of them laughing.

"You're a disaster," Calder said.

"Well, at least I managed to get you back in a bath."

"I know, you much prefer me in the bath."

"For obvious reasons," Quinn said. He flailed a bit until he knelt between Calder's legs, which were now spread wide, his calves up on the edges of the bathtub to give him room. Calder helped him peel his wet clothing off, tossing it to the floor next to the drain. Quinn rose on his knees to get out of the tub, but Calder stopped him, tugging on his trousers. "Not quite yet," he said.

Calder unbuttoned the fall of Quinn's trousers and released his blood-thickened cock to his greedy hands, shifting forward until he could get his mouth around him, and when he did, Quinn grabbed the edges of the bathtub to hold himself upright. Calder's legs slid from the edges of the tub, wrapping around his thighs, holding him solidly. He took him deep, pulling unholy sounds from Quinn as he drew the seed from his bollocks.

The water splashed around them, licking at his hips and thighs as Calder drew and played, and Quinn heard a symphony of beauty as sparks flew behind his eyelids. When he came off, Calder wrapped his hands around his hips and dug his fingers into his arse, shoving his cock down his throat as he swallowed. The heaven he found there was like a cleansing. His head dropped back, and the only thing keeping him from collapsing were Calder's strong arms wrapped around his thighs.

"Fuck. Devil. Fuck." Quinn slid his hands through Calder's hair and held on through the last of his spasms until there was nothing left and he leaned back, Calder licking and kissing and soothing his flesh. Then he pulled Quinn down to his chest, both of their legs slipping out of the tub as Quinn lay there, his trousers yet around his knees, the water low and cooling.

"We should get out," Quinn said. "We've made a terrible mess."

"Not yet," Calder said as reached up with his foot and turned the spigot on. Warm water splashed between Quinn's legs, and Quinn scooted to avoid it as the cool water heated. Once the tub was sufficiently refilled, Calder helped push his trousers off his legs.

"You have the most talented toes I've ever had the pleasure to know."

"Lucky man that you know me, then," Calder said, and Quinn felt his smile at the back of his head.

It was the perfect moment. Quiet and peaceful, a melting of worries and frustrations.

Calder's hand moved restlessly over Quinn's chest, and Quinn tangled his fingers with it. Then he turned his head to the side and closed his eyes. They needed to speak with Celeste, but after everything, and knowing how patient she was prepared to be, Quinn wasn't about to disturb Calder in what was possibly the first moment of true peace he'd had in quite some time.

"I love you," Calder said, and it vibrated through his skin and sank into his bones. The water cooled, and Calder released the drain, then warmed it once again, and still Quinn didn't stop him.

Calder

That Quinn's patience with him was so genuine bound his heart. He was prepared to do his best by Quinn and Celeste. No matter how difficult it would be for him. After seeing Grayson, with the knowledge of all he'd been through and all he now faced, Calder was even more determined to that end—but he wasn't quite ready. He ran a finger down Quinn's shoulder to his elbow and back up again, lazily tracing that ridge of muscle he adored so very much.

That was when it hit him. Quinn's patience; he hadn't seen a calm like this in Quinn in years. "Quinn?" he asked, not wanting to wake him if he slept. The man mumbled, then nodded against his chest. "When was the last episode?"

Quinn squeezed the hand he held against his own chest and shifted in the water. "The boat, Alexandria. When I left for the telegraph office. That's the closest I've come to an episode in…weeks now."

"Why is that?" Calder asked.

"I cannot pretend to know for sure, but…"

"Tell me."

"When you agreed to try…when you showed yourself to being committed to it…I felt a certain tension that I'd carried for so very long dissipate."

"Just like that?"

"Well, not just like that. There are quite a few factors. Lulu helped. She taught me something that has helped me to ward off the worst of it, and that the majority of our family is supportive of us helps. That Celeste is supportive of us, that we have somewhere to be, somewhere safe…but…"

"Yes?"

"But having you back, having you with me, knowing you're safe again… knowing you were willing to try—"

"I should have done so long ago…tried, I mean. I should have listened more. I should have done so many things differently," Calder said, only now realizing just how much he and Quinn had missed in life for being at odds. He closed his eyes and pressed the heels of his palms against his eyes. He told himself there was nothing to be done about it, but it didn't change the frustration he had with himself.

"I wasn't ready, you know. I never thought you would go and not return, until you did, and that's what broke me, ultimately. That I had to follow to get you back. That I had to truly lose you in order to stand up to my mother. It wasn't fair to you either, what I'd done," Quinn said.

Calder opened his eyes and stared at the single candle left burning in the room, the light from the sun finally gone. He just sat there, simply absorbing the shift and sway of the large muscles of Quinn's back against his chest as he considered it all, and Quinn spoke softly.

"You're the devil."

The memory of their first night together came to him from nowhere, as though it had happened only moments before, and he closed his eyes again, wrapped his arms around Quinn, and whispered the same words he had so many years ago. "What does that make you?" Calder asked as his voice caught, and he hoped, hoped that Quinn remembered as well as he did.

"If you're the devil, that makes me an angel," Quinn whispered, and Calder felt lightheaded in the realization that Quinn knew exactly what he was supposed to say.

"Perhaps a fallen angel," Calder said, his voice breaking.

"Still an angel," Quinn said with a smile to his voice.

"And I brought you down to earth?"

"Or perhaps…" Quinn paused, and Calder knew he was considering something. "Perhaps I raised you up?" Quinn said, and it was more of a question this time.

"Perhaps you did," Calder replied. "You're painting yourself in a much better light than you are me."

"Of course I am. I'm the good one. I'll always be the good one."

Calder said quietly, "And so I've ruined you."

"No, you haven't ruined me. I fell from grace long ago. I've been waiting for you. You're lucky I came." Quinn said the last so softly he almost didn't hear it.

"Hey, that's my line," Calder complained, his throat tight against the words as he forced them out.

Quinn flipped over in the bath, coming back up to his knees and bracketing Calder's head with his hands against the edge of the tub. "I will wait for you forever," he said, his lips brushing Calder's mouth as he spoke the words and stole Calder's breath.

"And I—I will always come." Calder darted his tongue out to Quinn's lips, enticing him forward until they were pressed together, not even room for water between them. He braced them at the end of the tub with one foot at the edge as Quinn slid his hand down Calder's back to tease his arse.

"Take me to bed, Quinn. Take me to bed."

"As you wish." Quinn pushed away from him, and the sudden chill sent a shudder through his system. They stood and dried each other off with warmed towels, then Quinn turned Calder and walked him backward toward the bed. His thighs hit the soft bedding, and he scooted back to the headboard, laying himself among the pillows as Quinn looked on.

Calder sat up, and Quinn stopped. He considered whether or not he could manage… He looked away, unable to meet Quinn's eyes as he thought about the possibility. Then he turned back and met his gaze.

"Go get Celeste," Calder said.

Quinn stared at him. He glanced over his shoulder toward the door, then looked back to Calder. "What—what do you mean?"

"I mean to start as we…intend to go on. Go get Celeste."

"I'm not—I'm not sure that…" Quinn palmed himself, and Calder knew that Quinn's cock had become inordinately hard since he'd spoken of her. "What do you intend?"

"She wants to watch…let her watch. Let her, this time, see how much I love you. How much you mean to me. Let me thank her for what she's done for you by gifting her with her desire. Quinn, go get Celeste."

Quinn looked to the door once again then back to Calder. "You're serious?"

"Quite. Now hurry before I lose my nerve."

"Perhaps we should—"

"Quinn," Calder said in his best argument-stopping voice, and Quinn, naked as the day, walked out of the bedroom. Calder stared up at the canopy on the bed, forcing himself to breathe steadily. He imagined Celeste sitting in the parlor waiting for them, only to have a naked Quinn walk in and drag her to bed with them. Perhaps this wasn't a good idea.

He started to shift, trying to pull the blankets from beneath his arse, when the door slowly opened and Quinn returned. Calder froze, his breath stilled, his lungs unable to take in the air he desperately wanted. Celeste didn't follow him immediately, but Quinn left the door wide open so Calder knew she was there. Quinn was very carefully not touching her in any way before leaving her at the entry and walking to the bed.

Calder pointed at a chair across the room, and she went to it. Then Calder's view was obstructed by his lover's body. He reached forward, and Quinn—God, he was beautiful, his dark hair still wet and falling across his forehead, the strength of his shoulders that could carry him anywhere should he need it, the smooth lines of his belly that all led to that beautiful cock, standing proud between his hips.

Calder took his hand and pulled him to the bed and forgot there was anyone in the room, anyone in the house, anyone in the entire world besides Quinn.

He worshiped him, flipped him to his back, and pushed him into the heavy pillows as he once again took him in his mouth and savored his early seed. He rolled the soft globes of his bollocks and chased the seam of his cods to his arse, teasing gently before pushing his legs wide and tilting his arse up for his tongue to explore.

He heard the quiet scrape of wood against wood, and he ignored it in favor of Quinn. He wrapped his hand around Quinn's cock, and between his hand on his cock and his tongue in his arse, he brought him off quickly.

"I understand you like the sight of a man's mettle," Calder said to her without taking his eyes from Quinn. Then he slid his belly against Quinn's, his seed covering them both before he reached for the bottle of oil he had next to the bed. He sat back on his knees between Quinn's widespread

thighs and dribbled the oil, making Quinn shudder and jerk as it ran his torso, mixing with his mettle. He dribbled more across his cock and shifted slightly to be sure she could see it come to fullness once again. Then he put his hand under Quinn's arse and dribbled the oil down the root of his cock so it ran his cods and gathered in Calder's palm as he worked first one finger and then two into his arse.

Calder heard her breath catch, and it gave him pause. He slowed his movements. Slid down until he was on his belly as Quinn relaxed his legs and Calder lay between them to catch his breath. He wasn't sure how he felt yet about this. About any of it.

"I'll go," she said, and he shook his head. His hair brushed Quinn's inner thighs, making him jump.

"Stay," he whispered.

Then Quinn's hands came down to his shoulders, and he looked up to find Quinn sitting above him, his face the perfect picture of concern tempered with lust. It was ridiculous, really, what that expression on Quinn did to him. Before all of this between them had happened, it would have sent Calder into a rage, but tonight it did quite the opposite. Tonight it meant something completely different. It meant Quinn loved him and cared about how he was treated, how he felt, how he was affected by all of this indefinable…whatever this was. They were making new rules, breaking the old, learning about each other, and finding ways to move forward together.

He came back up to his knees and scooted closer, draping Quinn's legs over his folded knees as he kissed him. He ran his hands up and down his thighs, and Quinn's hands came around his waist, holding his ribs, his thumbs dancing across his skin.

"We can stop," Quinn said against his skin, but Calder shook his head.

"No, I want you, and I want this."

Quinn kissed him in earnest then, and Calder felt that kiss all the way to his toes. He pushed Quinn back to the bed and started anew.

When Quinn had come to the parlor bare naked, Celeste hadn't known what to think, and now? She was simply overwhelmed. This wasn't at all what she'd expected from tonight; this wasn't at all what she'd expected from their relationship. But she wasn't going to walk away until Calder told her to, because to be a witness to this? She very much wanted that. She'd offered to go once, and she wasn't going to do it again.

She was, however, going to attempt to be more silent so as not to distract him.

"Celeste," Calder said, and she froze in place, her hands in her lap.

"Yes?"

"Move the chair over here, by the side of the bed where I can see you."

Her muscles jerked as though trained to move on command, but her mind told them to stay because she'd only just determined to not be intrusive. "All right," she said finally, but the words were practically inaudible for the lack of strength behind them. She was weak and overwhelmed, a bit lightheaded at the idea of being here. She stood and scooted the chair, which sounded extremely loud to her ears as she dragged it across the floor next to the bed. Then she sat down and pulled her feet up beneath her and held on to the chair with both hands.

Calder gazed at her then. Caught her eye as Quinn kissed his way down his neck.

"Is this what you want?" he asked quietly, and it wasn't at all judgmental, it wasn't harsh, as she might have expected in this moment, it wasn't cruel. He was simply asking this of her; he wanted to know. This wasn't the same

man she'd last seen on a night very like tonight with both of these men naked and wrapped up in each other.

"What I want doesn't matter," she said. "Only what you want matters." She withered under his glare.

"What I want matters," he said definitively. "What Quinn wants matters. And for this to work…what you want also matters."

"But what is this?"

"Whatever we make it," he said, then his neck moved on a swallow as he closed his eyes and put his head back when Quinn wrapped a hand around his cock, and it was the most glorious thing—she wanted to cry out…but she held it in, she held it all in. Her muscles vibrated from the tension she managed to constrain.

"Celeste," he said again, and his voice was like carriage wheels over a gravel road. "Is this what you want?"

Her throat was suddenly dry and scratchy, and she couldn't seem to swallow past the sudden lump that had formed there. She nodded and heard someone whimper, and he opened his eyes to challenge her to speak, as if he knew, and perhaps he did; perhaps that small noise she'd heard was actually her. "Yes," she whispered. "I want this."

Calder pushed Quinn to the bed and rose over him, spreading Quinn's thighs wide as he seated his hips between them. He tested his arse once again then lined himself up and thrust slowly forward as he licked Quinn's mouth until it fell open and he caught his gaze. "I love you," he said, and Quinn wrapped his arms around his torso as he shifted to allow for more depth. "I love you," Calder repeated. "I've loved you from the day I became aware of you. I've been helpless in the want of you. I always will be." Calder slowed, the muscles of his hips flexing slowly, rocking him against Quinn in the most languid and decadent of ways.

Desire rushed her skin and flushed her chest, and Celeste couldn't help but groan. She closed her eyes from the sheer power of the moment. A tear slid down her cheek, dropped to the crest of her collarbone then dissipated, and she reached up and ran a finger along that hard line. Her other hand snaked down to press against her mons, soothing the ache that built there.

She opened her eyes to see both of them staring at her, their eyes black with lust, and she froze again. Calder turned back to Quinn, but Quinn—he kept his gaze on her. "Lift your skirt," he whispered. She crawled her fingers up her legs and held on to her skirts as she lowered her legs to the floor, bunching the fabric at her knees. Once she reached bare skin, she stopped. "Keep going," he said.

She pulled the skirt up, dragging the fabric up her sensitive skin, her thighs shaking from the tension created by the slide of the fabric; the sudden cool air as the heat that had been trapped beneath her skirt dissipated, leaving her blood-heated body shaking against it.

"Go on," Quinn ground out. Calder's hips thrust at his words, closing his eyes and making him arch against the bed. "More," he said. Calder leaned into him, wrapped a hand under his shoulder, pinning him against his own body as Quinn reached down and grabbed his arse and pulled him in. "Devil," he whispered. It seemed the word was swept away by Calder's

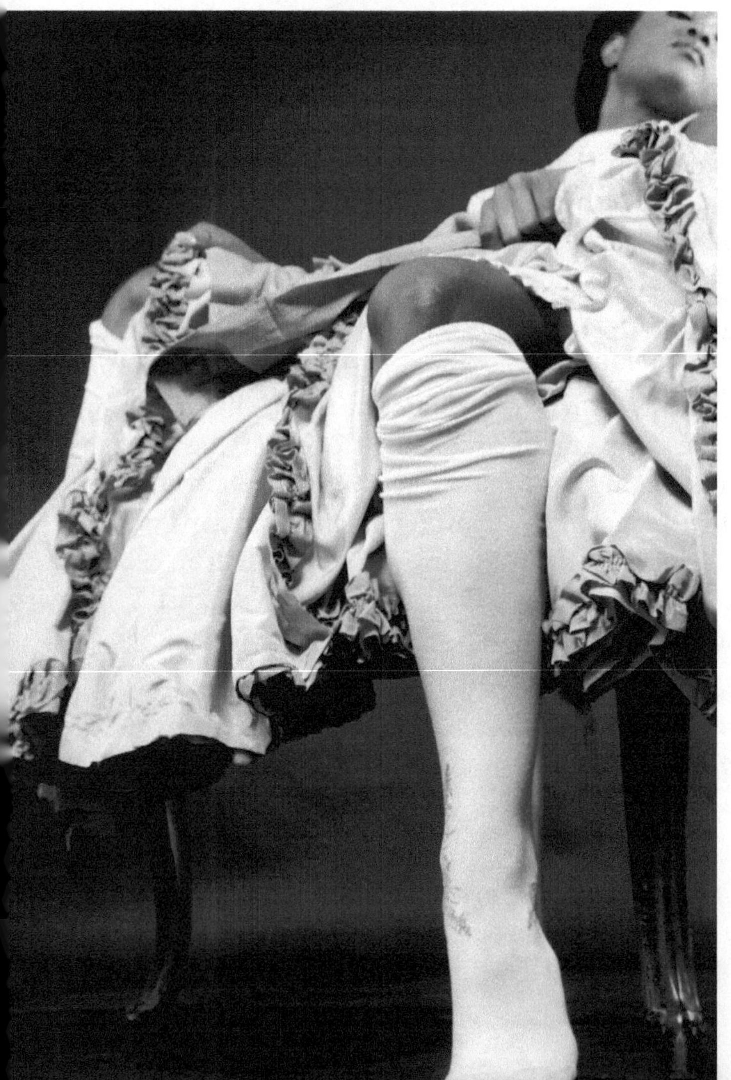

breath taken into himself as he leaned in and bit his lip. "Harder," Quinn said, and Calder grunted on a thrust that slid them both up the bed and stopped Celeste's breath.

Calder held him there, their eyes on each other, the emotion passing between them a tangible thing to her, so powerful she could feel the love as though it were her very own, and her chest hitched in a sob. Then Calder relaxed and slipped free of Quinn. He pulled him up to his knees, rotating him until he faced Celeste directly. They sat there a moment, Quinn presented to her, on his knees, wide open and gazing at her while Calder's hands searched his body, stroked his cock, teased his nipples, presented his neck so he could lick and kiss it. Then Calder pushed between his shoulder blades until Quinn went to all fours, and Calder poured more oil into his palm and took Quinn's arse again with a feral moan.

"Are you watching?" Calder groaned, and Celeste met his glassy gaze and nodded. Calder thrust hard, forcing Quinn's chest to the bed, his elbows buckling beneath the weight. His face came down at the edge of the bed, and he turned his head to look directly at her, and she slid her hand up her inner thigh and finally, finally touched her own hot, wet, skin, and with that touch, her breath quickened, her heart raced, her blood pushed through her veins, trying to get to the places that needed it most.

This time Calder stole her gaze, and she followed him. He ran his hands over Quinn's back, and she ran one hand up her abdomen, pulling her bodice down until her breast came free and she took it in her hand, pinching her nipple as her other hand continued to play. Calder held tight to Quinn's hips, pulling him back into the cradle of his thighs and grinding against him as Quinn groaned mercy into the linens.

She slid one finger into her pussy, added a second finger, and threw one leg over the arm of the chair as the other came up to the edge of the bed, bracketing Quinn and his hot gaze. Her breath quickened, her heart raced, and she saw nothing but red.

"Come off for us, Celeste, can you?" Calder asked, and she nodded. He grinned, thrust twice more then pulled his cock from Quinn and spread his seed across Quinn's hips and back. Her body shook then exploded, and she shuddered with a scream as she was overcome. Quinn straightened his legs between Calder's, and Calder lay down atop him, his chest against Quinn's back, his legs straddling him as Quinn's hand reached back and played with Calder's thigh.

"You're so beautiful when you come off, Celeste. I'd forgotten just how beautiful," Quinn said.

Celeste's legs slipped to the floor as she released her breast and stood on wobbly legs. "I should—"

"No," Quinn said, and he reached out and tugged her hand then Quinn pulled the towel from the floor and handed it to Calder. He cleaned his belly and Quinn's backside then rolled from the bed. Quinn heard the water rush before Calder returned from the water closet and came back to the bed. Quinn shifted into him until they were fitted together perfectly. "Come on," he said to her.

She started to shake her head, but he tilted his head and raised one eyebrow, and she lost all thought. She was exhausted. Quinn sat up and turned her around, making quick work of her dress, corset, and petticoats, leaving her in her drawers and chemise. Then he pulled her to the bed with them, and as she fell asleep in Quinn's arms, and he in Calder's arms, and she thought how like an odd set of spoons they were—all different designs, yet fitted so perfectly together in the drawer.

Quinn

In his life, Quinn had never thought to find himself falling asleep between the two people he cared for most in this world. But here he was, and he felt nothing but blessed as he closed his eyes, Calder's arms wrapped around him, their legs tangled together, with Celeste carefully curved into his body.

Tonight had been difficult for Calder, of that he had no doubt, and Quinn imagined he'd still need time to become familiar with Celeste for various reasons. But this was a start, and Quinn thought it could be the beginning of something truly beautiful. He had no intention of sharing every intimate moment between he and Calder, but he imagined Celeste wasn't so terribly interested in being a part of their life in such a full and complete way either.

Tomorrow they needed to use words to find solutions instead of bodies, but tonight, using their bodies had worked. He and Devil, she and Calder, the three of them. Tomorrow they needed to begin the journey they'd started down the path together tonight.

Tomorrow, unexpectedly, was full of possibility.

Q

When Quinn woke, he was alone. He couldn't believe he'd slept so soundly that both Celeste and Calder had managed to disappear without waking him. He stretched like a cat in the sunshine after a long nap then rose and went to clean up and get dressed. He didn't worry too terribly about his clothes; they were alone here at the dower house. No servants had been retained, and the stable master had returned the horses and carriage to the main stables.

He pulled on trousers and a white lawn shirt, not bothering at all to tuck the tail or put shoes on. He wanted to find Calder and Celeste. The house was so incredibly quiet as he descended the main staircase that his heart picked up a beat. But then he smelled breakfast in the dining room and followed it. He found an entire service, hot and ready under covers— but nobody had touched it.

He saw a movement from the corner of his eye and walked to the windows that overlooked the back gardens. Celeste and Calder were squared off, both of them stiff and formal, roughly four feet away from each other as they spoke. The sight of them so formal upset him, and for a moment he wanted to go outside and fix everything. But he didn't. He walked back through the dining room and across the entry to the library, where he found a snifter of Lucas and Beau's smuggled French brandy and sank into the overstuffed club chair before the fireplace.

Quinn pulled his feet up to the chair, sitting cross-legged, resting his forearms on his knees, sipping brandy as he waited for Calder and Celeste to come find him.

It seemed an inordinate amount of time before Celeste could meet his eyes and attempt to answer the question he'd posed. In fact, she'd yet to meet his eyes since he'd found her here in the gardens. He would have taken a step toward her to attempt some sort of comfort, but it was quite clear his proximity was what unsettled her.

His eyes dropped to her chest, and she took a deep breath, then he watched her lips as her mouth dropped open. "Yes, my lord, I love him," she said, and Calder allowed her to drop her gaze. He wanted to correct her, tell her to call him Calder, as everyone else did, but chastising her now…one step at a time.

"This is not easy for me," he said quietly as he inspected the toes of his boots. He wasn't entirely sure why he'd dressed so formally today. He imagined that none of them was going anywhere, but having the formality between them after last night helped. He also felt better knowing that he could leave at any moment, and he supposed that was part of it. The whole of his life he'd been concerned with having an exit strategy in case of… whatever. He paused to think about that, that Quinn, his brilliant Quinn, would have noticed that Calder was always looking for a way out. He closed his eyes and filed that thought away for the moment.

He wouldn't leave today. Not unless Quinn told him to go, and even then he intended to fight. Right now, however, he wanted to try to speak with Celeste. Try to get to know her. It wasn't exactly going well.

"He has this smile," Calder said and kicked an errant weed in the lawn. "When he doesn't think anyone is looking, and he tries to stifle it before someone sees it. It's the most beautiful thing I think I've ever seen in my life."

He heard her take a swift breath and looked up to find her expression so filled with recognition and love he wasn't sure what to do with it. He couldn't categorize it. Some small piece of him reached for her, but it shied before it got too cozy. He tamped it down, held on to his jealousy-born fear of her.

"That's one of my favorites," she said. "That and the wicked little half grin he gets when he has some sort of plan he knows could get him in trouble but he intends to see it through regardless."

"Yes," he said, and the tension in his shoulders seemed to drain through his arms and out his fingertips like rain. "I'm never sure what to think when he's got that crooked smile on. Everything is about to go so terribly wrong or—"

"Or incredibly right!" she cut in excitedly.

Calder couldn't help but laugh. Goddamn, but Quinn was right. She was magnificent for a woman. She turned and started walking through the garden, and he strolled next to her. "I don't know how this works. I don't know how any of this works. What I do know is that I owe you an apology for my behavior and my thanks for what you've done for him—and therefore, what you've done for me."

To her credit, she didn't speak. She didn't stop him and try to stifle his apology, and neither did she gloat over his appreciation. She simply walked on in silence with a small nod of her head. This was what true grace looked like. Quinn had not been blind, or perhaps Calder was slowly coming under her spell as well.

He said, "Do you intend to—"

She stopped walking suddenly, stealing the words from his lips, and he forgot what he was about to say. "I have no intentions whatsoever," she said. "Beyond ensuring that you and Quinn are together, there is nothing I want from him nor you. I want to say that, first and foremost."

"And yet we will take care of you. We will…somehow manage all of this," he said. "You are his lawful responsibility—at the *very* least—so in that regard we will ensure you are kept comfortable and safe." He knew he was using *we* too much, that his conscience was forcing it out as though it flaunted some small victory before her. He really needed to control his jealousy.

He saw a small bench under an old apple tree and walked her to it, allowing her to sit before he joined her. He remembered that Quinn had said she spoke more freely to him when he wasn't looking directly at her, so Calder leaned forward on his knees and wove his fingers together, because this next part would be uncomfortable for the both of them.

"Last night," he said quietly. "I'm not sure—" He heard her take a sudden breath as if to speak, and he turned his head and caught her gaze to stay her words, quite effectively, then he turned forward again. "I'm not sure I'm entirely comfortable with what happened last night. Not necessarily because you were there, but more for my own feelings. My intention was to invite you to our life, to show you how important he is to me, and to prove to you in action how much I care for him. Particularly since the last time you saw us together, it wasn't so very cordial." His throat went dry, and he cleared it, swallowing several times to clear the lump in his throat. "That wasn't exactly how it ended up. It was perhaps too soon for us…for that. You must understand how very possessive of him I am. He has always been mine, and mine alone. I intended for him to always be mine, and mine… alone."

"He's had mistresses," she said.

"You are no mistress, my dear, and we both know that," he said, turning to her so she knew the depth of his resolve on that opinion.

She fell silent, and he considered his next words carefully. He stared down at the toes of his boots, shining against the green of the lawn. "I need to be sure I'm not harming him in my actions, and last night—I know I bordered on trying to prove something to you as opposed to giving him everything that I am…which is as it should be. So I would very much appreciate some time to reconcile everything that has happened. I would appreciate it if we could keep that part of our lives together separate, for the time being at least. If you don't mind." He closed his eyes and pinched the bridge of his nose, his eyebrows coming together there as he tried to stave off the headache that threatened.

"You will have whatever time you need. As I told Quinn, I've no intention of being a witness to your intimacies. I didn't want to join last night—" He turned and narrowed his gaze on her to ask that she be absolutely truthful with him, as he had been with her. As difficult as it was, it was all he asked at the moment. She swallowed hard and gave a single nod, and he turned away again. "I didn't want to…*intrude* last night—I believe is more accurate. I do not want to feel my presence in your life is an intrusion. Something Quinn had a very difficult time understanding about me is that I can, more than adequately, manage myself," she whispered the words, and Calder gave a quick laugh and she stilled.

"Apologies, that's simply exactly what Quinn said you called it, and he thinks it's adorable, and hearing it from you…I believe I concur."

"Would you prefer me to be vulgar?" she asked, cocking an eyebrow when he turned his head toward her.

He considered it a second, imagining those lips uttering words like "coming off," "cock," "pussy"…"fucking."

"Not always," he said, "but a bit of vulgarity once and again isn't necessarily out of the question."

"Duly noted," she said with an acquiescing nod. "I can, you know. I can be vulgar. I simply choose not to be, for the most part. At any rate, as I was saying…I don't believe that I need to be witness to your intimacies. I'm fine on my own with my—my…"

He heard her swallow hard and turned back again. "Memories?" he asked, and she closed her eyes and nodded, her brown cheeks pinking in such a subtle way he wanted to rub his thumb across them as if he could smudge the pink like fresh paint. He turned away again. "Memories of us… together."

"You are so beautiful, the two of you. I don't understand what it is. I certainly don't know why I'm so enamored of you. But I have quite a vivid memory, and I'll be fine, please believe me."

"I will endeavor to be better than Quinn in this. I will trust you to know yourself, as there is no possible way for me to get to know you as quickly as we may find necessary. Not to mention that the inner workings of women tend to baffle me for various and sundry reasons. I will happily leave your inner workings for you to deal with. And perhaps in time we may find our relationship such that I would be amenable…to…refreshing your memories." He heard her breath catch and knew he'd brought her arousal at just the thought of seeing them together again. Much like he'd aroused Quinn with the simple mention of her coming off for him. Fancy that, a man like him making a woman swoon. It intrigued him.

"Thank you," she said, and he could see her press her thighs together beneath her skirts, her hands twisted tight in her lap. He watched as she suppressed the reactions, then her hand came out to his arm and rested there for a second. She started to pull away, and he put his hand over it to keep her.

"Would you mind too terribly if I asked you to spend the afternoon with Lilly?"

"Not at all," she replied without the least bit of hesitation. It drew a smile from him without effort that she was so willing to respect his wishes where he and Quinn were concerned.

"I very much appreciate it. I need to speak with Quinn about…well, all of this. I know he enjoyed last night, and I don't want to disappoint him, but I need to be sure he understands I am simply not yet comfortable with it. Though…"

"Yes?"

"The sleeping part of it, I didn't mind that so terribly," he said quietly. "One of my favorite things in the world is Quinn's face when he realizes just how much he loves…well, myself—or you. It's a beautiful thing to see that pure realization come to him. Your sleeping in the same bed with us gave him so much joy I'm hard-pressed to deny that, and since I was sleeping and didn't much notice your presence, I figure we can continue with that. Some nights."

"I think that would be lovely." Celeste smiled. "Thank you."

"For?"

"For sharing yourself with me. For being understanding, for being open and considerate, for giving me another chance, for listening to Quinn and giving him the opportunity to explain himself. Just…for everything. For trying."

"I should have done it sooner. I regret that I didn't, but in consideration of where we are now, I cannot be too terribly frustrated by it."

"No, don't. I think I like where we are and where we're going. Quinn said you may have found a property for me?"

"For us," he said quietly. "For us."

"Oh," she said, and it sounded patently defeated.

He looked over to her again. "Celeste, this *us* includes you."

She smiled, and he tugged her hand gently until she turned back to him with tears limning her eyes with the gold of the sun.

He did raise his thumb then and run it across the crest of her cheek, making that pink shine in the warmth of the sun. "Don't cry, sweet, sweet

girl, don't cry." He dropped his hand and stood, drawing her up. He placed a single kiss on her forehead, then her hand on his elbow. He looked at her hand and realized everything Quinn had said about her, everything he'd told him had been absolutely true and genuine. She was to be held and protected at all cost. Something inside him made him think about that day in Hyde Park, and he turned her toward him once more.

"There's something else…" He tried to gather his thoughts as he contemplated eyes the color of a forest. "But perhaps not…" He was unsure how to proceed.

"What is it?"

"Around ten years ago, Quinn and I were in Hyde Park—" He stopped when her eyes widened, and she turned away. "It was you," he said.

She put her back to him. He waited patiently until she turned around. Then she lifted her chin and met his gaze. "It was me."

Rather suddenly that small piece of him that had reached out before, but shied, reached out once again. It took hold of her and pulled her to him and refused to release her. It was a mere slip of a silken thread, so thin and delicate…but it was something he meant to guard and protect. Perhaps Quinn had been right; perhaps she'd been brought here for the both of them…in different ways.

"You…you're like Francine and Lulu," he said, and she nodded. "Quinn doesn't know about them," he said, and she nodded again. "That doesn't mean he shouldn't—he should. I just mean to say that this is a delicate situation."

"I understand," she said quietly. "I would like to be the one who tells him, if you don't mind."

"It's your story to tell, though I would like to hear it as well someday."

She nodded once more. "You are just as beautiful as I remember from that day," Celeste said, and they turned together toward the house.

"We should find Quinn before he gets carried away trying to figure out what we're talking about," Calder said.

"You don't think he's still sleeping?"

"I know he's awake. He came to the dining room and he saw us out here."

"You've never once looked back to the house."

"I didn't need to," he said.

"My lord—"

"One more thing today, and then we'll leave all this difficulty for the moment," he said, and she looked up to him.

"All right."

"You will call me Calder, as the rest of the family does," he said then.

"Calder."

"Yes."

"I will...follow your lead, for now. I will not invite myself to spend time with either of you, but please do not think it because I don't wish to. What I wish to do, for now, is to defer to you, until you are comfortable with me. Is that...is that acceptable?"

"It is, and I appreciate it. But if you need something from us, either of us, you will ask. You are *not* to go wanting simply out of deference to me," he said.

"I will," she said. "I will ask."

eleste decided to walk up to the main house on her own, even though Calder offered to escort her. She wanted him to be with Quinn. It was such an oddly fulfilling feeling in her that she was happiest when she knew them to be happy. These feelings weren't anything like what she was brought up learning about love and marriage.

She was taught the usual—she would love her husband, if she was lucky, at some point after marriage. That she would wish to be with him as much as possible, but as a man he would have things that needed doing, and she'd need to find ways to preoccupy herself so as not to become a nagging pain in his side out of boredom. Children were a good way to do that. Children. She wondered what they'd do about Calder and his title. She brushed it off for the time being. They could figure that out when they managed to figure out the small things, like, where they would live and how. The minor details.

Even so, this feeling she carried wasn't solely due to them, it was because she felt this certain freedom to be who she wished to be, that they accepted her for who she was and they didn't wish for her to change a bit. Even Quinn had accepted her finally. This entire family, all of these people she'd spent time with over the past couple of months, they'd been so lovely and so welcoming…she was truly blessed.

Celeste knocked on the large front entry and rushed through without waiting for the butler. In the entry she was met with the smell of eggs, meat, and coffee, and as her belly rumbled, she realized she hadn't even eaten breakfast yet. She made her way to the dining room to find Perry and Lilly huddled together at one end of the table, and she cleared her throat as she stood in the entry.

Lilly looked up and smiled then waved her in. "Come on, have you eaten? We sent breakfast down to the dower house."

"Yes, actually I was the first up and heard them at the service entrance and let them in to set it up. It smelled wonderful, but I got distracted and wasn't able to partake. I thought perhaps we could spend a bit of time together today? After breakfast?"

"Of course," Lilly said then motioned to the sideboard. "Come and join us. We only sat down a few minutes ago." Lilly walked over and handed Celeste a plate, then filled another and brought it to the end of the table where they were sitting.

"Did Warrick and Lulu leave? I was hoping to see her," Celeste asked.

"Not yet," Perry said.

"They're in the old guest suites in the north wing. We haven't heard from them since Calder left yesterday. The news he had…Gray didn't particularly take it well," he said finally.

"Quinn said he would tell me about it when he was able, so don't feel you're obligated," Celeste said.

"Thank you," Perry said as he turned his face to the window, his gaze distant.

"What would you like to do today?" Lilly asked.

"Perhaps a ride? Would that be something we could do? I haven't ridden in a while, and I do miss it."

"Absolutely."

They turned toward the main hall when they heard boots running down the steps in the entry, then Gray walked in the breakfast room and Perry stood.

"Thank you for your hospitality," he said. "We'll be quitting for London as soon as the carriage can be readied."

"Warrick—"

"Don't." He shook his head, and what she saw in his eyes froze the blood in Celeste's veins. She wasn't sure she'd ever get used to the sheer force of power this man exuded.

"Gray," Perry said carefully. "You're more than welcome to stay here for however long you wish. There's no reason to hurry back to London."

"You know bloody well there's reason," he said, and Celeste put the plate down and walked toward Lilly, needing to be closer to someone and farther from him. He cut a glance at her, and she shuffled quickly away, then was instantly regretful when he dropped his gaze to the floor and rubbed his palm across his forehead.

She mouthed *I'm sorry* to Perry, but he waved her off.

Perry approached him. "Gray, let's… Can we go to my office for a moment? The queen knows you're here. If anything must be done, she'll send for you. Just come with me and give me a moment." Warrick nodded, and Perry put a hand on his shoulder as he turned him for the main entry.

Celeste quietly went back to the sideboard and picked her plate back up. No sooner had she filled it, when Lulu walked in. Her eyes were puffy and red; she wore naught but trousers and a shirt that was probably Warrick's.

"Lulu?" Celeste said. She put the plate down and walked to her, wrapping her up in her arms.

"Hi, sorry. Hi," she said, and Celeste leaned back and looked at her.

"Are you all right? Can I do something?"

Lulu shook her head, and her chin wobbled as tears began to run her cheeks.

"Oh, Lulu, no, what's wrong?" she said, wrapping her back up in her arms.

"I can't," she said. "I'm so frightened. I've only just found him, and if I were to lose him… I can't," she said. "I simply can't lose him."

"Why would you lose him?" Celeste asked as she pulled her to a chair at the table. "I don't understand. Calder couldn't have told him something so terrible…I don't understand," she repeated. "The two of you…you belong together."

"Yes, well, apparently there's something out there more important than me." Lulu hid her face behind her hand.

"There can't be," Celeste said quietly, but what did she know, honestly? Not much. Warrick was quite obviously disturbed by what Calder had told him, and Lulu…she was a wreck. She took Lulu's hand and held it between her own, just trying to soothe her as best she could. "Perry has him in the study. He's trying to convince him to stay here for now."

"That would be good."

A door slammed in the main entry, and all three of them stood and turned toward the doorway. A moment later, Warrick walked in and Celeste took a step back.

"Are you coming or not?" he said. Lulu simply dropped her hand, following him from the room. Lilly came up next to Celeste, and they held hands just for some sort of elusive comfort as they watched them go.

Perry returned to the dining room, and Lilly went to him, where he wrapped her in his arms and held on for a while. Celeste wished she had someone to comfort her ragged nerves. She would have to tell Calder and Quinn about this. She imagined Calder wasn't going to be too happy about Warrick leaving.

A warm hand ran up and down her arm, and she turned to see Perry and Lilly standing there. He put his arm out, and she walked into his embrace, accepting the comfort offered.

"Perhaps we should simply stay home today," Celeste said then.

Lilly nodded, and Perry squeezed her. "We'll do whatever you both wish to."

"Someone should tell Calder, but at the moment…I'm not sure…it's just, if we don't let him know what's happened—"

"I'll send a missive. He can open it or not, but it won't intrude. Will that work?"

She nodded against him. "Yes, thank you."

When he released her, she walked once more to the sideboard and took up her plate. Her stomach was in knots at this point, but she had to try to eat something. The rest of the meal passed rather quietly, as did the rest of the day. They did stay home, and they played cards and had a late supper.

Celeste wondered whether she should return to the dower house tonight or stay with Lilly and Perry.

"One more hand?" Lilly asked, and Celeste smiled absentmindedly, nodding.

"One more hand," she said.

Quinn

alder had been right about Quinn and the book. He hadn't expected to find the snifter of brandy, though. "It's a bit early for this, isn't it?"

Quinn shrugged. "Is she well?"

"She is. She's spending the afternoon with Lilly."

"Your request?" Quinn asked, and he nodded. "Last night was too much for you," he said, and Calder nodded again. "I'm sorry," Quinn said, and Calder went to his knees in front of the chair as Quinn lowered his legs to the floor, his knees bracketing Calder's chest.

"Don't be," Calder said. "I don't want you to be sorry. It was my choice, and I'm glad to have done it, but it was too soon, because at some point I made it about me instead of concentrating on you. Would you let me make it up to you?" he asked, and Quinn smiled.

"If by making it up to me, you mean going back to bed…" Quinn started.

"No—I'm hungry," Calder said then laughed.

Quinn stood, blatantly displaying his manhood at Calder's eye level, palming himself once before stepping over him to go to the breakfast room. Two could play at this tease. "As you wish."

Calder stood and followed Quinn, and they followed breakfast with long, slow strokes and heavy, wet kisses. They didn't speak much, instead spending the day between the sheets. And on top of the sheets. And next to the sheets. And in the bathtub far from the sheets.

Once they fell asleep, they stayed that way until the sun rose and Quinn knew he needed to find Celeste.

"She's the girl from the park," Calder said, and Quinn rolled over to face him.

"You asked her?" Quinn said.

"I did, yesterday."

"What else did you talk about?"

"Quite a bit, actually. We aren't going to do…what we did the first night…again. At least, not for some time. I am not in full control of my emotions, and it's unfair to you, and to her, and frankly to myself. Perhaps one day. But not soon."

Quinn nodded. He was shocked they'd even done it to begin with, and he'd considered the entire experience a gift wrapped up in an apology. He wasn't going to push the issue. All he wanted for was his Devil in his bed and Celeste safe. "She was well?" he asked. "I mean—" He wasn't sure what he meant.

"She's well. Your wife is lovely, Quinn," Calder whispered, and Quinn had no more words for him. He simply stretched toward him and took his mouth as though he had every right to do as he wished.

EPILOGUE

Celeste watched out the carriage window as it bounced down the rutted road toward Eildon Hill manor. It had been a while since they were here last, and they still had a while to go before they reached it, but just the trip brought back so many strong memories that she had to push her finger to the tip of her nose to stop the tears.

Quinn took her hand and pulled it to his lap, massaging her palm. "My love?" he said quietly.

"It's just…" She took a deep breath then let it out slowly. "So much happened here. So much and I'm just overwhelmed by the memories, I think."

"Happy memories?"

"Mostly."

Calder reached out from across the carriage where he'd been sprawled lazily—having the bench to himself—and put his hand on her knee, sweeping his thumb over the side, soothing her.

"I thought you were napping," she said.

"Me? No. This ride is much too much to manage any sleep," he said, but he didn't move or open his eyes. His body was on the bench, his hips canted to the side so his legs could cross the center, resting on the bench next to Quinn. "How long until we arrive?"

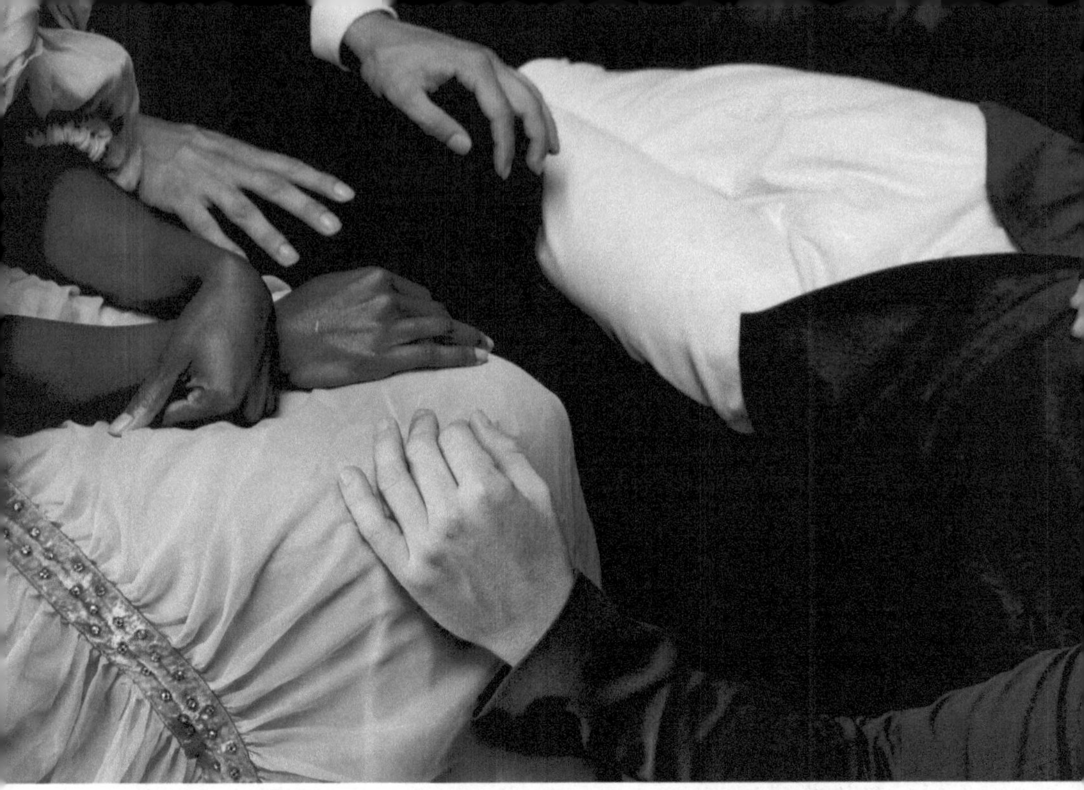

Quinn looked out the window. "Perhaps half an hour, perhaps a bit more."

Calder smiled a devilishly heated grin and caught Quinn's gaze, and a streak of electricity shot her spine. She put her head back on the squabs and closed her eyes, trying to regain her composure. "Celeste, how about we make some new memories, then?" Calder said as he squeezed her knee.

She couldn't respond, turning her face to the sun through the window without opening her eyes.

"It's time to refresh your memories. You don't want to miss this, my sweet," Calder said. She opened her eyes, and he sat up as Quinn went to his knees between Calder's legs, releasing his trousers and taking him in his mouth.

He was right, she didn't want to miss this. She would take all the memories she could get.

Quinn

When the carriage came to a stop at the entry, Celeste threw the door open and jumped down, running into the house without a backward glance. Quinn and Calder watched her go as the footman stared after her, his hand on the door as he wondered if he still had a job to do.

Quinn laughed, still inside the carriage, and the footman turned back when he realized she hadn't been alone and dropped the step for him, holding the door wide. "My lord," he said.

Quinn stepped out first, followed by Calder. He turned Calder and straightened his waistcoat and coat, a bit better now that he was standing, pulling his heavy capes closed around his shoulders when he was done. Calder took a step toward him, much too close, and Quinn's breath left him in a rush, ruffling his creamy white cravat. "Back off, you improper beast," he said.

"Certainly improper, but am I sufficiently presentable?" he asked, and Quinn rolled his eyes.

"I can't tell at this distance, to be honest," Quinn said.

"Is that so?"

"It is," Quinn said under his breath as he looked around. The footman and butler seemed to have disappeared.

"Well, it isn't important enough for me to step away, so I suppose we'll just have to deal with it."

"It's not fair, you know?"

"What's that?" Calder asked.

"I swallowed your mettle, my lord, yet mine is still waiting for attention." He jerked the hem of Calder's waistcoat down, then turned toward the entry, but Calder's laugh stopped him in his tracks.

"Listen, it's just a baby, Quinn. How long could it possibly take to see it? I've heard they're rather small, and slightly boring. We'll be done in no time, then we can…disappear for a bit. Nobody will mind. Certainly Celeste will wish to stay with Francine and the babe for a bit while we go settle our things in the suite?"

Quinn grinned. "I will definitely have some things that need to be settled by then."

"I have no doubt I'll be prepared to settle."

"Well, then, shall we?" Calder asked, his hand out to the entry of the manor.

Quinn laughed.

When the carriage had rolled to a halt, Celeste had thrown the door open and jumped down, picking her skirts up and running to the door as the butler opened it. She pushed past and searched the foyer, listening carefully.

Celeste had never thought about babies, really, because the context of babies had always been in the realm of the ones she'd be forced to bear for her future husband.

This baby, however, *this baby* was the newest member of this family, and she meant so very much to them all. That no matter what, life did go on. The pure innocence of this child…Celeste felt such a strong need to protect her, to keep her safe, to see her happy, and she didn't even know her full name yet.

Celeste wasn't familiar with such a strong emotional response. She heard the smallest noise, no more than a squeak, come from the spring parlor, followed by a quiet shushing, and she followed it.

Roxleigh stood there, his massive frame bouncing and swaying in the window over the garden, the quiet shushing so drastically different from anything she'd ever heard him utter, and Celeste simply dissolved into tears. It was the most beautiful thing to witness.

She must have made too much noise, because Francine stood from the chaise at the back of the parlor, and Roxleigh turned toward her. His eyebrows were drawn down in concern, but when he saw Celeste, his entire face lit up with his smile.

"Celeste," he said. "Come, come. Come meet our Evalina."

Celeste felt a tug at her shoulder and realized the butler had followed her through the entry. "I'm so sorry," she said.

"Not to worry, my lady, I've always appreciated a good chase," he said, then took her capes and gloves and left.

Francine stood and walked slowly to her.

"No, Francine, please sit," Celeste said.

"I'm okay. I've been sitting for a while. I needed to stretch my legs a little." She wrapped her arms around Celeste and squeezed her so tight that if she hadn't already been crying, she would have started then. Francine released her and took her hand, pulling her toward her husband and baby. "Hey, Daddy, are you ready to share yet?"

Roxleigh turned to Francine. "Unfortunately, yes. I have to check the new foals. Two dropped last night, and I haven't yet been to the stables."

Babies everywhere. "Quinn and Calder should be in momentarily," Celeste said.

"I'll catch them on my way out. They can come with me to the stables and meet Eva later so the two of you can have some time to catch up." He was so sweet it hurt. "Do you want to sit?" This Roxleigh was so foreign to her, and she was fascinated.

"Does she like to be bounced?" she asked. "I could stand, if she wants to bounce," Celeste said and realized she was already bouncing, so she stopped herself.

He grinned. "She's perfectly happy. Here, have a seat."

Celeste sat, and Francine sat next to her, then Roxleigh sat on her other side. He was so close, so warm, so big, it was unnerving. She turned to him, and he reached out with his daughter and placed her in Celeste's arms.

"Oh dear God, she's so tiny, she weighs nothing," she said.

"She's a bit of a pixie," he said as he leaned over her, his big hand smoothing the hair on the baby's head, his arm wrapped behind Celeste.

"I don't want to break her," she whispered.

"You won't," he whispered back.

Francine leaned back against the settee with a massive grin. She shook her head. "Go on, Daddy, go get some work done. We'll be here when you return."

Roxleigh nodded but didn't shift.

Francine laughed.

"Fine, fine. I'll be back in time for luncheon. Mrs. Weston said she would have them put it in the family parlor so you can show off your Christmas tree," he said.

"That sounds perfect," Francine said, and Roxleigh stood and walked to her, kissing her softly, then turning. He paused at the doorway and turned back, gave a small wave, and ducked out of the room.

"Wow," Celeste said.

"Yeah," Francine replied. "He's a mess. It's absolutely the most adorable thing I've ever seen. He's completely smitten."

"If I hadn't seen it for myself…"

"Yeah, nobody would believe me. I know."

Celeste turned back to the tiny blanket-wrapped thing in her arms. The baby just lay there, her eyes closed, her fist at her chin, a tiny pout on her lips. "She's beautiful, Francine, the most beautiful little thing I've ever seen."

Francine sighed and shifted, finding a more comfortable spot on the sofa.

"And how are you?" Celeste asked.

"I'm doing well. Would have given anything for an epidural, but Gideon was amazing through the whole thing, and he's still amazing now. I'm more in love with him than I've ever been, Celeste. I know this is where I was meant to be."

"I'm learning to reconcile it. I've remembered so much, and I'm still writing, processing, trying to figure out what's real and the things I cannot place. It's difficult, but I wouldn't be where I am without your help. I've missed you."

"I've missed you too. I'm so glad you could come for a visit. How long will you be able to stay?" Francine asked.

"Oh, as long as you'll have me, I suppose, though I think Calder has business in London, so he'll have to leave within a sennight, and I'm certain Quinn will accompany him."

Francine smiled. "You're more than welcome to stay, but I think those two will miss you."

"Perhaps."

Evalina squeaked, and Celeste bounced her gently. "She might be getting hungry," Francine said.

Celeste leaned forward, handing Evalina to her mother. Francine leaned back and held her daughter close, cooing and clucking her tongue, and she rained kisses on her face to wake her up, then she put her to her breast. Francine was desperately in love; you could just see it in her every expression.

"What's her full name? We left before the official announcement arrived," Celeste said.

Francine smiled. "Melisande Evalina Grace Trumbull."

"What?"

"I wanted to name her after two people I love but never had the chance to meet. We grieve Gideon's mom and for that small girl who came here and slipped through the cracks. I wanted to honor her, and your bravery."

Celeste turned to look out the windows. She'd accepted what had happened, and she was happy to be here now, happy to have found her place with Quinn and Calder, and for once she was looking forward to the future. That much was true, but it was still difficult. Most days, she put it from her mind as if the future had never happened. Someday, she thought, she would truly understand it all. Francine had helped.

She took her hand and squeezed. "Hey," Francine said.

"I'm quite honored. I am. Thank you."

"Hey, hey, peanut, wake up now. Time to switch." Francine lifted her daughter and kissed her face until the baby wiggled, her little bottom poking out as she stretched and complained, but the complaint was nothing but the cutest little squeak of annoyance that burrowed into Celeste's heart and took up residence.

"Thank you, for everything."

"No, Celeste, thank you. I am so happy to have you as a friend. I love you."

"I love you too," she said. She leaned toward Francine, putting her head on her shoulder as she watched Evalina nurse.

Mrs. Weston came in with a tray of tea and set it up in front of them, then she reached her arms out and wiggled her fingers. Francine laughed and handed Evalina to her. "Have some tea and cakes," Mrs. Weston said, "then I'll return this little bean to you."

Celeste laughed and poured, ready to spend the afternoon with one of her dearest friends.

"And Quinn and Calder?" Francine asked.

"Quinn and Calder," Celeste said. Just their names brought joy to her in a way she couldn't define. "Quinn and Calder." She smiled at Francine.

"I take it Giggleswick is treating you all well?"

"It will. We've been staying at Canford while Shaw is working on the manor. But it's beautiful, it's so… You'll have to come visit, perhaps in the spring when it will be safer to travel with Eva?"

"Absolutely. I'd love to see your new home."

"Quinn planned the renovations. I have an entire suite, my own library, a ballroom for dancing…it's perfect. Just perfect."

"It sounds perfect."

"It is."

"And you're all doing well, together?" she asked.

"We are. Calder has…he's coming to be as important to me as Quinn, which I thought patently impossible, really. I never thought I could care for someone as much as I do Quinn, but…I think I will. And he cares for me more than I'd considered possible for him, all in all. He's become the most thoughtful and lovely…I don't know, whatever he is to me. We don't have words for any of it. I find myself looking at them and trying to categorize what we are to each other, but it just… Our relationship falls outside of any categorization."

"What a beautiful sentiment, Celeste," Francine said. "Someday, perhaps there will be words for it. Someday, perhaps those words may even come to you. But until then, simply enjoy this new thing that you have. Hold it and cherish it."

"Oh, I will. I very much intend to."

"It is truly so fantastic to see you so happy," Francine said.

"It feels good," Celeste said. "It feels really good."

They stood with their arms on the stable wall, watching the little black wobbly things that were more legs than anything, and Calder laughed. "Gangly beasts," he said. Roxleigh turned to him, and Calder held his hands up in surrender. "Apologies, I won't speak on your children in such a way."

"No, you won't," Roxleigh said. "Especially since these two are meant to be raised matched for your carriage."

"You can't mean it," Quinn said.

"I do mean it," Rox replied. "I'm already much too fond of them to see them sold to a man such as Dunphre who named my four after devils."

"I'm rather fond of devils," Quinn said quietly, and Roxleigh turned his glare to him. "All right, it's just one particular Devil, and we promise not to name your chattel for demons," he said, and Calder wrapped his arms about his waist and pulled him tight to his chest, kissing his neck.

Roxleigh grunted then looked behind them.

"Apologies," Calder said, releasing Quinn.

"No," Roxleigh replied, "I just wanted to be sure we were still alone here."

Calder nodded.

"I want you to be as comfortable as anyone else who is welcome in my home, but I also want you to be safe here. My staff is the best possible staff, I trust each one of them with my life, but out here anyone can show up, particularly with the new foals dropping. So I wouldn't bet either of your lives on it being absolutely secure. There's only so much mitigation we can manage. I've heard talk of Labouchere attempting to criminalize…" He didn't finish the sentence, but he also didn't motion with his hand or look meaningfully at the two of them, or any other myriad demeaning moves he could have done. "The amendment we've been working on, the one associated with the men we just shut down. As you know, we passed the amendment in Lords, but Commons failed to pass it. My fear is other amendments may get tacked on to convince those currently uninterested in simply protecting women and girls. Because protecting women and girls is simply not reason enough to pass an amendment."

"After everything we've been through over the past three years to provide further protections and shut down that skin trade…it's going to come back on me?" Calder said.

"I hope not, but I'm watching Labouchere. I simply do not trust him."

"Of course," Calder said as Quinn's hand slipped into his and squeezed it.

"Has the abdication been finalized?" Roxleigh asked.

Calder nodded, then shrugged. It was as final as it could be until his brother received the Letters Patent from the queen. His stomach twisted at the thought. Jerrod had never been particularly interested in a title; he'd always been much more interested in scientific pursuits than governmental, but Calder knew Jerrod understood the need for the title to pass to him. The logic was irrefutable, and Calder's guilt lay more in the fact that he'd used his brother's own sense of reason against him. Jerrod's rational mind and extreme intelligence had forced his hand.

It had also been somewhat painful, giving up that piece of himself. He'd been raised to be St. Cyr. He'd retained the marquessate and the entailments in Canford, but that was all, and his title would eventually pass to Jerrod's sons, as he would have no heirs himself. Quinn's arms wrapped around him from behind, and Calder leaned back against him, borrowing his strength.

"I can't imagine the difficulty in that decision," Roxleigh said.

"Actually," Calder replied, "it wasn't the decision that was difficult. Abdicating the title was the easiest thing I've done, in some respects. It's all the rest surrounding it that was difficult. What I gained by doing it is truly immeasurable. I can still be active in the House, and nobody cares about the lesser title. Nobody's going to look to me and expect me to carry on the Marquessate of Canford."

"It's still second to a duke," Roxleigh said.

"Yes, but a duke, it is not," Calder replied.

Roxleigh nodded and turned back to the foals. "I only need to finish some tending here. You two should go settle in. How long will you be staying?"

"I'm required in London next week to complete documents, and I should be there when Jerrod accepts his Letters," he said, and Roxleigh nodded.

"Then we have time. Go on. You'll meet Evalina this afternoon." And with that they were dismissed.

They didn't hold hands as they walked across the property to the manor house, but they did walk much too closely. Calder couldn't help it, though; he needed Quinn's warmth, his strength.

"Are you sure about this? Are you sure you don't want to be St. Cyr?" he asked.

"We've been over this too many times, Quinn. I don't want to be St. Cyr. I want to be yours." He stopped and turned to him. "Listen to me, and understand this. I won't say it again. There's nothing in this world I want for, nothing I covet or seek, nothing that could possibly take the place of having you at my side. This guilt I carry is for my brother, not for the title. Do not *ever* feel that you've taken something from me. What you've done in my life is give me everything. I would not have a life to live if it weren't for you."

Quinn took his hand and pulled him as he ran across the snow-dusted lawns toward the manor. He pulled him under the walkway supported by the buttresses and through the door to the orangery. He took a cursory glance around the room, then pushed Calder up against the closest wall, his fists on his lapels crushing the fabric, his knee shoved between his thighs, pinning him there.

Then Quinn took his mouth, glory be.

He didn't ask permission. He didn't wait until it was passively given. He took, and Calder gave. He lifted his hands, threading his fingers into his hair and holding the fabric of his coat at his back. It was everything Calder could have asked for in that moment. It was Quinn taking what he wanted and with the realization that his Quinn, the Quinn he'd fallen in love with so very long ago, had fully returned to him, Calder's tears fell, flavoring the kiss between them.

Sodomy was illegal in England beginning with the Buggery Act of 1533. It was commuted from a hanging offense to a life term in prison in 1861.

The Criminal Law Amendment Act of 1885 was originally written to protect women and girls from sexual offenses. One of the original intents of the bill was to protect girls who were being transported to the continent for immoral purpose. It took four years to research and write the bill that would eventually pass in the House of Lords in 1883, but dropped in the House of Commons.

One of the effects of the act would raise the legal age of consent from thirteen (thirteen!!) to sixteen. In England, indecent exposure or attempted rape of a child between the ages of ten and thirteen was a misdemeanor. If the child was under ten, it was a felony. The law raised the age of felonious assault to thirteen and misdemeanor to sixteen and included mentally impaired women and girls. It also made it illegal to procure girls using drugs, fraud, or intimidation. Included penalties for those who allowed underage sex on their properties. Made kidnapping for the purposes of carnal knowledge illegal for girls under eighteen. It gave the government the power to remove a girl from her parents if they condoned her seduction, or her sale into prostitution.

The bill was reintroduced in Parliament again in 1884, and again it languished.

Then in 1885, it was once more introduced into Parliament. The move was prompted by an article by W.T. Stead who investigated the flesh trade. He even purchased a thirteen-year-old child to prove his point. The child,

Eliza Armstrong, was examined medically to prove she was still a virgin then drugged and taken to a brothel for delivery to Stead.

The article enraged Parliament enough that the bill was reintroduced. Three days before reintroduction, Labouchere added an amendment that would criminalize homosexuality—in a bill written to specifically protect women and girls.

The bill passed.

The Labouchere Amendment was incredibly vague, calling for a two-year term of imprisonment for any man found guilty of gross indecency with another man whether in public, or in private.

This is the amendment under which Oscar Wilde was charged.

This is the amendment under which Alan Turing was convicted and subjected to chemical castration in lieu of prison.

The amendment was not repealed until 1967.

There's another piece of history that played a big part in this story, and that's gay marriage. I touched on this with Calder and his refusal to break the vows Quinn has with Celeste, vows he would never be able to take himself, and mean, in any way. Marriage was important to him, but he was never allowed to marry the person he was meant for. I think it would make him happy that finally, after all this time, he *could have* been married to Quinn. And for that matter, Celeste would happily give up her hand to him without pause.

It's important to me to relay this history and where my storylines come from. Though the majority comes from extensive research and is knitted together from countless sources, learning about this bill was one of the main reasons I wrote *The Rake and The Recluse* to begin with. There were crimes committed against women and girls, and they were absolutely horrific, and not considered crimes at all.

In that novel, Madeleine is sold, by her parents, as a chaste bride to Lord Hepplewort. Now with this novel I'm able to bring the final piece of this bill to the story.

I've been asked about Calder since that first book came out. Invariably—*who will his heroine be?* So let me be clear, if it wasn't quite clear in the other books: Calder was born gay. There isn't a moment in my mind in which he was not gay. As people are born gay in real life, Calder was born gay in my mind, even if, at times, he attempted to pass.

Calder has always been very dear to me, and I hope you've enjoyed his story.

"And what is the use of a book,"
thought Alice,
"without pictures or conversations?"

Alice's Adventures in Wonderland
-Lewis Carroll

find me:

If you loved this book you can join my newsletter to be notified of releases before they come out, and to participate in fun giveaways.

JennLeBlanc.com

@JennLeBlanc

IllustratedRomance.com

Facebook.com/IllustratedRomance

9 781944 567156